THE IM

The Impossible Fortress

JASON REKULAK

First published in the UK in 2017 by Faber & Faber Ltd
Bloomsbury House, 74–77 Great Russell Street
London WC1B 3DA

First published in the United States in 2017 by Simon & Schuster
1230 Avenue of the Americas, New York, NY 10020

Printed and bound by CPI Group (UK) Ltd, Croydon, CR0 4YY
Interior design by Lewelin Polanco

The maps on pages 53 and 75 were illustrated by Doogie Horner.

This book is a work of fiction. Any references to historical events, real people, or real places are used fictitiously. Other names, characters, places, and events are products of the author's imagination, and any resemblance to actual events or places or persons, living or dead, is entirely coincidental.

A CIP record for this book is available from the British Library

ISBN 978–0–571–33062–1

2 4 6 8 10 9 7 5 3 1

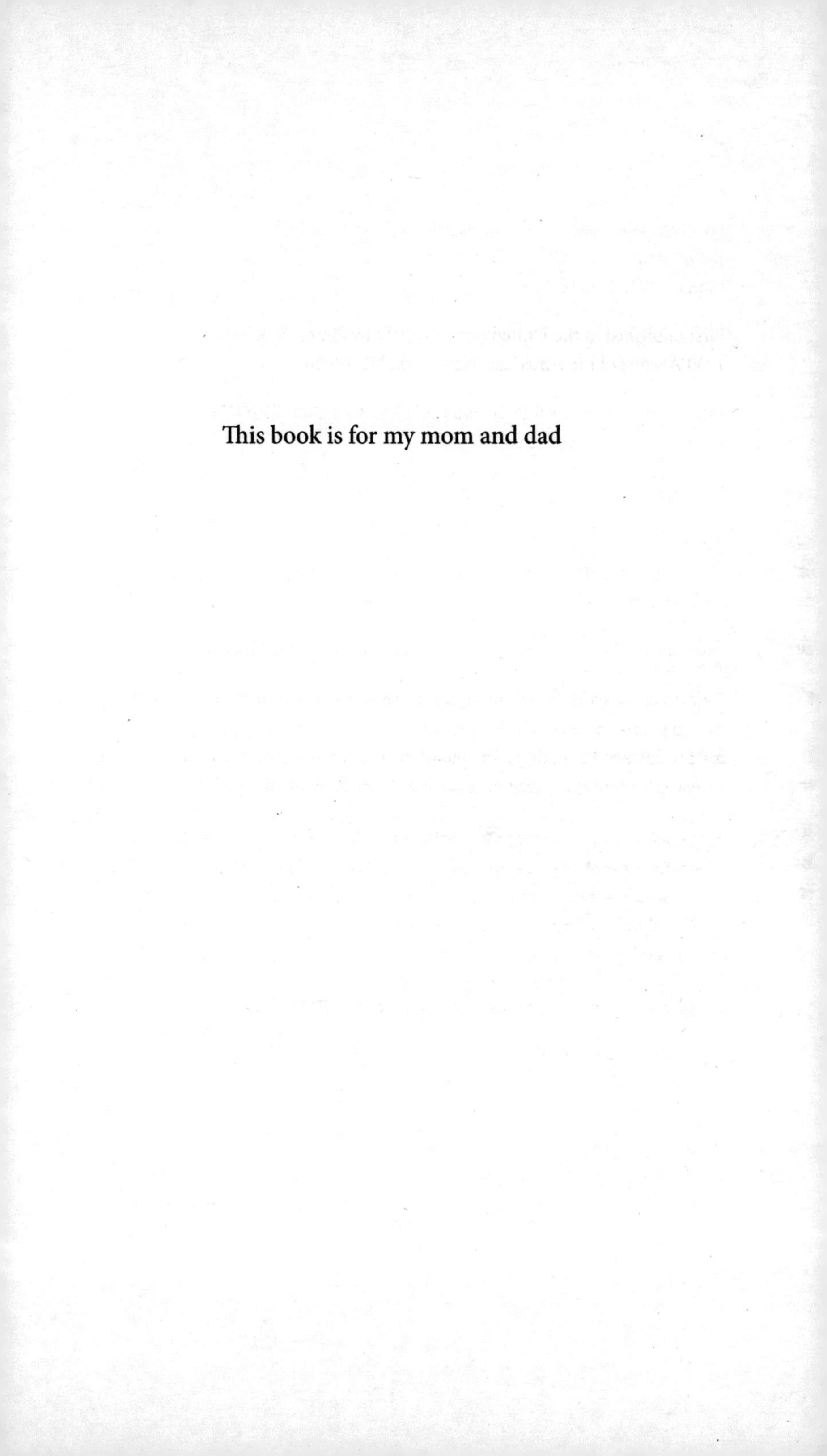

This book is for my mom and dad

THE IMPOSSIBLE FORTRESS

1

```
10 REM *** WELCOME SCREEN ***
20 POKE 53281,0:POKE 53280,3
30 PRINT "{CLR}{WHT}{12 CSR DWN}"
40 PRINT "{7 SPACES}THE IMPOSSIBLE FORTRESS"
50 PRINT "{7 SPACES}A GAME BY WILL MARVIN"
60 PRINT "{9 SPACES}AND MARY ZELINSKY"
70 PRINT "{2 CSR DWN}"
80 PRINT "{7 SPACES}(C)1987 RADICAL PLANET"
90 GOSUB 4000
95 GOSUB 4500
]■
```

MY MOTHER WAS CONVINCED I'd die young. In the spring of 1987, just a few weeks after my fourteenth birthday, she started working nights at the Food World because the late shift paid an extra dollar an hour. I slept alone in an empty house while my mother rang up groceries and fretted over all the terrible things that might happen: What if I choked on a chicken nugget? What if I slipped in the shower? What if I forgot to turn off the stove and the house exploded in a fiery inferno? At ten o'clock every evening, she'd call to make sure I'd finished my homework and locked the front door, and sometimes she'd make me test the smoke alarms, just in case.

I felt like the luckiest kid in ninth grade. My friends Alf and Clark came over every night, eager to celebrate my newfound freedom. We watched hours of TV, we blended milk shakes by the gallon, we gorged on Pop-Tarts and pizza bagels until we made ourselves sick. We played marathon games of Risk and Monopoly that dragged on for days and always ended with one angry loser flipping the board off the table. We argued about music and movies; we had passionate debates over who would win in a brawl: Rocky Balboa or Freddy Krueger? Bruce Springsteen or Billy Joel? Magnum P.I. or T. J. Hooker or MacGyver? Every night felt like a slumber party, and I remember thinking the good times would never end.

But then *Playboy* published photographs of *Wheel of Fortune* hostess Vanna White, I fell head over heels in love, and everything started to change.

Alf found the magazine first, and he sprinted all the way from Zelinsky's newsstand to tell us about it. Clark and I were sitting on the sofa in my living room, watching the MTV Top 20 Video Countdown, when Alf came crashing through the front door.

"Her butt's on the cover," he gasped.

"Whose butt?" Clark asked. "What cover?"

Alf collapsed onto the floor, clutching his sides and out of breath. "Vanna White. The *Playboy*. I just saw a copy, and her butt's on the cover!"

This was extraordinary news. *Wheel of Fortune* was one of the most popular shows on television, and hostess Vanna White was the pride of our nation, a small-town girl from Myrtle Beach who rocketed to fame and fortune by flipping letters in word puzzles. News of the *Playboy* photos had already made supermarket tabloid headlines: The SHOCKED AND HUMILIATED VANNA claimed the EXPLICIT IMAGES were taken years earlier and most definitely not for the pages of *Playboy*. She filed a $5.2 million lawsuit to stop their publication, and now—after months of rumors and speculation—the magazine was finally on newsstands.

"It's the most incredible thing I've ever seen," Alf continued. He climbed onto a chair and pantomimed Vanna's cover pose. "She's sitting on a windowsill, like this? And she's leaning outside. Like she's checking the weather? Only she's not wearing pants!"

"That's impossible," Clark said.

The three of us all lived on the same block, and over the years we'd learned that Alf was prone to exaggeration. Like the time he claimed John Lennon had been assassinated by a machine gun. On top of the Empire State Building.

"I swear on my mother's life," Alf said, and he raised his hand to God. "If I'm lying, she can get run over by a tractor trailer."

Clark yanked down his arm. "You shouldn't say stuff like that," he said. "Your mother's lucky she's still alive."

"Well, *your* mother's like McDonald's," Alf snapped. "She satisfies billions and billions of customers."

"My mother?" Clark asked. "Why are you dragging my mother into this?"

Alf just talked over him. "Your mother's like a hockey goalie. She changes her pads after three periods." He had an encyclopedic knowledge of Your Mother jokes, and he unleashed them at the slightest provocation. "Your mother's like a Japanese steakhouse—"

Clark flung a pillow across the living room, hitting Alf square in the face. Enraged, Alf threw it back twice as hard, missing Clark and toppling my glass of Pepsi. Fizzy foam and soda went sloshing all over the carpet.

"Shit!" Alf exclaimed, scrambling to clean up the mess. "I'm sorry, Billy."

"It's all right," I said. "Just grab some paper towels."

There was no point in making a big deal. It's not like I was going to ditch Alf and Clark for a bunch of new and more considerate friends. Nine months ago, the three of us arrived in high school and watched our classmates dive into sports or clubs or academics. Yet somehow we just orbited around them, not really fitting in anywhere.

I was the tallest boy in ninth grade, but I was not the good kind of tall; I wobbled around school like a baby giraffe, all skinny legs and gangly arms, waiting for the rest of my body to fill in. Alf was shorter, stouter, sweatier, and cursed with the same name of the most popular alien on television—a three-feet-tall puppet with his own NBC sitcom. Their shared resemblance was uncanny. Both Alfs were built like trolls, with big noses, beady eyes, and messy brown hair. Even our teachers joked they were twins.

Still, for all of our obvious flaws, Alf and I knew we were better off than Clark. Every morning he rolled out of bed looking like a heart-throb in *TigerBeat* magazine. He was tall and muscular with wavy blond hair, deep blue eyes, and perfect skin. Girls at the mall would see Clark coming and gape openmouthed like he was River Phoenix or Kiefer Sutherland—until they got close enough to see the Claw, and then they quickly looked away. A freakish birth defect had fused the fingers of Clark's left hand into a pink, crab-like pincer. It was basically useless—he could make it open and close, but it wasn't strong enough to lift anything bigger or heavier than a magazine. Clark swore that as soon as he turned eighteen, he was going to find a doctor to saw it off, even if it cost a million bucks. Until then, he went through life with his head down and the Claw tucked into a pocket, avoiding attention. We knew Clark was doomed to a life of celibacy—that he'd never have a real flesh-and-blood girlfriend—so he needed the Vanna White *Playboy* more than anyone.

"Is she on the centerfold?" he asked.

"I don't know," Alf said. "Zelinsky has it on a rack behind the cash register. Next to the cigarettes. I couldn't get anywhere near it."

"You didn't buy it?" I asked.

Alf snorted. "Sure, I just walked up to Zelinsky and asked for a *Playboy*. And a six-pack. And a crack pipe, too, because why not? Are you crazy?"

We all knew that buying *Playboy* was out of the question. It was hard enough buying rock music, what with Jerry Falwell warning of satanic influences, and Tipper Gore alerting parents to explicit lyrics. No shopkeeper in America was going to sell *Playboy* to a fourteen-year-old boy.

"Howard Stern says the pictures are incredible," Clark explained. "He said you see both boobs super close-up. Nipples, milk ducks, the works."

"Milk ducks?" I asked.

"*Ducts*, with a T," Clark corrected.

"The red rings around the nipples," Alf explained.

Clark shook his head. "Those are areolas, dummy. The milk duct is the hollow part of the nipple. Where the milk squirts out."

"Nipples aren't hollow," Alf said.

"Sure they are," Clark said. "That's why they're sensitive."

Alf yanked up his T-shirt, exposing his flabby chest and belly. "What about mine? Are *my* nipples hollow?"

Clark shielded his eyes. "Put them away. Please."

"I don't have hollow nipples," Alf insisted.

They were always vying to prove which one knew more about girls. Alf claimed authority because he had three older sisters. Clark got all of his information from the *ABZ of Love*, the weird Danish sex manual he'd found buried in his father's underwear drawer. I didn't try to compete with either one of them. All I knew was that I didn't know anything.

Eventually seven thirty rolled around and *Wheel of Fortune* came on. Alf and Clark were still arguing about milk ducts, so I turned the TV volume all the way up. Since we had the house to ourselves, we could be as loud and noisy as we wanted.

"Look at this studio, filled with glamorous prizes! Fabulous and exciting merchandise!" Every episode started the same way, with announcer Charlie O'Donnell previewing the night's biggest treasures. "An around-the-world vacation, a magnificent Swiss watch, and a brand-new Jacuzzi hot tub! Over eighty-five thousand dollars in prizes just waiting to be won on *Wheel of Fortune*!"

The camera panned the showroom full of luggage and houseboats and food processors. Showing off the merchandise was the greatest prize of all, Vanna White herself, five foot six, 115 pounds, and draped in a $12,000 chinchilla fur coat. Alf and Clark stopped bickering, and we all leaned closer to the screen. Vanna was, without doubt, the most beautiful woman in America. Sure, you could argue that Michelle Pfeiffer had nicer eyes and Kathleen Turner had better legs and Heather Locklear had the best overall body. But we worshipped at the altar of the Girl Next Door. Vanna White had a purity and innocence that elevated her above the rest.

Clark shifted closer to me and tapped my knee with the Claw. "I'm going to Zelinsky's tomorrow," he said. "I want to see this cover for myself."

I said, "I'll come with you," but I never took my eyes off the screen.

2

```
200 REM *** ESTABLISHING DIFFICULTY ***
210 PRINT "{CLR}{15 CSR DWN}"
220 PRINT "SELECT SKILL LEVEL"
230 PRINT "EASY-1  NORMAL-2  EXTREME-3"
240 INPUT "YOUR CHOICE? ";SL
250 IF SL<1 OR >3 THEN GOTO 200
260 IF SL=1 THEN PK=10
270 IF SL=2 THEN PK=15
280 IF SL=3 THEN PK=20
290 RETURN
]■
```

WE LIVED IN WETBRIDGE, five miles west of Staten Island, in a geographic region known to stand-up comics as the Armpit of New Jersey. We had factories and fuel refineries, dirty rivers and traffic snarls, densely packed single-family homes, and plenty of Catholic churches. If you wanted to buy anything, you had to go "downtown," a two-block stretch of mom-and-pop businesses adjacent to the train station. Downtown had a bike shop, a pet shop, a travel agency, and a half-dozen clothing stores. All of these places had thrived during the fifties and sixties, but by 1987 they were slowly and stubbornly going out of business, squeezed by competition from all the new shopping malls. Most days I was free to race my bike along the sidewalks, because there were never any shoppers blocking my way.

Zelinsky's Typewriters and Office Supplies was the only store in town that sold *Playboy*. It sat opposite the train station on Market Street, a two-story brick building with antique typewriters in the windows. The awning over the door advertised "Manual * Electric * Ribbons * Repair," but most of Zelinsky's business came from the newsstand just inside the front door. He sold cigarettes and newspapers and hot coffee to commuters rushing for their morning trains.

We left our bikes in a heap on the sidewalk, and Clark went inside to confirm Alf's story. He emerged moments later, face flushed, looking dazed.

"Did you see it?" I asked. "Are you okay?"

Clark nodded. "It's on a rack behind the register. Just like he said."

"And her butt's on the cover," Alf added.

"And her butt's on the cover," Clark admitted.

We squeezed onto a bench to discuss strategy. It was three thirty in the afternoon and it felt good to be outside; it was the warmest day of the year so far, and summer was just around the corner.

"I've got it all figured out," Alf said. He glanced around to make sure the coast was clear. "We'll hire someone to buy it."

"Hire someone?" I asked.

"The magazine costs four dollars, and we need three copies. So that's twelve bucks total. But we'll pay someone *twenty* bucks to buy them. We get the *Playboys*, they keep eight dollars in profit. Just for buying magazines!"

Alf spoke like this was a magnificent revelation, like he'd hatched a plan to steal gold from Fort Knox. But when Clark and I looked around Main Street, all we saw were moms pushing baby strollers and some old people waiting for the bus.

"None of these people will help us," I said.

"None of *these* people," Alf corrected, putting the emphasis in its proper place. "We just need to be patient until the right person comes along. Operation Vanna is all about patience."

Alf was the mastermind of all our greatest capers, like Operation Big Gulp (in which we shoplifted music cassettes using sixty-four-ounce soda cups from the 7-Eleven) and Operation Royal Dump (in which we destroyed a school toilet using M-80 fireworks). He got a thrill from breaking rules and challenging authority, and when he set his mind on a goal, he would pursue it for weeks with dogged determination. It was only a matter of time, my mother warned, before Alf was imprisoned or dead.

We sat huddled on the bench, watching the cars drift along Market Street, scrutinizing every pedestrian. We all agreed that we needed a man—but that was the problem, there were no men walking around Wetbridge at three thirty in the afternoon. All the men were busy at work. And every time a guy did come along, we'd invent a reason to disqualify him:

"He looks too young."

"He looks too old."

"He looks too mean."

"He looks like an undercover priest."

This was Alf again—his family was Catholic and he was always warning us about undercover priests, holy men who dressed in plain clothes and patrolled Wetbridge looking for troublemakers. Clark and I told him this was bullshit; there was no mention of "undercover priests" in the dictionary or the encyclopedia or any book in the library. Alf insisted this secrecy was deliberate; he claimed that undercover priests lived in the shadows, completely anonymous, by strict order of the Vatican.

We sat on the bench for well over an hour, and Clark started getting impatient. "This is hopeless," he said. "Let's go to Video City. We can rent *Kramer vs. Kramer*."

"Not again," Alf said.

"It beats sitting here all night," Clark said.

Video City checked for ID and refused to rent R-rated films to anyone under the age of seventeen. But Clark researched their inventory and discovered a number of PG movies with shocking amounts of female nudity: *Barry Lyndon*, *Barbarella*, *Swamp Thing*. The best of these was *Kramer vs. Kramer*, the 1979 Oscar winner for Best Picture, starring Dustin Hoffman and Meryl Streep. The story—something about two grown-ups getting divorced—was insanely boring, and we always fast-forwarded to the forty-four-minute mark, when Dustin Hoffman's hot one-night stand gets out of bed to use the bathroom. What follows are fifty-three seconds of jaw-dropping full-frontal nudity filmed from multiple angles. We had rented the movie a dozen times, but never watched more than a minute of it.

"I'm tired of *Kramer vs. Kramer*," Alf said.

"I'm tired of sitting on this bench," Clark said. "None of these people are going to help us. Operation Vanna isn't working."

"Traffic's picking up," I pointed out. "Let's give it a little more time."

In the late afternoon, the trains started arriving every fifteen minutes, discharging dozens of age-appropriate male passengers, most of them carrying overcoats and briefcases. They filed past Zelinsky's on their way out of the train station, and a few ducked inside the store for cigarettes or scratch-off tickets. But we watched them march past without saying a word. We couldn't bring ourselves to ask any of them for help. They looked way too respectable.

"Maybe we *should* call it quits," I suggested.

"Thank you," Clark said.

But Alf was already pointing across the street to the train station. "There," he said. "*That guy.*"

Emerging from a crowd of suits and ties came a young man dressed in denim cutoffs, a red flannel shirt, and Ray-Ban sunglasses. I felt like I'd seen him before, maybe hanging around the parking lot of Wetbridge Liquors. He had hair like Billy Idol, bleached white and spiky, sticking straight up.

"He looks . . . fishy," I said.

"Fishy is good," Clark said. "We *want* fishy."

"Excuse me, sir!" Alf called.

The guy didn't miss a beat. He veered toward us like fourteen-year-old boys flagged him down all the time. The mirrored shades made it impossible to read his expression, but at least he was smiling.

"What's up, fellas?"

Alf held out the twenty bucks. "Can you buy us some *Playboys*?"

His smile widened. "Vanna White!" he said knowingly. "I heard about these pictures!"

"Three copies is twelve dollars," Alf explained. "You could keep the change."

"Shit, man, you don't have to pay me. I'll do it for nothing!"

We stared at him in disbelief.

"Seriously?" Alf asked.

"Sure, I grew up around here. My name's Jack Camaro, like the car." He shook hands with all of us, like we were old friends. "I'm glad I can help. You guys need anything else? *Penthouse*? Cigarettes? Maybe some Bartles and Jaymes?"

Alfred counted twelve dollars into his palm. "Just three *Playboys*."

"We really appreciate it," I told him. "Thank you."

"Three *Playboys*," Jack Camaro repeated. "No problem. You guys sit tight."

He stepped inside Zelinsky's, and the three of us stared after him, slack-jawed. It was like we'd summoned a magical genie to obey our every whim and command. A moment later Jack Camaro exited the store and returned to us, still clutching the twelve dollars.

"I just had a crazy idea," he said. "Are you guys sure three copies is enough?"

"Three is plenty," I said.

"One for each of us," Alf said.

"Just hear me out," Jack Camaro said. "I bet your school is full of horndogs who want to see these pictures. If you bought a couple extra magazines, you could charge whatever you wanted."

We all realized the brilliance of his proposal and everyone started talking at once. Most of our male classmates would happily spend ten or fifteen or even twenty dollars to own the Vanna White photos for themselves. Jack Camaro suggested that we allocate "rental copies" for everyone else; we could loan them out for one or two dollars a night, just like the movies at Video City.

"You're a genius!" Clark exclaimed.

Jack Camaro shrugged. "I'm an entrepreneur. I look for opportunities. This is what we call supply and demand."

We dug deep in our pockets and pooled the rest of our money—another twenty-eight dollars. Jack Camaro would buy ten copies for a total of forty bucks, but we insisted that he keep one of the magazines as a service fee.

"That's too generous," he said.

"It's the least we can do," Alf insisted.

He took our money into the store and we returned to our bench. Suddenly our futures seemed alive with hope and possibilities. With Jack Camaro's help, we could *all* be entrepreneurs.

"And make a fortune!" Alf exclaimed.

"Take it easy," Clark told him. "Let's not get carried away." He urged us to be sensible and invest our profits into more magazines—not just *Playboy* but *Penthouse*, *Hustler*, *Gallery*, and *Oui*. "I'm talking hundreds of copies. If we have enough inventory, there's no limit to this thing!"

Alf announced his plans to buy a Ford Mustang; Clark said he would pay for surgery to remove the Claw; and I would help my mother with bills so she wouldn't worry all the time.

These dreams lasted all of six or seven minutes.

"Sure is taking a while," Clark finally said.

"It's rush hour," Alf reasoned. "The store gets crowded."

But we'd been watching the door the whole time, and no other customers had entered or left the building.

"Maybe he's an undercover priest," I suggested. "Maybe he and Zelinsky are calling the Vatican."

Alf turned to me, angry. "That really happens, Billy! You don't hear about it because undercover priests don't want the publicity, but it happens!"

"Take it easy," Clark said softly.

We counted to a hundred Mississippis before sending Clark into the store to investigate. He promised he wouldn't say or do anything to upset the plan. He would simply locate Jack Camaro and report back. He disappeared through the door. Alf and I remained frozen in place. The second hand on my Swatch ticked off a full minute, then another, then another. We didn't move. We just watched the door, waiting for Clark to return.

"Something's wrong," Alf said.

"Something's definitely wrong," Clark said.

Suddenly he was standing behind us, like Doug Henning or David Copperfield escaping from a locked box.

Alf whirled around. "What the hell? How did you—"

"There's a rear entrance, dummy. You can park behind the store."

"So where's Jack Camaro?" I asked.

My question hung in the air as the truth settled in. Jack Camaro was long gone and forty dollars richer. Our dreams of entrepreneurship and financial prosperity went spiraling down the toilet. Between the three of us, we had just $1.52 left over, barely enough to rent a movie.

"*Kramer vs. Kramer*?" Clark asked.

We trudged off to Video City.

3

```
300 REM *** TRANSFER CHARACTER SET ***
310 PRINT "SETTING UP THE GAME..."
320 PRINT "PLEASE WAIT..."
330 POKE 56334,0
340 POKE 1,51
350 FOR ADDRESS=2048 TO 6143
360 POKE ADDRESS,PEEK(ADDRESS+51200)
370 NEXT ADDRESS
380 POKE 1,55:POKE 56334,125
390 RETURN
]■
```

BEFORE I GO ANY further, I need to stop and tell you about *Strip Poker with Christie Brinkley*. This was a video game we played on my Commodore 64 computer, a simulation that pitted human against supermodel in five-card stud. The machine acted as Christie Brinkley, the most beautiful woman in the world before Vanna White came along, and she stood center screen throughout the game. Every time she lost a hand, her blouse or skirt or bra would disappear; the goal was to win her clothes before she won yours. The most remarkable thing about *Strip Poker with Christie Brinkley* was that you couldn't buy it in any store. My friends and I were the only people who'd ever played it. I created the game myself by typing many hundreds of lines of BASIC code into the computer.

Alf loved to mock the game's simplicity. I'd illustrated Christie Brinkley using ASCII characters—a mix of punctuation and mathematical symbols—so she wasn't much more than a stick figure:

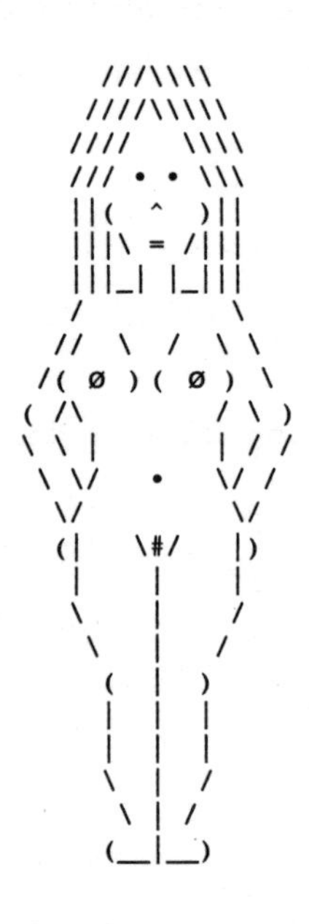

I knew I hadn't illustrated the Mona Lisa, but I was proud of the game anyway. I'd spent weeks trying to teach the computer the difference between two pair, three of a kind, and a royal flush. I even found a way to make random cards "wild." Alf didn't appreciate any of this. He just complained that Computer Christie didn't have any pubic hair; she didn't even have wrists.

"Plus her legs aren't long enough," Alf complained. "She's not contortionated."

"You mean proportional?" I asked.

"Exactly. It's terrible!"

I tried not to take Alf's criticisms personally. I reminded myself that he had no idea what went into making a computer game—none of my classmates did. Our high school had a lab full of new TRS-80 computers, but this was 1987 and none of our teachers knew what to do with them. They used the machines to teach typing skills and drill vocabulary words.

Most kids still didn't have computers at home. I was one of the lucky ones. My mother won the Commodore 64 through a contest at the Wetbridge Savings and Loan. When she first brought it home, I thought it just a fancy game machine—a turbocharged Atari 2600. But after plugging everything together and reading the owner's manual, I was astonished to learn that the Commodore 64 allowed you to *create* your own games—space adventures, fantasy battles, race cars, anything you wanted. And just like that, I was hooked.

While my teachers droned on about algebraic equations and the American Revolution, I sat in the back of the classroom, sneaking looks at the *Commodore Programmer's Reference Guide* and sketching 8-bit images on graph paper. I subscribed to hobbyist magazines filled with pages of dense BASIC code (FOR X=1020 TO 1933 STEP 3) that readers could type directly into their machines. I often stayed awake inputting programs until one or two in the morning. It was slow, tedious work, but every program taught me something new, and I'd sometimes copy patches of code into my own games. Alf and Clark were the only people who ever played my creations, and *Strip Poker with Christie Brinkley* was my most ambitious game to date—custom-designed to win their approval.

"Her nipples are zeros!" Alf complained. "That's the worst part. Who wants to play strip poker with a zero-nippled Christie Brinkley? Can't you round them off a little?"

This was a few days after the Jack Camaro incident, and we were gathered around the computer in my bedroom, guzzling RC Cola and bored out of our minds.

"I could switch them to asterisks," I suggested, but Alf and Clark agreed that asterisks looked even worse.

"Forget it, Billy," Alf said. "Let's just play something else."

He ejected the floppy from the disk drive. I tried to grab it before he could see the label, but I wasn't fast enough. This is what it said:

STRIP POKER WITH CHRISTIE BRINKLEY
A GAME BY WILLIAM MARVIN
COPYRIGHT © 1987 PLANET WILL SOFTWARE

Alf read the label and snorted.

"*William* Marvin?" he asked.

I blushed. "That's my name."

"What, like William Shakespeare?"

Clark leaned over to see. "What's Planet Will Software?"

"My company," I said.

Alf laughed even harder. "Your *company*?"

It was one of those ideas that doesn't sound stupid until someone says it out loud.

"Never mind," I said.

But Alf was just getting warmed up. He gestured around my tiny bedroom, pointing at my wall posters of Spuds MacKenzie and bikini supermodels. "Is this your corporate headquarters? Can I be CEO?"

"It's just a goof," I told him. "I wrote it on the label to be funny."

Alf didn't seem convinced, so I grabbed the closest distraction at hand—the 1987 *Sports Illustrated* Swimsuit Edition—and flung it into his lap. "Check out page ninety-eight. Kathy Ireland's swinging from a jungle vine, like Tarzan."

The ruse worked—Alf opened the magazine and stopped teasing me—and I was relieved. Even though he and Clark were my best friends, I hadn't told them about my secret plan to grow up and make video games for a living. I wanted to be the next Mark Cerny, the whiz kid game designer hired by Atari when he was just seventeen years old. I wanted to partner with visionaries like Fletcher Mulligan, the legendary founder of Digital Artists, and I wanted to have my own software company. These all seemed like crazy things to say out loud—like announcing you were going to be an astronaut or president of the United States. When adults asked me what I wanted to do with my life, I just shrugged and mumbled, "I don't know."

Alf stuck his nose in the magazine, trying to inhale the scent of Kathy Ireland, but Clark was still pinching the floppy disk in his claw, as if he'd been seized by a remarkable idea.

"Planet Will *is* a real business," he said.

"It's just a joke," I insisted.

"But it could be real," he explained. "There are real teenagers who make video games and sell them. They run real businesses out of their garages. And they buy their office supplies at stores like Zelinsky's."

Clark opened my closet and started removing clothes that I hadn't worn in years—the sports coat from my sixth-grade graduation, the slacks I wore to church on Christmas and Easter, scuffed black shoes that couldn't possibly fit me anymore.

"Put these on," he told me.

"What are you talking about?" I asked.

"Operation Vanna, take two," he said. "I've got a better idea, and this one is going to work."

4

```
400 REM *** PLAY THEME MUSIC ***
410 L1=54272:POKE L1+18,128
420 POKE L1,75:POKE L1+5,0
430 POKE L1+6,240:POKE L1+14,12
440 POKE L1+15,250:POKE L1+24,207
450 FOR L=0 TO 25:POKE L1+4,17
460 POKE L1+1,PEEK(L1+27)
470 FOR T=0 TO 100:NEXT T
480 NEXT L:POKE L1+4,0
490 RETURN
]■
```

EVERYONE KNEW YOU HAD to be eighteen years old to legally purchase *Playboy*, but we never stopped to wonder if the law was state, federal, or local, or which government was responsible for enforcing it.

Clark insisted that we dress up. He said that a proper coat and tie would age anyone's appearance by eighteen months.

"But that only gets me to fifteen," I said. "Fourteen plus eighteen months is fifteen, maybe sixteen."

"You'll be close enough," Clark promised. "We'll have so many other distractions, Zelinsky won't think twice."

My shirt was too small and my shoes pinched my feet; every step hurt and I wobbled like a woman in high heels. Clark had the opposite problem; he wore a teal polyester suit that was two sizes too large. Ever since his father went out of work, Clark survived on hand-me-downs shipped from weird relatives in Georgia. These items arrived once a year in black plastic trash bags, reeking of mothballs and adorned with mysterious brands we'd never heard of: U-Men, Bootstrap, Kentucky Swagger.

Alf was the only kid on our street who always dressed in new clothes. Both of his parents worked—his father hung wallpaper and his mother was a secretary in a Realtor's office—so they were rolling in dough. For our trip to Zelinsky's, Alf dressed up-to-the-minute in the latest *Miami Vice*–inspired fashion—white linen pants, a mauve jacket, and a blue T-shirt, no belt or socks. We were supposed to be businessmen coming off the train after a long day in Manhattan, but Alf looked like he was ready to seize cocaine from a Colombian drug lord.

"This is all about confidence," Alf assured me.

"Exactly," Clark said. "If you act like you're old enough, Zelinsky is going to think you're old enough."

It was easy for them to say. Even though Clark hatched the plan and Alf was the oldest of our group, they agreed that I *looked* the oldest and had the best chance of purchasing the magazine. We arrived at Zelinsky's at four in the afternoon, long after school let out but before the evening rush hour. An empty store was vital to our mission. I knew that if I found myself in a long line of customers, I'd probably lose my nerve.

"Are you ready?" Clark asked.

"Give me the money," I said.

Alf pushed a wad of wrinkled bills into my hand. He had pilfered the cash from the dresser drawer of his oldest sister, Janice, who spent all of her free time babysitting. "This is thirty-seven bucks," he said. "Make sure we don't go over."

A tiny bell dinged when I pulled open the door. Zelinsky's had existed in some form or another since World War II, so entering the store was like stepping into the past; the air was heavy with the smells of pipe tobacco, fresh cedar, and ink. The first thing you noticed was the enormous wall rack of newspapers and magazines—everything from the *Wall Street Journal* to *Good Housekeeping*. The second thing you noticed were all the signs around the display, handwritten in an angry Sharpie marker scrawl:

NO ONE UNDER 18 ALLOWED DURING SCHOOL HOURS!
ATTENTION STUDENTS: This is NOT Your LOCAL LIBRARY!!
We DON'T SELL COMICS so please STOP ASKING!!!

Sal Zelinsky stood behind the checkout counter, fifty years old with ruddy skin and the high-and-tight crew cut of a U.S. marine. He wore a shirt and tie under a filthy ink-smeared apron. He was skewering a long screwdriver through the back of an IBM Selectric; scattered all around him were greasy knobs and levers and keys. It looked like he'd slaughtered the typewriter and ripped out its guts.

At the sound of our arrival, Zelinsky adjusted his bifocals with blackened fingertips, studied our faces, and frowned. There was a swollen artery on his forehead, zigzagging from his hairline to his right eyebrow, throbbing like he'd just finished an arm-wrestling contest. He couldn't have looked more pissed off.

"Help you?" he asked.

"We just need a few things," I said, then forced myself to spit out the rest, because Clark insisted these words were crucial: ". . . for our office."

"Your office." Zelinsky said it the way another person might say "Your pirate ship" or "Your space shuttle." Just over his shoulder, behind the cash register, I saw Vanna White on a rack of magazines labeled ADULTS ONLY, and sure enough, her butt was on the cover. My heart did a little flip.

"Just some odds and ends," I said, but the words came out all mumbled.

Zelinsky turned the Selectric facedown and speared a second screwdriver into its bottom. "This isn't a toy store," he said. "You get what you need and you leave."

"Right," I said.

"No problem," Clark said.

"Understood," Alf said.

We were barely through the front door and already I wanted to turn back. But Alf and Clark were grabbing wire baskets and moving ahead with the plan. I grabbed a basket of my own and followed them.

I'd shopped at Zelinsky's dozens of times but never ventured past the magazine rack. Behind the checkout counter, the store divided into three long aisles filled with office supplies: calendars and stationery, staples and staple removers, markers and mailers, and a million other doodads. We spread out and went to work.

Clark's plan was to fill our baskets with many large but inexpensive items. I grabbed a three-ring binder, a pack of A13 batteries, and a massive tub of Elmer's Glue. If it cost less than a buck or two, I put it in the basket. There were no other customers. The store was silent except for the radio; Phil Collins was repeating the fade-out chorus of "Invisible Touch." But as soon as the song ended, it inexplicably started from the beginning all over again.

At the back of the store was a large showroom designed to look like a working office, complete with desks and swivel chairs, typewriters and wall clocks and file cabinets. Everything had a price tag; the whole showroom was available for purchase.

A fat girl sat at one of the desks, typing on a Commodore 64 computer.

The monitor was full of code and I was too far away to read it, but I could hear the results streaming from the speakers: a tinny, synthesized version of "Invisible Touch," the same song playing on the radio. The melody wasn't quite right—there were a few wrong notes—but as a copy, it was pretty damn close.

The girl looked up. "Can I help you?"

I grabbed the closest item on a shelf—it looked like a white paper hockey puck—and dropped it in my basket.

"No, thanks."

I turned down the next aisle but felt her eyes tailing me; none of the shelves were taller than my shoulders, and her desk in the showroom allowed her to observe the entire store. I grabbed some #2 pencils and then topped off my basket with old, bulky typewriter ribbons that were marked down to fifty cents apiece. Alf was in the next aisle over, scooping Styrofoam peanuts into a plastic bag. Clark walked past him with a dozen mailers wedged beneath his arms. They'd already gathered more stuff than we could carry.

I knelt down to grab a handful of erasers, and suddenly the fat girl was right beside me, straightening a display of Post-it Notes. She spoke in a low whisper: "My dad will call the cops."

"What?"

"He has zero tolerance for shoplifting."

She pointed to a sign on the wall:

We have ZERO TOLERANCE for SHOPLIFTING!

We WILL call the COPS!

"Thieves will not enter the kingdom of God." —First Corinthians, 6:9,10

"I'm not stealing anything," I said, but I started blushing anyway, because we were clearly guilty of *something*.

She reached into my basket for the batteries. "These are for hearing aids. And this"—she grabbed the paper hockey puck—"this is receipt tape for an adding machine. Nothing you're buying goes together."

She was leaning over to whisper, and I could smell her perfume, fresh and clean, like soap in the shower. Long black hair fell past her shoulders. She wore an oversize Genesis concert T-shirt, and her wrists were covered with purple jelly bracelets. A small gold cross hung from the chain around her neck.

"Is that your 64?" I asked.

"It's the store's. Technically it's for sale, but my dad lets me use it."

"I've got one at home."

She seemed skeptical. "Disk drive or tape storage?"

"Disk," I said, allowing a touch of superiority to creep into my voice. Programmers on a budget could store their data on cassette tapes, but the process was slow and unreliable. I gestured to the stereo speakers in the ceiling—*She seems to have an invisible touch, yeah*—and asked, "Was this song playing on your computer?"

"Yeah, I'm messing with the waveform generator. The SID chip has three sound channels, but to do the song properly, you need four. That's why you didn't hear any drums."

I would have been less astonished if she'd answered me in Japanese. "You programmed your 64 to play 'Invisible Touch'?"

"My 'Sussudio' is way better. I'm coding all of his greatest hits on the 64, one track at a time. So I can listen to them on my computer."

"Are you a musician?"

"Nah, I just really like Phil Collins. British bands are the best, you know?"

I did not know. Most people in our neighborhood viewed the words *Made in America* like a badge of honor. "What about Van Halen?" I asked. "Could you do Van Halen?"

She shrugged. "Maybe? Guitars are tough."

It was my first time meeting another programmer, and I had a lot more questions: Was she working in BASIC or Pascal or something else? Was each song its own standalone program? How long did it take to load a song into memory? But across the store, Alf was already glaring at me. This wasn't part of the plan. We were supposed to move swiftly and purposefully. Operation Vanna was going off the rails.

"Do you go to Wetbridge High?" I asked.

"St. Agatha's," she said. "My father's raising me to be a nun."

"Do they teach you how to use waveforms?"

She laughed. "If you want to see something hilarious, you should come to my school and watch nuns teaching computer science. We spent all winter learning how to draw a cross. No functions, no calculations, no animation. Just graphics inspired by the holy gospels."

"At least you're programming," I told her. "My school put a typing teacher in charge of the computer lab. I've seen her use a floppy disk sideways."

"That's impossible."

"Not if you push hard enough."

She laughed. "Are you kidding?"

"Swear to God," I insisted. "She broke the disk *and* the drive."

Alf and Clark moved behind the girl, invading my sight line. They were pantomiming furiously, waving their shopping baskets and pointing toward the cash register.

"What about you?" she asked. "Do you program?"

I thought of *Strip Poker with Christie Brinkley*. "I made a poker game last month. Five-card stud. Human versus computer."

"You taught your 64 to play cards?"

"It's not very good. It only wins maybe half the time. But I did teach it how to bluff."

Now she looked impressed. "That must have taken forever!"

And it felt so good, hearing somebody say that. Because it *had* taken forever! I'd spent all winter on the game, painstakingly teaching the 64 to recognize the difference between a straight, a flush, and a straight flush—only to have Alf mock the game because digital Christie Brinkley didn't have enough pubic hair.

"You're the first person I've met with a 64," I told her. "And you're a girl."

"Is that strange?"

"I didn't think girls liked to program."

"Girls practically *invented* programming," she said. "Jean Bartik, Marlyn Wescoff, Fran Bilas—they all programmed ENIAC."

I had no idea what she was talking about.

"And don't forget Margaret Hamilton. She wrote the software that let Apollo 11 land on the moon."

"I meant programming video games," I said.

"Dona Bailey, *Centipede*. Brenda Romero, *Wizardry*. Roberta Williams, *King's Quest*. She designed her first computer game at the kitchen table. I interviewed her for school last year."

"For real? You talked to Roberta Williams?"

"Yeah, I called her long-distance in California. She talked to me for twenty minutes."

King's Quest was a landmark computer game, an undisputed masterpiece, and now I had even more questions. But Alf was clearing his throat so loudly, it sounded like he was choking. "Look, I gotta go," I told her. "My friends are in a hurry. But we're going to pay for all this stuff, I promise."

She took another look at my shopping basket, well aware there was something wrong with my story. "Suit yourself," she said. "Have fun with your hearing aid batteries."

I followed Alf and Clark to the front of the store, and we unloaded our baskets on the checkout counter. Now that we were actually spending money, Zelinsky's mood brightened. He swept aside the greasy typewriter parts to make room for our purchases. "All right, gentlemen, do you want separate bills? Or shall I put it all together?"

"Together is fine," I said, flashing my thirty-seven dollars in wrinkled bills.

Zelinksy bagged the items as he punched prices into the cash register. It was a beautifully ornamented brass chest with mechanical buttons, big and clunky and nothing at all like the electronic models at Food World.

"Must be some business you guys are running," he said. "What kind of work is it?"

"Computer software," I explained. "We make our own games."

"Smart thinking," Zelinsky said, and he bagged my hearing aid batteries without blinking an eye. "You don't want to be in the typewriter business, I can tell you that. All the money's in word processing now. And laser printers. Have you ever seen a laser printer? They're like magic."

The subtotal on the cash register crept higher and higher—$23.57, $24.79, $28.61—and I worried one of us had overspent. But after everything was bagged, the total with tax came to an even thirty dollars—exactly where we hoped to be.

"Is there anything else?" Zelinsky asked.

This was the moment of truth—the moment I'd rehearsed with Alf and Clark again and again. They'd coached me to keep my pitch exactly the same—to speak the words like I used them all the time: "Just some Tic Tacs," I said, "and a *Playboy*."

"Hang on," the fat girl called, and she came running to the front of the store, waving a sheet of paper. "There's a contest at Rutgers this month. For high school programmers. Anyone under eighteen can enter."

I didn't move. None of us did.

"First prize is an IBM PS/2," she explained. "With a sixteen-bit processor and a full megabyte of RAM. You should enter your poker game."

I couldn't look at the girl, and I couldn't look at Zelinsky, so instead I looked at the paper. She had found the rules on a CompuServe forum and spooled them through a dot matrix printer; the skinny perforated "tractor feed" strips were still clinging to the sides of the page.

"The judge is Fletcher Mulligan from Digital Arts," she continued. "He's coming all the way from California to judge the contest."

"Seriously?" I asked. For a moment, I forgot all about the magazine. "Fletcher Mulligan is going to be there?"

Fletcher Mulligan was a god among computer programmers. My classmates worshipped athletes like Cal Ripkin and Michael Jordan, but my teen idol was the founder of Digital Artists and the best game designer in the world. I'd often daydreamed about going to California to meet him, but never imagined that he'd come to our weird little corner of New Jersey.

Zelinsky cleared his throat, and the girl seemed to understand that she had wandered into something awkward.

"What's the matter?" she asked.

"Nothing's the matter," Zelinsky said. "I was asking these *businessmen* if they needed anything else."

The artery in his forehead was still throbbing like crazy. His tone made it clear that requesting a *Playboy* in the presence of his teenage daughter was a terrible idea, on par with unzipping our pants and exposing ourselves. Alf and Clark were taking little steps toward the door, ready to bolt. Zelinsky glared at them, and they froze like baby rabbits. "So answer my question," he said. "Is there anything else?"

"Nope," Alf said.

"Not me," Clark said.

"Just the Tic Tacs," I said.

Zelinsky flung a box of orange mints into the bag, took my money, and counted out the change.

"Well, the deadline's in two weeks, if you're interested," the girl continued. "These PS/2s look incredible. They have twenty-megabyte hard disks. Twenty megabytes!"

"I'll think about it," I said.

Zelinsky shoved the bag into my chest. "Go think someplace else."

As soon as we hit the sidewalk, the guys ripped into me.

"Why the hell did you pay him?" Alf asked. "We went over this, Billy. You were supposed to run! If he freaked out, you were supposed to ditch the crap and run!"

"I didn't see you running," I pointed out.

"I couldn't move!" Alf said. "I was paralyzed by your stupidity!"

I pulled off my tie and stuffed it into my pants pocket. Then I wriggled out of my sports coat and slung it over my shoulder. Outside the bike shop stood a pair of teenage girls, both dressed in tank tops and cutoff denim shorts. They tracked Clark with their eyes as we walked past, then exploded into giggles. He was too upset to notice.

"We were supposed to bring home Vanna White," Clark said. "Instead we've got thirty dollars of pipe cleaners and thumbtacks. What are we gonna do with all this crap?"

We all agreed that the only appropriate course of action was an Amtrak Sacrifice. We walked over to the train station, followed the platform to its western end, then hopped a fence and continued hiking alongside the tracks. After a half mile or so, we reached a patch of woods where no one was likely to bother us, and then dumped our entire shopping spree onto the tracks. Since we had no use for typewriter ribbons or adding machine tape, we could at least take some small pleasure in watching everything get destroyed by a two-hundred-ton locomotive. We positioned the biggest items directly on the rails, using smears of Elmer's Glue to hold them in place.

"You should have stuck with the plan," Alf said. "'Get in and get out.' That's what we agreed. But instead you start chatting up Two-Ton Tessie."

"She thought we were robbing the place," I explained. "She saw right through the whole plan."

Alf emptied a sack of Styrofoam peanuts between the rails, then shaped them into a neat pile. "That girl was hot for you, man."

"No, she wasn't."

" 'Oh, Billy, you should enter this contest!' " He mimicked her voice in a high falsetto, then placed his hands on his hips and wiggled his bottom. " 'And when we're done, you can take off my clothes and make little piggy babies with me!' "

"She never said that."

"It's what she *meant*," Clark said. He was kneeling beside the tracks, Scotch-taping the hearing aid batteries to the top of a rail. The sun was low in the sky; it was almost dinnertime. I was tired of their teasing and ready to go home.

"We were talking about computers," I insisted. "She's using the SID chip on the 64 to make pop songs."

"She's in love with you, man," Clark said.

Alf nodded. "All three hundred pounds of her."

"She's not three hundred pounds."

"Are you kidding?" Alf asked. "She's so fat, she shows up on radar."

"For real," Clark said. "She's so fat, her blood type is Ragu!"

They were on a roll now, volleying zingers back and forth.

"She's so fat, the zoo goes to visit her!"

"She's so fat, her scale says 'to be continued'!"

"She's so fat, her clothes have stretch marks!"

"She's so fat . . ."

They might have continued like this forever if the 5:35 Amtrak to Philadelphia hadn't materialized out of nowhere, blasting its air horn and streaking past at 125 miles an hour. Its sudden arrival knocked all three of us to the ground. I huddled in the gravel with my hands over my head, afraid to open my eyes, afraid I'd see the great grinding wheels inches from my nose. The train was so loud, I felt certain it was running over part of me, and I braced myself for a pain that never came.

My ears kept ringing long after the train was gone. Eventually the earth stopped shaking and I dared to open my eyes. All around us, the woods were calm. Clark was sitting up and picking gravel from his hair.

Alf spat out some dirt and debris, then finished his earlier statement: “She’s so fat, the horse on her polo shirt is real.”

We rose to examine the wreckage. The items we glued to the tracks were gone, scattered, pulverized into nonexistence. All that remained were a handful of Styrofoam peanuts.

And the rules of the Game of the Year Contest for High School Computer Programmers, which I’d safely stored in the back pocket of my pants.

5

```
500 REM *** INTRODUCE VARIABLES ***
510 SCORE=0:LEVEL=1
520 LIVES=3:TIMER=300
530 HX=24:HY=50:AA=1:BB=256
540 W1=54276:W2=54283
550 W3=54290:H1=54273
560 H2=54280:H3=54287
570 L2=54279:L3=54286
580 V=53248
590 RETURN
]■
```

I WENT HOME THAT afternoon, hurried into my bedroom, and started flipping through my collection of floppy disks, looking for a game that would be worthy of Fletcher Mulligan's attention. *Strip Poker with Christie Brinkley* was out of the question. Fletcher wouldn't be impressed by a simple poker simulation. I needed something bigger, more ambitious—something that would really dazzle him.

His company, Digital Artists, was famous for building massive, fully realized worlds within 64 kilobytes of RAM. Every game took players to new and surprising destinations: Egyptian pyramids, alien planets, pirate ships, and gothic mansions, all rendered in beautiful, blocky 8-bit graphics. Fletcher never made the same game twice, and he never copied popular hits. Anytime you saw the Digital Artists logo on a package, you knew you were buying something completely original.

Unfortunately, most of *my* homemade games were rip-offs of arcade classics. I gave them names like *Gobbleface* (a *Pac Man* rip-off), *Toadally Awesome!* (a *Frogger* rip-off), and *Monkey Kong* (you get the idea). I learned a lot by making these games, but I wouldn't dare submit them to the contest.

I also had a dozen half-finished programs that never went anywhere. I once started a game called *Mission Zero* because I liked the name "Mission Zero," but I never got past creating the title screen. I started an adaptation of the Stephen King novel *Cujo*, in which you played a Saint Bernard and tried to bite as many people as possible—but stopped when Clark warned that Stephen King would probably sue me.

The best of these half-finished efforts was a game called *The Impossible Fortress*. I got the idea after seeing a drawing by a guy named M. C. Escher. He'd created this crazy castle full of hallways and staircases that doubled back on themselves. My idea was to set a jumping-and-climbing game in an Escher-like setting. Players had three hundred seconds to climb a mountain and enter a giant fortress with a princess hidden in its center. There were guards and guard dogs swarming all over the place; if they collided with the player, or if the time ran out, then the hero was imprisoned in the fortress for all of eternity. To win the game, you had to free the princess and then follow her out of the castle to safety.

I'd used a sprite with six different frames to animate my hero. The graphics weren't terribly detailed, but he bent his knees and elbows when he ran, and the animation looked fairly realistic:

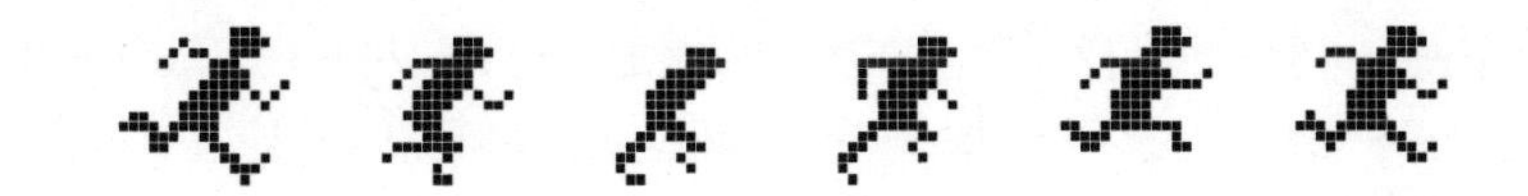

There was just one problem: All the fancy graphics and animation were overtaxing the 64, so the game was painfully slow. The hero lumbered across the screen and the guards trudged after him, like they were slogging through mud. Playing the game was like listening to a 45 record at 33 RPM—you could make out the basic idea, but after a minute or so it would drive you crazy.

I knew that if I could speed up the action, I'd have a pretty decent game. But when I flipped the power switch on my 64, nothing happened. I got down on my knees and studied the tangle of wires underneath my desk. The computer wasn't plugged into the wall. In fact, the entire power supply box was missing. This could only mean one thing.

I found my mother in the kitchen, making me a grilled cheese sandwich for dinner. She was already dressed in her white Food World uniform; her shift started in twenty minutes, but for some strange reason she wasn't rushing to get out the door.

"Have you seen my power box?"

She didn't answer. She just pressed the sandwich into the pan with a metal spatula.

"It looks like a black brick," I explained. "With wires coming out of it."

I studied her more closely and realized she was upset. It looked like she was channeling her anger into the sandwich; she was leaning so hard on the spatula, I thought the handle might snap.

"I saw it in your bedroom," she finally said. "Under your computer desk."

"It's not there anymore."

"You're damned right it's not."

She flipped the grilled cheese onto a plate and then dropped it on the table. I realized my report card was waiting there with the rest of the day's mail. This is what it looked like:

NAME: WILLIAM MARVIN GRADE: 9 DOB: APRIL 27, 1973

COURSE DESCRIPTION	QUARTER				FINAL GRADE
	1	2	3	4	
CONCEPTS OF MATH	C	D	D		
READING FUNDAMENTALS	C	C	C-		
INTRO TO HISTORY	C	D	D		
PHYSICAL EDUCATION	C	C	D		
ROCKS AND STREAMS	C-	D	F		
WOODWORKING	B-	C	D		

3RD QUARTER GRADE POINT AVERAGE:
0.83

"I can explain," I said.

"Go ahead," she said. "Tell me how you get a D in gym. Tell me how you *fail* a class called Rocks and Streams."

"I'm sorry," I said.

"Don't apologize to me. You're not hurting *me*. Three months ago we sat at this table and you promised me you would do better. But look at these marks. You've gone from Ds to Fs. You're failing Rocks and Streams!"

At the start of my freshman year, my mother dragged me into the principal's office to protest my new class schedule. She explained I had no place in a class called Reading FUNdamentals. "Billy knows how to read," she said. "He belongs in Honors English, not a bunch of dummy classes."

Mr. Hibble, the principal, smiled and nodded with the patience of a man who had heard it all a thousand times before. When my mother finally finished, he directed her attention to my eighth-grade transcripts (all Cs and Ds) and my state assessment tests ("lowest 25th percentile"). He suggested that a little remedial work would raise my academic performance, and offered to make a deal: "When we get to the end of the first quarter, we'll look at Billy's grades. If he earns a B+ or better in any of these classes, we'll bump him up to the general level equivalent. And if he succeeds there, we'll bump him up to Honors."

My mother shook his hand, satisfied that she'd solved the problem. She felt confident I would be taking Honors Everything by the middle of ninth grade. On the way home we stopped at Dairy Queen and Mom treated us to ice cream. I sat on the hood of our Honda, licking a soft-serve vanilla cone, while she paced back and forth in the parking lot, giving me an animated pep talk. "We'll show that Mr. Hibble, won't we? As soon as you get that report card, we're going to march right back into his office. And I can't wait to see the look on his face!"

The next day I returned to school determined to please her. I wanted to bring home a report card that would impress her, the sorts of grades that mothers post on refrigerators. I sharpened all my pencils and organized my Trapper Keeper notebook for maximum efficiency.

But every time I walked into a classroom, my willpower vanished. I'd try to focus on the teacher; I'd try to listen and take careful notes. But after five or ten minutes I'd be doodling, and eventually one of my doodles would morph into a sprite, an animated shape constructed of 504 bits in a 24-by-21 grid. Or I'd just scribble down a few lines of BASIC code, something to test on my computer when I got home from school. I'd mastered the art of hiding reading material underneath my notebook so I could study the *Commodore Programmer's Guide* while my classmates drilled the parts of speech or hunted for common denominators. As long as I sat in the back and kept quiet, my teachers were happy to ignore me ignoring them.

And now I was failing Rocks and Streams.

"These teachers think you're an idiot," Mom told me. "And all you're doing is proving them right."

"I'll do better," I promised.

"Yes, you will. And I'm keeping that power box until you do. You're playing too many games."

"I'm not playing games," I said. "I'm *making* games."

"Not anymore. Not until your grades improve."

I started to feel nervous. Normally she was too tired to argue with me, but that night she seemed unshakable.

"Look, Mom, I promise As and Bs, all right? But I really need my computer. Fletcher Mulligan is coming to New Jersey and he's the king of video games—"

"I said no more games! You're fourteen years old, Billy. You're not a little kid anymore." She checked the clock—now she was really late for work—then grabbed her car keys and hurried for the front door. "I am busting my butt to take care of you," she said. "I cook your food, I clean your clothes, I even give you an allowance. But you're not keeping your end of the deal."

She was right, I knew she was right, and I felt terrible. My mother was much younger than all the other moms at my school, only thirty-three years old. Her long brown hair was streaked with gray. All she ever did was work and take care of the house. She never went out for fun; she didn't really have friends. On her nights off, she watched *Dallas* and *Dynasty*, and gabbed on the phone with my aunt Gretchen, who was married to a big-shot Realtor in Manhattan and sent checks every month to keep us afloat.

"I'm sorry," I told her. "I'm going to do better."

She was so angry, she left the house without saying good-bye. I watched her car pull out of the driveway before going into her bedroom. Most of our house was pretty tidy, but she reserved the right to leave her room an absolute mess. The bed was unmade and there were dirty clothes all over the floor. An ironing board lay toppled on its side; it looked like a tornado had swept through the place.

I opened her closet and pulled on the light. I reached deep into the back, past shoes and sandals that she hadn't worn in a decade, and grabbed the handle of the fire safe. It was a heavy white chest with a four-digit combination lock. I set the tumblers to 1129; I had guessed the combination years ago, after learning that November 29 was my father's birthday. I'd never spoken to my dad; he left Wetbridge before I was born and supposedly moved to Alaska to drill oil wells. He didn't call or write or send money, and Mom rarely spoke of him, but that birthday combination never changed. This fact led me to wonder if maybe he'd reenter our lives someday. Maybe he'd show up on our doorstep with flowers and money and a plausible explanation for his fourteen-year absence. Because I felt certain he'd have a good explanation. I would be willing to listen.

But in the meantime, we were on our own.

I popped the latches on the fire safe and lifted the lid, and there was my power supply box, resting atop tax returns and bank statements. I carried it back to my bedroom, plugged in my C64, and went to work.

6

```
600 REM *** INSTRUCTIONS ***
610 PRINT "SAVE THE PRINCESS! SHE IS"
620 PRINT "IMPRISONED IN A DANGEROUS"
630 PRINT "FORTRESS. YOUR MISSION IS"
640 PRINT "TO AVOID THE GUARDS, ENTER"
650 PRINT "THE FORTRESS, AND FIND THE"
660 PRINT "PRINCESS BEFORE TIME RUNS OUT."
670 PRINT "HIT ANY KEY TO BEGIN."
680 GET A$:IF A$="" THEN 680
690 RETURN
]■
```

I SPENT THE NEXT few nights sneaking the power box out of my mother's fire safe and sneaking it back before bedtime. Yes, this was dishonest, and yes, I felt bad about lying. But I knew that winning the $4,000 IBM PS/2 was more important to my future than anything I'd learn about Rocks and Streams. If I was serious about Planet Will Software, I couldn't work on a Commodore 64 much longer. Newer computers offered more memory and better graphics, and C64s would be obsolete in another year or two. I needed to upgrade to the latest technology, and the contest was my best chance to do it.

To keep Alf and Clark from coming around my house, I said I was grounded for bad grades. They came around anyway, tapping on my screen door as soon as my mother left for work, suggesting we watch *MacGyver* or play Trivial Pursuit or crank-call the girls in our homeroom. I explained that Mom had the neighbors keeping an eye on me, that Mrs. Digby across the street was watching through her lace curtains, so I had to close the door.

I worked on the code all night, and spent my days editing printouts during class. None of my changes made a difference. *The Impossible Fortress* was still maddeningly slow. I tried everything. I crunched the code as tight as possible, rearranging my subroutines and deleting REMarks and eliminating spaces between commands. In a moment of desperation, I even vacuumed the crevices of my keyboard, on the off chance that dust was slowing the circuitry.

And I thought many times about going back to Zelinsky's and asking the girl for help. I knew anyone capable of programming Phil Collins on a SID chip would probably have great ideas for speeding up animation. She seemed funny and smart and cool, and I really needed some good advice. But I knew the flak from Alf and Clark would be ridiculous. All the little piggy baby jokes. All the she's-so-fat put-downs. They would never let me hear the end of it.

So I worked alone, staying up late every night, getting more and more frustrated. By Friday evening, I was ready to quit—and then I heard a familiar squeak of bike brakes outside my window. I peered out through the blinds and saw Alf and Clark riding into my driveway. They were dressed all in black, like girls in a Robert Palmer video, minus the bright red lipstick.

"What's with the costumes?" I asked.

"Operation Vanna," Alf said.

"Take three," Clark said. "We've got a new plan."

I realized they were still talking about the *Playboy* magazine, about the Vanna White photos. I'd been so wrapped up in my game, I'd forgotten about them.

"You guys are obsessed," I said.

Clark looked like I'd hurt his feelings. "You said you wanted to see them, too. You said she was the most beautiful woman in America."

"I know."

"You said she was a perfect ten!"

"I *know*."

"So why aren't you interested?"

I thought of Fletcher Mulligan, of the $4,000 IBM PS/2, of my hopelessly inept game that still needed hours of work. "Because I'm grounded, remember? My mom has Mrs. Digby watching me."

Clark peered across the street to Mrs. Digby's tiny two-bedroom bungalow. Her porch was empty; her windows, dark. "That old lady went to bed three hours ago. She'll never know you sneaked out."

"And you don't want to miss this," Alf promised me. "The sooner we get there, the sooner we start getting rich."

This set off plenty of warning bells. Over the years, I'd learned to be skeptical of Alf's get-rich-quick schemes. Like the time we spent a week pulling a wagon all over Wetbridge, collecting aluminum cans for resale, because Alf read that the scrap metal yard paid ten cents a can. We collected more than eight hundred cans before discovering that Alf didn't know how to read digits after a decimal point, that the actual rate was just .01, a penny a can.

"What's the idea?" I asked.

"It's simple," Alf said. "Do you know the story of Jesus and the fishes?"

I stared at him, thoroughly confused, trying to understand how a Bible story could relate to photos of Vanna White.

"It's like this," Alf continued. "Jesus goes to this party at Galilee, or wherever, and five thousand guys show up. And everyone's starving, it's the middle of a desert, but all they have is one fish. One scrawny little perch on a plate. But Jesus is like, 'Don't worry, guys, just pass it around, there's plenty for everyone.' And he's right, it's a miracle, they keep passing the plate and somehow there's enough for everyone. He feeds all five thousand people with one fish. That's the story. But now ask yourself something: What if Jesus *charged money* for the fish? What if he had a magic machine that turned one fish into five thousand fishes, and he charged two bucks a fish? That's what I'm talking about, Billy. The magic machine exists! It's real!"

I turned to Clark. "Translate to English?"

Clark gave me a sheet of paper, and I held it under the dim glow of the porch lamp. It was a photograph of Alf's face, smooshed behind a pane of glass. His eyes were closed, and a blinding white light illuminated the zits on his forehead. It looked like he'd copied his face on a Xerox machine—except the image was rich with color, like a picture in a glossy magazine. I'd never seen anything like it.

"How did you make this?" I asked.

"Color Xerox machine. My mother's office just got one. Copies anything you want in full color."

Suddenly I put it all together.

"You're going to copy the Vanna White pictures?"

"Bingo," Alf said.

He handed me an index card listing the prices:

UNCENSORED! VANNA WHITE! UNCENSORED!

1 photo - $2

3 photos - $5

All 10 photos - $10

Its America's Sweatheart

Like You've Never Before Seen Her

"ORDER TODAY"

"I hate to admit this," I told Alf, "but you're a genius."

Alf took a little bow. "Thank you."

The tabloids and television shows had been talking about the Vanna White photos all month. Every boy in the eighth and ninth grade would be lining up to give Alf their lunch money. He would take a simple four-dollar magazine and Xerox it into a fortune. There was just one problem.

"Where's the magazine?"

"We're getting it tonight. Tyler Bell wants to help."

I was certain I'd misheard him. Tyler was three years older than us, a senior. He was the only kid in town with a motorcycle—a beat-up 1968 Harley with a shovelhead engine. He wore leather in the winter and denim in the summer and he rotated a wardrobe of heavy metal T-shirts all year round: Iron Maiden, Metallica, Megadeth, Slayer. His pants were fringed with safety pins, and his boots were always scuffed because he didn't give a shit.

"Since when are we friends with Tyler Bell?" I asked.

"He's actually really cool," Alf said. "Most of the stories about him aren't true."

"Except he *did* have sex with a teacher," Clark pointed out. "Señora Fernandez. That story's totally true."

Sex-with-a-teacher was minor-league compared to the other rumors I'd heard. It was said that Tyler rode into New York City on weekends, that he got into fistfights with metalheads and had sex with hookers in Times Square. Surprisingly, none of this prevented the girls in my class from going berserk over him. When Tyler came swaggering past their lockers, they'd fall all over themselves, like he'd just stepped off the cover of a Harlequin romance novel. In another life, he was probably a pirate or a Viking.

"Why is Tyler helping you?" I asked. "How does he even know your names?"

"Me and Alf were getting dressed after gym," Clark explained. "We were talking about Zelinsky in the locker room, and Tyler overheard us. He said for twenty bucks he would get us the magazine."

"And you paid him?"

"No, not yet," Alf said. "We're meeting him right now. At the train station."

"I didn't want you to feel left out," Clark explained. "I thought you'd want to be there when we saw the pictures."

Clark was pretty thoughtful that way. Anytime he had good luck, he was always quick to spread it around. In my earliest memory of him, we were little kids, walking home from kindergarten in a snowstorm, and Clark stumbled across a pristine Hershey's chocolate bar. Any other kid would have pocketed the candy for himself. But five-year-old Clark knelt down in the snow, unwrapped the Hershey bar, and used his claw to snap it into three evenly sized pieces. The chocolate was frozen solid, dusted with perfect white snowflakes, and maybe the purest, most delicious thing I'd ever tasted.

"I'll be right out," I said.

By the time we reached Market Street, it was nearing eleven o'clock and all of the stores and restaurants were closed. The sidewalks were empty, and there were few cars on the road. At Alf's direction, we ditched our bikes behind the bank because we'd look cooler meeting Tyler on foot. Motorcycles were badass, but pedal power was for little kids.

Tyler was slouched on a bench in front of the train station. The illustration on his T-shirt depicted a toilet bowl with a dagger emerging from the water; a caption in a satanic typeface read "Metal Up Your Ass." He didn't say anything when we approached, just stood up and walked around the side of the train station. It was the tallest building in Wetbridge—a three-story structure ornamented with multiple roofs and gables and balconies.

Tyler stopped in the shadows of the building, a narrow gap between a Dumpster and a chain-link fence.

"Who's this?" he asked.

I realized he meant me.

"This is Billy," Alf said. "He's cool."

Tyler seemed skeptical. "You look familiar," he told me. "How do I know you?"

"My locker's next to yours. You're A29. I'm A28."

"You're shitting me. Seriously?" He shook his head in disbelief. "I always thought that locker was empty, no offense."

None taken. I tried to make myself invisible around guys like Tyler Bell, and apparently I'd been successful.

Alf held out a twenty-dollar bill. "Where's the magazine?"

Tyler pocketed the money but ignored the question. "If anybody comes, I want you guys to scatter. Everyone run in different directions. The cops can't catch all four of us, understand?"

No, I did not understand, not really. The train station was deserted. The ticket office was closed. No one was waiting on any of the platforms.

"The coast is clear," Alf assured him. "Just give us the magazine."

Tyler scowled. "I never said I'd *bring* you the magazine. I said I'd show you how to get it."

"What does that mean?"

"Watch and learn."

Tyler stepped onto the chain-link fence, wedged his boot into the diamond mesh, and started to climb. For all of his size and bulk, he moved quietly and gracefully, scaling the fence like Spider-Man. When he was eight feet off the ground, he swung a leg over the top rail, straddling it. Then he grabbed an overhanging tree branch, pulling himself into standing position, balancing himself on top of the fence like a trapeze artist.

"What are you doing?" Alf asked.

Holding the branch to steady himself, Tyler sidestepped across the top of the fence, then crossed onto the roof of the train station.

“Come on, ladies,” he said. “Let’s get moving. I don’t have all night.”

Alf didn’t need to be told twice. He leapt onto the fence, trying to mimic Tyler’s graceful movements, but he didn’t have any of Tyler’s strength or coordination. He thrashed and flailed like the coils were electrocuting him, and Clark and I had to push up on his ass to help him reach the top.

“I’ll go next,” Clark volunteered.

“What the hell are we doing?” I whispered.

“Just stay cool,” he told me. “Tyler doesn’t have all night.”

Clark squeezed his claw through the fence, anchoring the left half of his body, then used his good arm to pull himself up. Over the years he’d learned to compensate for his weaker side; he did nightly push-ups to keep his body symmetrical, and he was easily the strongest and most athletic of our group (which admittedly wasn’t saying very much). Clark could have been a varsity athlete in track, soccer, tennis, wrestling, maybe even baseball—but insecurity over the Claw kept him from attending tryouts. He hated any activity that drew attention to his hands.

One by one, we joined Tyler on the roof of the train station, and then followed him up a fire ladder to a second, higher rooftop. From there we scaled a steep gable on our hands and knees. This brought us to the very top of the train station—a small eave overlooking Market Street. We were fifty feet off the ground, lying flat on roof tiles that were cracked and spotted with bird shit. The rain gutter was full of stagnant water and smelled like farts.

“This place is awesome!” Alf whispered. “How’d you find it?”

Tyler shrugged. “My brother showed me. We bring girls here sometimes.”

“For sex?” Alf asked. He was practically salivating.

I was embarrassed by his question, but Tyler just laughed. “I’ve had more ass on this roof than you’ll see in a lifetime.” He gestured up at the night sky. “Girls see all these stars and it’s like their belts unbuckle themselves.”

I wriggled forward, peering out over the gutter. The top of the train station offered a bird's-eye view of all the neighboring buildings.

"So where's the magazine?" I asked.

"Look across the street," Tyler said. "You see General Tso's? The Chinese restaurant on the corner?"

General Tso's Mount Everest was the nicest restaurant in town, and the only place to take a girl if you didn't have a car. Every item on the menu came served in pint-sized or quart-sized containers.

"There's a fire escape ladder in the back of the restaurant," Tyler explained. "What you want to do is climb the ladder to his roof. You need to be quiet because the General lives above the restaurant. He's got the apartment on the second floor."

"Wait a second," I interrupted. "What are we talking about? What are we doing up here?"

Tyler sighed long and loud, like his worst fears about me had just been confirmed.

"Let's just hear him out," Clark said.

"Yeah, go ahead, Tyler," Alf pleaded.

As Tyler continued, Clark started taking notes. He brought out a pencil and paper and sketched the buildings along Market Street; from our perspective they seemed small and easily scalable, like obstacles in a video game. Most stores were crammed side by side, but General Tso's was separated from its neighbor by a narrow alley.

"You'll need to hop across the alley," Tyler explained. "That'll put you on the bike shop. They use their second floor for inventory, so you can be as loud as you want. And then you just walk east. Bike shop, travel agency, Zelinsky's. He uses his second floor for inventory, too. Old typewriters and shit. So you don't have to worry about noise."

I turned to Alf and whispered: "How does he know all this?"

"I worked there last summer," Tyler explained. "Now, you see that bump on the roof? The little square box? That's an exit hatch.

Zelinsky keeps it locked from the inside, but the whole door has gone to shit. The wood's rotten, the hinges are rusted. You could probably pry it off with your bare hands. With a crowbar it'll take two seconds."

At last I understood he was describing a burglary. "Are you kidding? You guys want to steal the magazines?"

A moment passed, and no one said anything.

"Well," Clark reasoned, "technically it's not stealing if we pay for them. We could leave money in the cash register. Four dollars for every copy we take."

"Then we fix the hatch on our way out," Alf said. "We'll bring a screwdriver and we'll put the hinges back on."

"No," I said. "No way."

"Why not?" Tyler asked.

"Because Alf just gave you twenty bucks! Why don't you just walk into a store and *buy* the magazine for him?"

"That would be illegal," Tyler said.

"*This* is illegal," I said. "You're telling us to break into Zelinsky's and steal the magazine."

I don't know where I found the courage to challenge Tyler Bell. He looked like he was ready to push me off the roof. But someone had to say something. His "plan" was ridiculous. It was straight out of *Mission: Impossible.*

And my friends were hooked.

"It's not stealing if we pay for them," Clark repeated.

"Yes, it is," I said.

"Nobody will ever know," Alf said. "Zelinsky finds some extra money in his cash register. We bring home Vanna White. It's a win-win."

"Exactly," Tyler said. Clark finished his sketch and held it up for review. Tyler looked it over and nodded his approval. "That's the plan right there. Three easy steps."

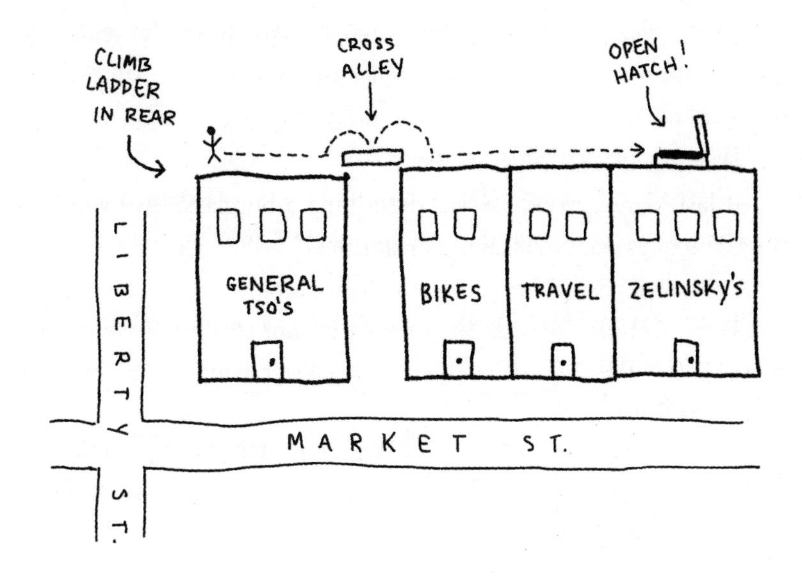

I turned to Tyler and made one last plea for sanity. "Look, what's in this for you? Why are you hanging with three freshmen on a Friday night?"

Clark drew in his breath, like my questions were unspeakably rude. "Jesus, Billy, he's being nice."

Tyler didn't seem offended. "I'm just killing time, chief. I'm meeting my friends at eleven thirty, and I figured I'd help you guys while I wait." He said this all very matter-of-factly, but the explanation stopped me cold: Tyler Bell was so badass, he didn't *start* hanging out until eleven thirty! "But if you guys don't want my help . . ."

"We do, we do!" Clark insisted.

"Let's go right now," Alf said. "Let's go tonight!"

"There's just one problem," Tyler said. "Zelinsky has the whole store wired. Front door, windows, and the roof hatch. So as soon as you pop it open, the alarm gets tripped. You've got sixty seconds to turn it off or the whole place lights up like the Fourth of July. Sirens, flashers, the works."

Down below, a police cruiser slowly drifted along Market Street. Even though we couldn't be seen, we all stopped talking until it reached a safe distance.

"How do we turn off the alarm?" Alf asked.

"There's a little keypad near the front door. Says 'Ademco Security.' You enter a pass code, and that's the problem. I don't know it."

"Who does?"

"Just Zelinsky. And his daughter, Mary." Tyler turned to Clark. "That's where you come in."

Clark blinked. "Me?"

"You need to smooth-talk her, Pretty Boy. Make her trust you."

Even though it was pitch dark on the roof of the train station, I knew Clark was blushing. "I can't smooth-talk anyone."

"Sure you can. You're a good-looking guy. You wear nice clothes. You're polite. If you had a little more confidence, you'd be getting tons of pussy."

Clark held up his claw. "What about this?"

"That's your secret weapon!" Tyler said. "You show Mary that ugly flipper every chance you get. Because it makes her trust you, understand? It makes her feel safe."

Clark wasn't having any of it. He was so shy around girls, he'd cross the street to avoid walking past one.

"Just hear me out," Tyler continued. "Mary works at the store every afternoon. And this chick is horny like a baboon, all right? I had to beat her back with a stick. She couldn't keep her hands off me. She is *desperate* for action."

"I'm not . . . I don't want action with her," Clark said.

"Just hang out," Tyler said. "Talk with her, tell some jokes. Act like she's interesting. Take her to the movies, play with her hair, kiss her—"

"I'm not kissing her," Clark said. "I want the magazine. Really, I do. But I'm not kissing her."

"Then we're done," Tyler said, rising to his knees. "And thanks for wasting my time. I thought you guys were serious."

"We are!" Alf said. "We're very serious!"

"Then you need the code," Tyler insisted.

By this point, I was wishing I'd never left my house. Tyler's plan was ridiculous. Its chances of working were zero. Any girl smart enough to program "Invisible Touch" on a C64 would never be stupid enough to give up the security code to her father's store. We had climbed all the way to the top of the train station for nothing.

"I won't do it," Clark insisted. "I'm sorry."

"Then *I'll* do it," Alf said grudgingly. "I won't enjoy it, and I'll have nightmares for life. But I'll suffer for the greater good."

Tyler shook his head. "She's fat, but she's not blind. It's got to be Bryan Adams here."

Clark didn't look anything like Bryan Adams, but I knew what Tyler meant; he had the natural good looks of someone you'd expect to see on a concert stage. Whereas Alf looked like the sweaty kid working the concert concession stand, selling soft pretzels and Polish sausage.

"I'm not doing it," Clark said.

They kept arguing back and forth, but I knew Clark wouldn't budge; he might be willing to rob a store, but he was too kind to risk hurting someone's feelings. I wanted to get off the roof and go home. I wanted to get back to programming my game. And that's when I had my big idea—the stupid brainstorm that set this whole sad story in motion.

"I'll do it," I said.

"You?" Tyler asked.

"Really?" Clark said.

"Yeah, I can do it," I said. "I'll get the code."

This was a lie. I didn't think anyone could get the code. I wasn't even planning to try. But *pretending* to try would give me a good excuse to visit the store and show *The Impossible Fortress* to Mary. Maybe she'd know how to fix it. I still had fifteen days before the contest deadline.

Tyler seemed skeptical, so I turned on the macho bullshit. "But I'm going to need some time. I can't just walk into the store and start grabbing her tits. It's going to take a week or two. Most likely two."

Clark stared at me in astonishment. He knew damn well that I'd never touched anyone's tits, that I'd never even passed first base. "Seriously, Billy? You'd actually kiss her?"

"Kiss her, fondle her, I'll bone her if I have to," I said. "You guys plan the other details while I make nice with Miss Piggy."

For the first time all evening, Tyler looked at me with respect and maybe even admiration. He clapped me on the shoulder. "You see! *This* is what I'm talking about. This is the kind of attitude that gets results!"

7

```
700 REM *** DRAW HERO SPRITE ***
710 POKE 52,48:POKE 56,48
720 FOR HE=0 TO 62:READ H
730 POKE 12888+HE,H
740 NEXT HE
750 POKE 2040,192:POKEV+21,1
760 POKE V+39,1
770 POKE V+0,HX
780 POKE V+1,HY
790 RETURN
]■
```

THE INTERNET AS WE know it didn't exist in 1987, but people willing to pay a thirty-nine-dollar membership fee and twelve bucks an hour could access CompuServe, which was the next best thing. If today's Internet is like a vast galaxy with billions and billions of blogs, CompuServe was more like a small, private social club. There were limited topics of discussion and just a handful of games. Everything was controlled by CompuServe, and only CompuServe members could get inside.

There were no videos or graphics or sound. There wasn't even color. Our 300-baud modems were barely capable of streaming ASCII characters, and the words filled our screens slowly, one c . . . h . . . a . . . r . . . a . . . c . . . t . . . e . . . r at a time. Every interaction was like waiting for a Polaroid to develop. After logging in to the site, I had to wait a full minute for the main menu to download:

```
CompuServe Information Service
23:12 EST      Friday 15-May-87

1. Newspapers
2. Finance
3. Entertainment
4. Communities
5. CompuServe User Information
6. Electronic Mail

Enter your selection number, or H for more
information.

>_
```

I chose option 6, ELECTRONIC MAIL—an easy way to contact Mary without visiting the store and facing Zelinsky. The contest rules had come from a CompuServe user's group, and Mary's member ID number was printed at the top of the page. All electronic mail on CompuServe had a maximum limit of twelve lines, so I kept my message brief.

```
TO: 59453,1
FROM: 38584,8

1: HI ARE YOU MARY ZELINSKY?
2: MY NAME IS WILL MARVIN.
3: I WAS IN YOUR STORE THE OTHER DAY.
```

4: YOU TOLD ME ABOUT THE RUTGERS CONTEST.

5: ARE YOU GOING TO ENTER?

6: I WANT TO . . . BUT MY GAME SUCKS.

When I finished, I hit Enter, and CompuServe presented me with a submenu:

OPTIONS

1. REVIEW WITH MINI-EDITOR

2. MODIFY

3. SEND

ENTER DIGIT FOR OPTIONS OR M FOR MENU, OR H FOR HELP.

>_

I chose option 3, SEND, and CompuServe promised the message would be delivered within four to twenty-four hours. Then I logged off fast before any more charges could be applied to my mother's credit card. I hoped that by the time she received her Visa statement, she'd have forgotten that I was forbidden to use my 64 anyway.

I checked CompuServe again the next night, but there was still no reply. This didn't surprise me. CompuServe was so expensive, most people (especially kids) could only afford to use it sporadically. Factor in the slow delivery time and you could understand why electronic mail conversations often stretched over weeks or even months. It was like casting a message in a bottle; there was no way of knowing when she'd receive it.

But when I got to school on Monday morning, I found that someone had pushed a 5¼ floppy disk through the vent of my locker. Affixed to the front of the disk was a small white label with my name on it. I skipped first period (Intro to History) and went to the school computer lab. Class was already in progress, and I ducked behind an empty terminal in the back row. The monitor was large enough to conceal my face from Ms. Grecco, the typing teacher, who paced across the front of the classroom, reciting letters for students to type: "A, A, A, A . . . S, S, S, S . . . D, D, D, D . . ."

I pushed the disk into the drive and opened the directory. There was just a single file titled PLAYME. So I loaded it into memory and typed RUN. The screen went black, then filled with text.

```
You are standing outside Zelinsky's Typewrit-
ers and Office Supplies in downtown Wetbridge.
You are carrying a brass lantern and a floppy
disk. On the ground is a hearing aid battery.
```

I realized it was a game, or at least a mini-game, modeled after text adventures like *Zork*. The player typed commands, and the game advanced the story using words instead of pictures. I tried typing:

```
>GET BATTERY
```

And the game replied with:

```
You reach down and pick up the hearing aid
battery (because you seem to have a thing for
hearing aid batteries. It's weird.) Your score
just went up by 50 points!
```

Encouraged, I leaned over the keyboard and kept playing.

```
>ENTER STORE
```

You enter the store. Sal Zelinsky is standing here, repairing a typewriter. To the north, a passage leads deeper into the store.

>WALK NORTH

Sal jumps up, blocking your way. "Can I help you?"

>ASK SAL ABOUT MARY

Sal squints at you and jiggles the plastic amplifier tucked inside his right ear. "I'm sorry, young man, I can't hear you. Can you repeat that?"

>ASK SAL ABOUT MARY

He shakes his head. "I'm sorry, I can't understand you. My hearing aid's not working right."

>GIVE BATTERY TO SAL

Sal cheerfully accepts your gift. (Your score just went up by 50 points!) He inserts the battery into his hearing aid. "Ah, much better!" he exclaims. "Now what were you saying?"

>ASK SAL ABOUT MARY

"She's in the back!" he says, and he steps out of your way. You realize that Sal Zelinsky is very nice once you get to know him. He only acts gruff to frighten potential shoplifters.

>GO NORTH

You walk to the back of the store and find Mary sitting at a computer. She is listening to Phil Collins's extraordinary solo album NO JACKET REQUIRED, yet seems unhappy. "Golly," she says wistfully. "I wish I had a good video game to play."

>INVENTORY

You are carrying a brass lantern and a floppy disk.

>GIVE DISK TO MARY

"Thank you," Mary says. She puts the disk into her computer and she is blown away by the sheer awesomeness of your game. The ceiling explodes into butterflies, the angels descend from heaven and sing hosannas, and you all live happily ever after.

THE END.

Your score is 100 out of 100, giving you a rank of Awesome.

(Seriously, come over after school and bring your game—Mary Z)

A trill of musical notes played through the computer speakers, and I recognized them as the opening chords of "Jump" by Van Halen. I laughed out loud. Apparently it *was* possible to program Van Halen on a 64.

Ms. Grecco interrupted her typing lesson to scream at me. "Billy Marvin! What are you doing back there? You're not even in this class!"

I grabbed the disk and ducked out the door. Later, at lunchtime, I used one of the computers in the school library to examine the program more carefully. Even though the game itself was fairly simple, the coding was remarkably complex. Mary had programmed the game to anticipate dozens of commands and requests that I hadn't tried. It was much more sophisticated than any of the programs in my hobby magazines—and she had somehow written the entire thing over a weekend.

When I returned to Zelinsky's that afternoon, there were no hearing aid batteries on the sidewalk and I wasn't carrying a brass lantern. But I did have a floppy disk and Sal Zelinsky was waiting just inside the front door, smoking a pipe and reading the *Wall Street Journal.*

"Help you?"

"Is Mary here?"

He set down his pipe, folded his newspaper, and looked me over. "You were here last week," he said, eyes narrowing. "Some bullshit about starting a software company."

"That wasn't BS. I make games for real."

"Why should I believe you?"

I showed him the disk. The paper label on the front read:

THE IMPOSSIBLE FORTRESS

A Game by Will Marvin

Copyright © 1987 by Planet Will Software

Zelinsky lifted the disk by its corner and observed it from multiple angles, like he was examining counterfeit currency. "This is just a label," he said. "Any joker could write their name on a label."

I'd also brought a printout of the code—eight pages, single spaced, in a dot matrix typeface. Zelinsky flipped through it, not really reading it, because of course it was all Greek to him. "You understand this stuff? All these PEEKs and POKEs and whatnot?"

"Pretty much."

He pointed to a random line. "What's this? POKE SC comma L?"

"That changes the value of SC, the screen color. If L is zero, the screen turns black."

"What's DS equals PEEK JY?"

"That checks the value of the joystick register to see which way it's pointing. If you're pushing up, the value is three. If you're pushing down—"

He handed back the printout. "No sodas on the desk," he said. "I don't want any spills. And I want you out by seven o'clock. She has homework."

The bell over the front door rang—new customers had arrived, two men in coats and ties—and Zelinsky turned to greet them. Apparently I was free to proceed. I hurried into the store before Zelinsky could change his mind.

Soft rock was playing on tinny speakers in the ceiling—Hall and Oates's "You Make My Dreams Come True." I found Mary in the same place back in the showroom. She was hunched forward in her chair, her eyeballs inches from the screen, like she was counting pixels. She was listening to a Walkman, so she didn't hear me approaching. The volume was so loud, I could hear the Phil Collins leaking out of her headphones. Sitting on the desk beside the 64 was an open can of Pepsi.

She saw me and pulled off the headphones.

"You got my message," she said.

I nodded. "How'd you find my locker?"

"I live next door to Ashley Applewhite. She said she knew how to find you."

I was surprised that Ashley Applewhite even knew my name. She was the kind of girl who took Honors Everything. Her father was superintendent of the entire Wetbridge school system.

"I really like the game," I told her. "The Van Halen was dead-on."

Mary shrugged and said it was no big deal. "I assumed you'd want old Van Halen, not new Van Halen."

I was impressed that she even knew the difference. "Totally."

She wore a black blouse, black skirt, black stockings, and black shoes. It would have been easy to mistake her for one of the gloomy goth girls who hung around the art room at my school, but Mary's face glowed and she looked like she was smiling even when she wasn't. Three hundred pounds was a ridiculous exaggeration. She was a little stocky, sure, but nowhere near obese. Mary rolled a swivel chair over to her desk so I could sit beside her.

"You want a soda?"

"No, thanks."

"We've got Pepsi, Slice, Dr Pepper, and Jolt Cola. Have you tried Jolt Cola? It's got twice the caffeine of Pepsi."

"Your dad said no soda on the desk."

Mary sighed and moved the Pepsi to the top of the computer monitor, balancing the can on its narrow, flat edge. "He always says that, but I've never had a spill."

The can immediately slid forward on a skin of condensation, tipping over the side. My stomach lurched; I reached out and caught it just in time. "Maybe we should put it on the floor."

"Whatever," she said. "Let's see this game."

I gave her the disk with the Planet Will logo and braced myself for the usual razzing à la Alf and Clark. Mary looked at the label and laughed. "Planet Will Software, that's a fantastic name," she said. "Have you trademarked it?"

"Not yet." I didn't even know what that meant. "Should I?"

"Absolutely. I've been trying to name *my* company all year. The best I've got so far is Radical Music."

"That's pretty good," I said.

"Planet Will is way better! It's bold, it says fun, and your name's in it. You better lock it up before somebody steals it."

Mary loaded the game into memory and typed RUN. To my surprise, I found that my arms were trembling; I was actually nervous. I'd never shared my games with anyone who knew how to program—let alone someone smart enough to design an entire mini-game in a single weekend.

The title screen appeared with an 8-bit illustration of a foreboding castle. The hero and the princess stood center screen as a tinny theme song played, and then an ogre hauled the princess over his shoulders and dragged her away.

"This is awesome!" Mary exclaimed. "How did you draw this?"

"Koala Pad," I explained. "Then I touched it up with Doodle."

She leaned into the screen, studying all of the finer details. "God, I wish I could draw like this. Her outfit is perfect. You even put a tassel on her hat!"

I couldn't believe she'd noticed. To research that outfit, I'd spent an entire hour browsing encyclopedias at the library, studying portraits of princesses all over Europe until I found just the right hat. It was called a hennin, and it looked like a giant pointy cone.

"Keep watching," I told her. "This is where it all breaks down."

The game began and the brave hero began his quest at the base of a mountain, while ogre guards swarmed all around him. The object was to guide the hero up the mountain, but everything moved in agonizingly slow motion. The characters looked like they were flailing about in zero gravity, a Super Bowl instant replay that never ended.

Suddenly I wanted to get as far from Mary as I could. I felt dumb for trying and even dumber for sharing. Planet Will Software! What the hell was I thinking?

But Mary didn't look disappointed. If anything, she seemed more engaged, like I'd presented her with a problem worth solving. She hit RUN/STOP and typed LIST, and all of my code spilled down the screen. Mary skimmed the lines, nodding as she went along, not reading but skillfully assessing the overall structure, the way a mechanic might circle an automobile, inspecting the surface and kicking the tires before diving under the hood.

For ten minutes she didn't speak. She read and reread the program, one subroutine at a time, mumbling to herself and occasionally jotting notes on a scrap of graph paper. She never asked me a single question; she didn't need to. Sometimes she'd exclaim "Hmph" and I'd lean forward to see what she was hmph-ing about, but she was always moving ahead to the next loop. There was nothing for me to do except sit back and wait.

The speakers in the ceiling went from Hall and Oates to Glenn Medeiros to Howard Jones, and then there was a station break for 103.5 WLOV, "Radio's Home to All Your Favorite '80s Love Songs." It was my mother's favorite station; me and Alf and Clark referred to it as "Home to Ten Crappy Songs in a Row." Bruce Hornsby started whining about "The Way It Is," and Mary leaned back in her chair.

"Sorry about the music," she said. "My father insists on it."

I realized this was a polite attempt to turn the conversation away from the game. "I told you it sucked."

"You weren't kidding." She restarted the game and guided the hero across the screen, groaning as she prodded him forward. "You could torture prisoners with this game. Strap them to machines and force them to play for hours. I've had more fun playing spreadsheets."

I forced myself to laugh, but it came out like a whimper. See, I knew the game was horrible. It was unplayable. It was awful! But even with its flaws, this horrible, unplayable, awful game was actually the best game I'd ever made.

"You want to know the worst part?" Mary asked.

I couldn't believe it. There was more? There was *worst*?

"The worst part is, your code's perfect. There's not a single wasted command. Every line is packed. And the way you toggle sprites to animate the guards? That's fantastic. I love it."

And there it was. After fourteen years of fumbling footballs and missing baskets and striking out, after fourteen years of miserable grades and bad rhythm and terrible fashion choices, after fourteen years of *being me*, I wasn't used to compliments. My face burned bright red. I couldn't help myself. I wanted to freeze time and linger over her exact phrasing:

Perfect.

Fantastic.

I love it.

"Your only problem is speed," she continued. "You need to rewrite this game in machine language."

I laughed. She had to be joking. Machine language (ML) was the computer's natural language—a hundred times faster than BASIC, so fast that programmers often built artificial delays into their games to keep the action from looping too quickly. But ML was famously difficult to learn. I'd studied passages in books and magazines, but the syntax was too cryptic, too complicated. BASIC used English words like PRINT and NEXT, but machine language used complicated acronyms: ADC, CLC, SBC, TSX. Numbers were inputted in hexadecimal format, so 11 looked like 0B and 144 looked like 90. There was nothing intuitive or natural about the language; it demanded the user to think and communicate like a machine.

"You know ML?" I asked Mary.

She shrugged. "I've always wanted to learn."

"The deadline's next Friday," I reminded her. "I can't learn ML in twelve days."

Mary LISTed the program again, letting the lines cascade down the screen until she reached the loop that moved the seven ogre guards.

Then she tapped the screen with her pencil. "This is the slowest part of the program. These fifty lines where you move all the guards. What if you wrote this part in ML? Not the whole game but just this tiny section?"

I don't know where she got her confidence. It was like saying, "We don't need to learn *all* of Mandarin Chinese. We just need to learn enough to translate the Gettysburg Address." Mary seemed to believe that anything was possible if we were only willing to try.

"You're crazy," I told her. "I'm not that good."

"I'll help you," she said. "We can work here after school. And when you win the PS/2—"

I laughed. "I'm not going to win the PS/2."

"*When* you win the PS/2," she repeated, "you'll give me your old 64. So I can have my own computer at home. Does that seem fair?"

She put out her hand to close the deal. Each of Mary's fingernails was painted a different color and detailed with zeros and ones—a rainbow of binary digits arching over her hands, 01111101010. We shook on the agreement, and a shock of static snapped between us.

"Twelve days isn't a lot of time," I said.

"I have a great book we can use." She jumped up, grabbed a heavy tome from the shelf, and showed me the cover: *How to Learn Machine Language in 30 Days*.

"Thirty days?" I asked.

"We'll read it really fast," she explained.

8

```
800 REM *** DRAW GUARD 1 SPRITE ***
810 POKE 52,48:POKE 56,48
820 FOR GU=0 TO 62:READ G
830 POKE 12352+GU,G
840 NEXT GU
850 POKE 2041,193:POKE V+21,2
860 POKE V+40,2
870 POKE V+2,GX
880 POKE V+3,GY
890 RETURN
]■
```

ZELINSKY KICKED ME OUT at exactly seven o'clock so Mary could finish her homework. Alf and Clark were waiting outside the store, perched on their dirt bikes and eating slices of pizza off greasy paper plates.

"Finally!" Clark exclaimed.

"Did you get the code?" Alf asked.

I had forgotten all about my mission. "Not yet. I told you I'm gonna need some time."

Clark reminded me that I'd rushed to the store straight after school, that I'd been in the showroom for nearly four hours. "What the hell were you doing back there?"

"Computer stuff."

Alf grinned, like this was some new euphemism for sexual activity. "Did you show her your joystick?"

"No—"

"Did you squeeze her software?"

I tried to explain myself, but Alf had stumbled upon a deep well of techno-innuendo and he wouldn't quit until it was all mined out. Just five minutes earlier, I'd been getting a decent grasp on hexadecimal numbers, but now I felt all of my knowledge slipping away, as if merely being in Alf's presence was making me dumber.

"Did you feel her Q-Berts?" Alf asked.

Clark joined in the fun. "Did she fondle your Zaxxon?"

"That doesn't even make sense," I told them. "You're just replacing body parts with names of arcade games."

They didn't care. They were laughing like crazy, staggering all over the sidewalk like drunks. All around us, commuters from the train station were giving us a wide berth. Alf grabbed a lamppost to keep from falling over, and pretty soon I was laughing along with them. I couldn't help myself. The guys were contagious.

"I don't want to brag," I told them, "but I did load a couple bytes into her accumulator."

Alf stopped laughing. "What?"

"I don't get it," Clark said.

"It's a machine language joke," I explained. "An accumulator is a register where you store data—"

"Never mind that," Alf said. Suddenly he was all business. "We've got a problem with Operation Vanna."

We walked west on Main Street, past the travel agency and the bike shop, and then we arrived at our destination: General Tso's Mount

Everest restaurant. The name on the sign promised a sort of grandeur, but inside it was just a regular Chinese restaurant with red carpet, greasy noodle dishes, and paper place mats illustrating the Chinese zodiac.

We could see General Tso through the window, dressed in his usual black tuxedo, escorting some customers to their table. He was owner, maître d', and head chef of the restaurant, and he worked 365 days a year without fail. Years later I'd learn that his real name was Hiraku, he was born in Oregon, and he and his wife were both Japanese.

Alf and Clark led us through the narrow alley separating General Tso's from the bike shop next door. There wasn't much behind the buildings—just a few parking spaces for employees, a narrow access road, and then a much larger commuter parking lot, a sea of Buicks and Oldsmobiles. We ducked behind a Grand Marquis and then turned to study the rear of General Tso's.

At the base of the building was a large metal Dumpster and a back door for deliveries. On the second floor were two curtained windows and a rusty fire ladder ascending between them. The sun was setting, but there was still plenty of daylight, enough to get a good look at everything.

"Last night, me and Clark took a practice run up the ladder," Alf explained. "We wanted to get the lay of the land. Check out the rooftop. Maybe get a closer look at the hatch. See what tools we need to pack."

"Only we never found out," Clark explained. "We got five rungs up the ladder and Schwarzenegger freaked out."

"Arnold Schwarzenegger?" I asked. "The Terminator?"

Alf pressed binoculars into my hands. "Second-floor window," he said. "Take a look."

I pressed the lenses to my face and scanned the building, but all I saw were red drapes ornamented with gold dragons.

"I don't see anything."

"Other window," Clark explained. "The left window."

I shifted the binoculars an inch. The left window had the same red-and-gold drapes, but squatting between them was a tiny black-and-white dog with a silky coat and a serious overbite. He was glowering at me, like we were making direct eye contact. Even from fifty feet away, the dog seemed to recognize me as a threat.

"That's Arnold Schwarzenegger?" I asked.

"The General's pet," Alf explained. "He's a Shit Zoo. It means little lion in Chinese."

The little lion barked a warning—a series of short high-pitched chirps. He sounded less like a dog and more like a smoke detector. The sound was so piercing, it traveled two stories and across the parking lot, reaching us loud and clear. Schwarzenegger didn't stop barking until I lowered the binoculars.

"So last night we're climbing up the ladder," Clark explained. "Total stealth mode. Super quiet. We're not making a sound. But as soon as we reached those windows, the dog flips out. Yap-yap-yapping his head off."

"The guard dog from hell," Alf said.

I looked through the binoculars again. Schwarzenegger was standing in a tiny pillowed bed, growling and anxiously pacing in circles. As if he remembered Alf and Clark from the previous evening.

We walked around the block, studying the architecture, looking for another way to access the roof. There were no other fire escapes or ladders on the bike shop or the travel agency; the only way to access Zelinsky's was the way Tyler had shown us. After viewing the building from every possible angle, Clark reached in his pocket for a pencil sketch of the downtown shopping district. He knelt on the sidewalk and drew a dog in the second-floor window of General Tso's restaurant:

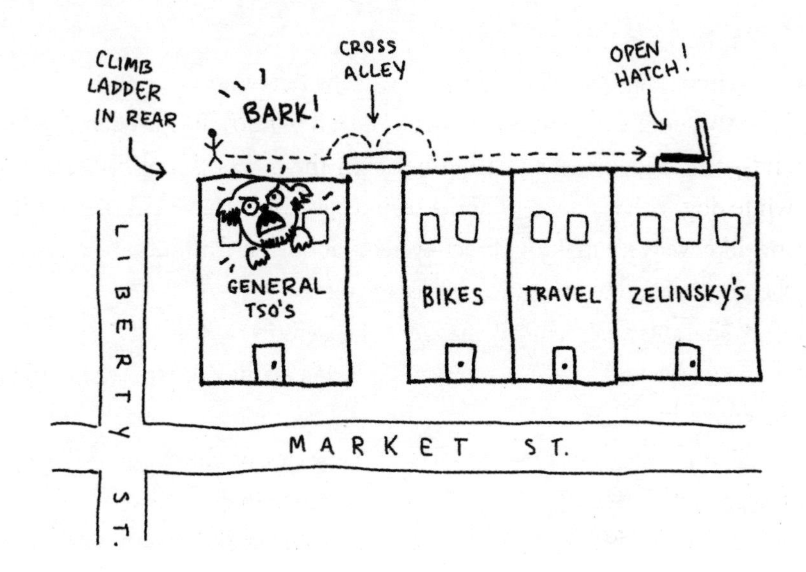

"I guess there's only one option," Clark said.

"Kidnap the dog?" Alf said.

"No," I told him. "No one's kidnapping anything."

Clark nodded. "We have to *distract* the dog. Get his attention on something else."

"Perfect," I said. "How do we do that?"

"Leave that to us," he said. "You keep playing with Mary's software, and we'll take care of the rest."

9

```
900 REM *** CONTROL HERO ***
910 JS=PEEK(56321) AND 15
920 IF JS=7 THEN HX=HX+2
930 IF HX>255 THEN HX=255
940 IF JS=11 THEN HX=HX-2
950 IF HX<24 THEN HX=24
960 IF JS=13 THEN HY=HY+2
970 IF HY>229 THEN HY=229
980 IF JS=14 THEN HY=HY-2
990 IF HY<50 THEN HY=50
995 RETURN
]■
```

THE NEXT MORNING I biked three miles to the nearest mall with a B. Dalton and bought my own copy of *How to Learn Machine Language in 30 Days* so I could study it during class. I didn't get to school until eleven o'clock, so I headed to the office to pick up a late slip. Over the years I'd become an expert at forging excuse notes from my mother. Normally the school secretary barely looked at them; she'd just check my name off the attendance grid and send me on my way.

But this day, something was different.

"Sorry I'm late," I said, pushing my note across the counter. "Doctor's visit."

The secretary raised her eyebrows. "Wait here."

She left her desk, tapped on the door of the principal's office, and ducked inside. A moment later, she returned. "Mr. Hibble wants to see you."

"It was a doctor's visit," I repeated.

She nodded. "You can go right in."

I hadn't spoken to Hibble since the beginning of the school year, when my mother dragged me into his office to protest my class schedule. I found him seated behind his desk, rereading my note with a bemused grin. He was short, barely five four, and my classmates nicknamed him "the Duke" because he wore jacked-up cowboy boots and spoke with a southern-fried twang. His walls were decorated with numerous diplomas and a framed photograph of Hibble standing beside Kenny Rogers.

"Don't just stand there," he called. "Come in and sit, Billy. We've been waiting for you."

I stepped inside. Sitting across from Mr. Hibble was my mother. Her eyes were puffy and she was clutching a balled-up Kleenex. In the middle of Hibble's desk was a brown paper bag with my name scrawled on the side. All at once I realized what had gone wrong: in my haste to get to the mall, I'd left the house without my lunch.

The only available chair in the office was beside my mother. I sat without looking at her. Hibble put on his glasses and read aloud from my note: " 'Please forgive Billy's tardiness. He had an appointment with our physician to discuss an ongoing medical debilitation.' " Then he sat back in his chair and nodded. "Very impressive note, Billy. Lots of big words."

I didn't say anything. One thing I'd learned is that no answer will ever satisfy an angry adult. Anything you say is bound to make them angrier, so the best response was always no response.

"School started three hours ago," Hibble said. "Where were you?"

"At the mall."

He nodded like this made total sense.

"Why were you at the mall? What's so important that you had to skip school and go to the mall?"

"Nothing."

I didn't dare mention the machine language book, not after my mother had taken away my computer privileges.

"Nothing?"

"I was just looking around and stuff."

Again he nodded, like this was precisely the answer he'd expected. My poor mother sighed long and loud. As bad as I felt, I knew she felt a hundred times worse.

"Your grade point average is zero point eight. A D-plus. You've been late to school nineteen times this year. Your teachers say you're bored, disinterested. You don't like learning. You don't like schoolwork. And that is totally fine, Billy."

I looked up, surprised. *Totally fine?*

"Academics aren't for everyone. Not everyone can go to Rutgers or Penn State or even community college. That's what I tried to explain to your mother last fall, when you asked about Honors classes. You're obviously not ready. And that's okay."

"It's not okay," Mom said. "If he worked harder, if he applied himself . . ."

Hibble shook his head. "'You can teach an elephant to tap-dance, but you won't enjoy the show and neither will the elephant.'" He spoke like this was some time-tested adage, but my mother stared back in bewilderment.

"I don't know what that means," she said. "Is that an expression? Is Billy the elephant?"

"These are his state assessment tests," Hibble said, pushing my transcripts across his desk. "Every child in New Jersey takes this test.

Eighty-three percent of ninth graders outperformed Billy on this exam. And that's okay. We're not here to blame Billy for his intellectual shortcomings."

My mother stared at the transcript like it was written in a foreign language, like she simply couldn't make sense of it. I'd always hated the state assessment tests, with their stupid questions and their fill-in-the-bubble answer sheets. After an hour of coloring the little circles, I felt ready to jump out the window—and the test lasted three days.

Mom pushed back the transcript. "So what happens now?"

"That depends on Billy." Hibble turned to me. "You're graduating in three years, son. What do you want to do after high school?"

I shrugged and looked over his shoulder, praying the whole thing would soon be over. I didn't dare tell him about Planet Will Software or my plan to become a successful programmer, like Fletcher Mulligan of Digital Artists. I knew Hibble would just laugh.

"Answer the question, Billy."

"I don't know," I said.

"He's only fourteen," Mom said.

"He needs a goal," Hibble said. "Work without a goal is just spinning wheels. It's wasting energy."

I tried to think of a bullshit answer that would satisfy Hibble and came up short.

"We're not leaving this office until we've found a goal," he said. "Have you thought about the army?"

I shook my head. I'd seen enough movies to believe the military was full of men like Hibble, that the army would be a lifetime of ugly encounters just like this one. "No army."

"How about Food World?" Hibble asked. "Do you want to work with your mother on the cash register?"

"Billy's not doing that," Mom said.

"He has to do *something*," Hibble said, raising his voice. "He's failing ninth grade, and the rules say I need to hold him back. Make him repeat the grade all over again. If you want me to ignore the rules and move him forward, I need to know what he's moving toward. Where is he going?"

The situation was more dire than I thought. I never realized there was any risk of repeating ninth grade. No one was ever held back at Wetbridge High—not even Greg Kuba, who came to school with a padded helmet and a diaper under his Wranglers. The threat scared me into telling the truth.

"I'm going to make video games," I said. "I'm going to start my own company, and I'll only hire cool people. Or I'll go work for somebody cool like Fletcher Mulligan of Digital Artists. He's in California, but I'd move there for the job."

Hibble was grinning before I'd even finished. I might as well have said that I wanted to be an astronaut, or president of the United States. "A computer programmer? Is that a joke?"

"He's serious," Mom said.

"You're failing math, Billy! Not Pre-Calc, not even Algebra. You're failing C-track! The basics! Pie charts and number lines!" I felt my face turning redder and redder. I *knew* I should have kept my mouth shut, because Hibble was really piling it on: "Think for a minute, Billy. What college is going to teach you programming?"

And he was right, sure he was right. I knew no college would ever want me—but that was okay, because *I* didn't want *them*. "I'll teach myself."

Hibble leaned across his desk and raised his voice, like he was desperate to get through to me. "That's not how it works. You think brain surgeons teach themselves? Or lawyers?" He gestured to the boxy TRS-80 computer on his desk. "I've spent three years on this machine, and I still can't get it to print. And I went to Brown, understand? The best of the Ivies! There are some things you can't teach yourself."

I knew TRS-80s were famously difficult to configure; I had read all about them in my hobby magazines, where readers disparaged the machines as "TRaSh-80s." The solution to Hibble's problem appeared to be "daisy-chaining" the peripherals—basically, connecting the printer to the computer via the stand-alone disk drive. This was not nearly as hard or as complicated as it sounds. But I sure wasn't going to tell Hibble the secret.

"Maybe Billy could try a programming class," Mom said. "If we encouraged this interest . . ."

Hibble shook his head. "Limited machines, limited enrollment. I save those seats for our best and brightest. Not kids flunking ninth grade. Not kids who cut class to go to the mall."

Round and round we went, in a discussion that seemed to last hours. Every time I opened my mouth, I was wrong. Out of nowhere, my mother started sobbing. She'd been awake all night, selling groceries to insomniacs, and this argument was way past her bedtime. Even *I* was worn-out, and I'd only been awake a few hours. I started agreeing with everything Hibble said. I just wanted to leave. When he finally said, "I think I have a solution," I nearly answered with *Yes, anything, please just get me out of here.*

Hibble produced two xeroxed flyers from his desk and gave one to each of us. The headline promised EXCITING CAREERS IN MANUFACTURING TECHNOLOGY. "There's a summer internship at the Cosmex plant on Route 9. It doesn't pay any money—you have to volunteer—but I want you to think of it like a foot in the door. If you show up on time, if you work hard and impress the right people, you can have a decent job waiting at graduation. They start full-timers at seven fifty an hour."

My mother turned the flyer front and back, searching for some missing component. "A makeup factory?"

"A world-class facility," Hibble said. "The operations manager is my brother-in-law. I've taken tours. They can make ten thousand lipsticks an hour. Can you imagine?"

The flyer featured photographs of men and women dressed in hairnets and standing over assembly lines, smiling cheerfully as they pressed tiny mirrors into tiny plastic compacts. The program ran for eight weeks, forty hours a week. At the end of it, I would receive a Special Certificate of Achievement. "Which will look very good on a resume," Hibble added.

"I've never heard of Cosmex," Mom said.

"They make high-quality generics at affordable prices. Like L'Oréal or Maybelline but half the cost. And Billy would be eligible for the ten percent employee discount." He winked at my mother, and she pressed her hands against the sides of her head, like she was trying to steady her thoughts.

So there were my choices: repeat the ninth grade or take the internship and advance to tenth grade. And I knew from my mother's sobbing that repeating the ninth grade was not an option. I accepted a gold-plated fountain pen from Hibble and completed the Internship Commitment form, agreeing to show up on June 28 for a summer's worth of volunteer work, and my mother countersigned.

Hibble's eyes followed our hands as they moved across the paperwork. "You're making the right choice," he said. "So I'm going to reduce your punishment to a single day's suspension."

"Punishment for what?" Mom asked.

"Playing hooky," Hibble said, gesturing to my brown bag lunch. "Remember?"

Mom spoke very slowly. "You're sending him home as a punishment for skipping school?"

"Actions have consequences!" Hibble said. "If you don't beat the cream, Mrs. Marvin, how do you expect it to froth?"

We left the school and drove home in silence. While climbing the steps to our front door, Mom tripped and nearly fell. "I have to go to sleep," she muttered. "I have to get up for work in three hours."

She trudged into her bedroom and closed the door. I was glad I didn't have to spend my suspension sitting across from her. I could easily pass the afternoon reading *How to Learn Machine Language in*

30 Days. But then her bedroom door opened and she emerged carrying the power box for my 64.

"You really know how to work this machine?" she asked. "You promise you're not playing *Pac-Man*?"

"I promise," I said. "I swear to God."

She gave me the box. "Then get to work."

10

```
1000 REM *** DRAW PRINCESS SPRITE ***
1010 POKE 52,48:POKE 56,48
1020 FOR PR=0 TO 62:READ P
1030 POKE 12416+PR,P
1040 NEXT PR
1050 POKE 2042,194:POKE V+21,4
1060 POKE V+41,3
1070 POKE V+4,PX
1080 POKE V+5,PY
1090 RETURN
]■
```

MARY TOLD ME THAT she started work right after school, so I biked over to the store at three o'clock. I didn't want to appear overeager, but the deadline was looming and every minute counted. I entered the store and the tiny bell signaled my arrival.

Zelinsky looked up from his work desk. He was busy prying apart another ancient typewriter; his hands and forearms were black with ink.

"She's not here," he said.

I was so flustered, I didn't know what to say. I never considered that Mary might bail on me, that her invitation was never less than completely sincere.

"She's at Crenshaw's," Zelinsky said. Crenshaw's was the pharmacy across the street, next door to the train station. "She'll be back in a minute."

"All right," I said.

I waited for Zelinsky to tell me what to do. Instead he just returned to work. He wedged a screwdriver in the open cavity of the typewriter and tugged backward, pulling harder and harder until something cracked and tiny plastic shards ricocheted off the walls. One of the fragments struck me in the forehead, just above my eyebrows. The pain was hot and quick, like a bee sting. I didn't mean to cry out but couldn't help myself.

"Careful!" Zelinsky snapped, shooing me away with his fingers. "Go stand someplace else. You're too close."

I decided this was an invitation to stick around until Mary returned. I paced in front of the news rack, reading the headlines on all of the tabloids and magazines. Bernard Goetz was on trial for shooting four youths on a subway train. Gary Hart resigned from his presidential campaign after admitting to an affair with Donna Rice. More and more people were dying from the mysterious AIDS virus. I didn't know the details behind any of these stories, and I didn't really care. The only magazines I read were full of computer code.

Beside the cash register were two glass cases—one filled with boxes of cigars, the other with new and antique cigarette lighters. There were all different colors and brands—Zippo, Dunlap, Penguin, and Scripto—and many were decorated with icons and military insignia. I was astounded to see that some of these lighters sold for as much as $300 or $400. I reached for the door of the case to take a better look, but it wouldn't open.

"No touching," Zelinsky said. "Don't touch anything you're not going to buy."

"Sorry," I told him.

"You don't have to apologize."

"Sorry," I said again.

I shoved my hands in my pockets and stood perfectly still. I didn't see how I could disturb him if I didn't move or touch anything or say anything. But Zelinsky looked up from his typewriter, exasperated. "Can you please not stand there? You're blocking the doorway."

I didn't know where to go. I couldn't stand next to Zelinsky. I couldn't stand by the door.

"Should I wait outside?"

Zelinsky nodded. "Maybe that's best."

I turned for the door as Mary returned, carrying a brown paper bag from the pharmacy. "Hey," she said, "where are you going?"

"Nowhere," I said, turning around yet again. "I was just waiting for you."

"Awesome. Let's get to work."

She passed the bag to Zelinsky and led me through the store. She was moving quickly, like she couldn't wait to get started. Hall and Oates were on the radio singing "You Make My Dreams Come True."

"You're not going to believe this," I said, "but the radio was playing the same song yesterday."

"It's not the radio," she said. "It's a mixtape. My mom's favorite songs. She taped them all off the radio." I nearly made a smart-ass comment, but I was glad I didn't because Mary continued, "She died two years ago. Stomach cancer."

She said this so matter-of-factly, I thought I'd misheard her. "Did you say stomach cancer?"

"Yeah. June 21, 1985. It was the last day of school."

Up until that moment, I assumed Mary and her father went home every evening to a warm dinner and a houseful of siblings, but Mary explained it was just the two of them. She was quick to steer the conversation back to the mixtape. "I know the songs are cheesy, but my dad likes them, so I put up with it."

"I don't think they're cheesy," I said, because I wanted to say something nice, but Hall and Oates hooted "ooh-ooh, ooh-ooh," and Mary laughed.

"This song has more cheese than a quesadilla," she said, "but I'm glad you're cool with it, because you're going to hear it a billion times. The stereo loops it automatically."

We arrived in the showroom, and I saw that Mary had rearranged the furniture so there were two chairs beside the computer. I brought out my own copy of *How to Learn Machine Language in 30 Days* so we could study side by side. The book was full of mini-programs to type and try, so I started keying one into the 64. But after a few lines, I noticed Mary frowning.

"What's wrong?"

"This is just a suggestion," she said, "but what if *you* read the code aloud and *I* do the typing?"

It took me a moment to catch her meaning.

"You think I type slow?"

"You're hunting and pecking. Your fingers are nowhere near home row."

"What's home row?"

"Exactly," Mary said, as if this proved her point. "Sister Benedict clocked me at ninety words a minute. She called my typing skills a miracle. And coming from a nun, that really means something."

We settled the debate by unpacking a second 64 from inventory, placing the machines side by side, and then racing to input the first paragraph of the user's manual word for word, no mistakes, on your marks get set go! I was lightning quick, my fingers flying all over the keyboard with perfect accuracy, but when I shouted, "Done!" I heard Mary echo me. We had finished together in a dead heat.

So our contest had settled nothing, but going forward we moved twice as fast, because Mary convinced her father that two computers increased the persuasive power of the store's showroom. "It's like walking into the Gap," she explained. "They never show just one T-shirt. There's always a table with six or seven. Products look better in groups."

I didn't totally buy her logic—for starters, T-shirts come in different colors—but Zelinsky seemed willing to try. "It's not doing anything sitting in a box." He shrugged. "Three months we've had these damn machines, and we've yet to sell a single one of them. 'The Most Popular Home Computer in America.' "

He glared at me like somehow I was responsible, like I had personally invented the 64 and then petitioned Zelinsky to stock the machines.

"I'm sorry," I said.

His glare intensified, and his eyebrows arched to epic heights. "Why do you keep apologizing?"

"Dad, we're on a tight deadline," Mary said.

"I want him out by seven o'clock," Zelinsky said. "You've got homework."

We spent the next three hours testing patches of code and reading aloud from *How to Learn Machine Language in 30 Days*. The mixtape looped from Howard Jones ("No One Is to Blame") and Bruce Hornsby ("The Way It Is") to Marshall Crenshaw ("Someday, Someway"). A pattern quickly presented itself: Mary would read aloud a dense and difficult passage, I would fail to understand it, and then she would re-explain the concept using her own words until it made sense to both of us.

This happened so often, I soon felt embarrassed. I knew Mary would be turning the pages much faster without me, that my "intellectual shortcomings" (or whatever Hibble had called them) were holding back our progress. I hunched forward in my chair, biting my cuticles and sighing and watching the clock. But Mary didn't seem flustered. She'd repeat herself three or four times without ever sounding aggravated. She acted like we had all the time in the world.

"I'm sorry I'm such a dummy," I said.

"This is tough stuff."

"But *you* understand it."

"Because I'm explaining it to you," she said. "Saying it out loud helps it make sense to me."

We ended the day with a practice exercise from the book. Each of us created a mini-program that utilized graphics in machine language. Mine flashed the words PLANET WILL SOFTWARE in different colors. Mary's featured a boy and girl dancing, popping and locking and moonwalking like Michael Jackson in the *Motown 25* special. I realized the boy was wearing a white shirt and jeans, and the girl had long dark hair. Mary had programmed them to look like us.

"How did you make this in forty-five minutes?" I asked.

"Yours is good, too," she said.

The crazy thing is, she actually managed to sound sincere. I listed the commands and studied her code, a long block of ideas I'd never considered and strategies I'd never tried, an entirely different approach to programming. I felt like I was finger painting next to Pablo Picasso.

11

```
1100 REM *** DRAW GUARD 2 SPRITE ***
1110 POKE 52,48:POKE 56,48
1120 FOR GU=0 TO 62:READ G
1130 POKE 12480+GU,G
1140 NEXT GU
1150 POKE 2043,195:POKE V+21,8
1160 POKE V+42,4
1170 POKE V+6,GGX
1180 POKE V+7,GGY
1190 RETURN
]■
```

ONCE AGAIN ZELINSKY BOOTED me out of the store at seven o'clock, and I left to find Alf and Clark waiting on their bikes. Alf had the Beast perched on his handlebars—this was our nickname for his massive Sony boom box, an enormous radio with giant speakers, twin cassette decks, and a hundred useless lights and levers. The Beast weighed a ton, but Alf had rigged a small platform onto his handlebars so we could bike around accompanied by movie soundtracks. He saw me coming and pressed Play on the cassette deck. Queen's "Fat Bottomed Girls" came blasting out of the speakers, turning heads up and down Market Street. Alf pantomimed a performance on the sidewalk, using a Coke bottle as a microphone—*Ohhh, won't you take me home tonight?*—until I hurried over to the Beast and spun down the volume.

"What's wrong with you?" I asked.

"Take it easy," Alf said. "She can't hear us."

He cranked the volume up, even louder this time—*fat bottomed girls, you make the rocking world go round!*

I ejected the tape and pocketed it.

"Hey, what's your problem?" Alf asked.

I stepped off the sidewalk into traffic, and the driver of an Oldsmobile stomped the brakes, screeching her tires and stopping just inches from my knees. I wanted to put some distance between us and the store. I didn't stop walking or say anything until we were across Market Street and around the corner.

Then I ripped into them. "You're being too obvious! If you keep hanging around the store, they're going to know something's up."

"Did you get the code?" Clark asked.

"Sure, I was like, 'Hey, what's the security code for your father's store?' And she told me, because she's an idiot."

"If you're not getting the code," Alf said, "what the hell are you doing in there?"

"We're working on a game," I explained. "I told you I needed time."

"My customers are getting impatient," Alf said.

"What about Arnold Schwarzenegger?" I asked. "How do we pass a guard dog that sits in the window all night long?"

"We're working on it," Alf said. "We've got a couple ideas we're testing."

Street traffic was already thin by seven o'clock—most of the commuters were home for the night—so we all noticed when two cute girls came walking down the block. They were fifteen or sixteen years old, with short-shorts and skinny legs. I recognized them from Video City, the store where we rented our movies. Clark stuck his claw in his pocket, and I stared at my sneakers, pretending I was too busy to notice them. Alf dropped the *Top Gun* soundtrack into cassette deck one so that "Danger Zone" by Kenny Loggins came thumping out of the speakers. Then he reached in his pocket for a bankroll of wrinkled bills. It was an enormous wad of cash, about the size of a hockey puck, and he counted it casually as the girls sauntered past.

"Where did you get that?" I asked.

"I'm giving an early-bird discount," he said proudly. Alf explained that fifteen of our classmates had already paid for their Vanna White photos in advance, with the understanding that the photos would arrive before the month ended.

I turned to Clark. "And you're okay with this? Are you selling to early birds, too?"

He shook his head. "Naw, I just want a copy for myself," he said softly. "But I don't see the harm in it."

Alf spread the bills into a giant fan of money, like he was Mr. Monopoly on a Chance card. Then he waved the bills in front of my face. "Smell the profit, Billy."

I slapped the money away. "Do not spend it," I warned him. "Not a penny."

"Why not?"

"In case you have to give it back," I said. "In case something goes wrong."

"What could go wrong?" he asked.

I wasn't ready to explain. I couldn't tell him there was no chance of getting the alarm code, not yet. I needed to keep trying, or pretending to try, until *The Impossible Fortress* was complete and submitted to the contest.

"Anything could go wrong," I said.

Almost on cue, a uniformed Wetbridge police officer rounded the corner of Market Street, walking toward us.

"It's Tack," Clark said. "Put the money away."

"Where?" Alf asked.

"Don't turn around!"

Tack's real name was long, Polish, and impossible to pronounce; we all called him Tack because he reminded us of young, super gung ho Eugene Tackleberry in the *Police Academy* movies. At six foot four, he was the tallest cop on the Wetbridge Police Department. Twice a year he visited our high school to screen horrifying movies on the dangers of drugs, alcohol, and Communism; he warned that movies like *Red Dawn* "could really happen." When he wasn't educating the children of Wetbridge, he patrolled downtown wearing a Kevlar vest and papered windshields with five-dollar parking tickets.

"Evening, boys," he said, shaking hands slowly and deliberately with each one of us. His grip left my hand feeling hollow and deflated, like a bike-tire flat. "Any signs of trouble tonight?"

This was his default greeting to all the little kids in Wetbridge; Tack warned there was an army of Dolph Lundgren clones just waiting to descend upon our town, and the patriotic youth of America were its last line of defense. At age fourteen we all felt like we were getting too old for this routine, but tonight we were happy to play along.

"No, sir," I said.

"No sign of trouble," Alf said.

"No Russkies for miles," Clark added.

"I'm not talking Russkies," Tack said. He gathered us into a huddle and lowered his voice to a whisper. "I'm being completely serious, boys. We had two attempted break-ins on Market Street last week. The pet store and the travel agency. Crowbar marks all around the back doors. Like someone tried to pry off the hinges."

We were all too panicked to respond. I worried even the slightest phrase might betray what we'd been planning. The bankroll of cash created a very conspicuous lump in Alf's Bermuda shorts, like he'd pocketed a tennis ball.

"And then last night someone broke a window at Video City. Ran off with a brand-new VCR and a bunch of those head-cleaning tapes. You boys hear anything about that?"

"No, sir," Clark said.

"Nothing," I added.

"But we'll be on the lookout," Alf promised. "Is there a reward if we catch the guy?"

"I'm sure they'd come up with something. The Merchants Association is freaking out. So city council has us doing night patrols until the 'crime wave' tapers off. Dusk till dawn. It's costing a ton of overtime."

"Dusk till dawn?" Clark asked.

"Our presence is what we call a deterrent. If a bad guy sees a police officer walking Market Street at four in the morning, he's likely to think twice. That's the idea, anyway. In the meantime I need you guys to keep your eyes peeled, understand? Let me know if you see anything squirrelly."

We all promised to stay vigilant. Tack thanked us for our service to the community and insisted on shaking our hands again before heading on his way. He walked down Market Street and turned left at the train station; minutes later, he arrived on Lafayatte, traversing the downtown shopping district in a figure-eight loop.

"Dusk-till-dawn patrols," Clark said.

"First Arnold Schwarzenegger and now Tackleberry," I said. "Maybe we need to rethink this plan."

"I'm not rethinking anything," Alf said. "You promised to get the code, Billy. We had a deal."

"Exactly!" Clark said. "You can't wuss out at the first sign of trouble. Are you saying you want to quit?"

"No," I said. "I'm not quitting." There were still eleven more days until the contest deadline. Eleven days to learn ML and get *The Impossible Fortress* into working order. "But I will need more time."

They both seemed relieved. Alf rewound *Top Gun* to the start of Side 1 and pressed Play, blasting Kenny Loggins and redlining the equalizer lights. "You just get that alarm code," he said, "and leave the rest to us."

12

```
1200 REM *** ADVANCE COUNTDOWN ***
1210 TIMER=TIMER-1
1220 PRINT "{HOME}TIME LEFT:",TIMER
1230 IF TIMER=0 THEN GOTO 1600
1240 IF TIMER<25 THEN ER=25:RETURN
1250 IF TIMER<50 THEN ER=20:RETURN
1260 IF TIMER<75 THEN ER=15:RETURN
1270 IF TIMER<100 THEN ER=10:RETURN
1280 IF TIMER<150 THEN ER=5:RETURN
1290 RETURN
]■
```

I STARTED GOING TO Zelinsky's every day. I worked with Mary from three until seven, when her father promptly kicked me out. At first we made nothing but mistakes. Learning machine language was the hardest thing I'd ever tried, and I'm sure I would have quit if Mary hadn't shown so much confidence. She acted like we'd already won the contest, and now programming the game was just a simple formality. I kept expecting her to lose interest in the project. Every time I arrived at the store, I expected her to tell me she'd made other plans—that she was going to the mall or babysitting or whatever normal fourteen-year-old girls did. But Mary never failed me. Every afternoon, she was waiting in the showroom, ready to work.

We fell into a routine. We started every afternoon with a Dr Pepper and a bag of pretzels. We took a Skittles break at five o'clock, when our energy flagged and we needed a sugar rush. Her mother's mixtape played on an endless loop, the same fourteen songs over and over. Soon I had the entire sequence memorized and I was quietly anticipating my favorites.

On our third day working together, Mary explained that her mother had created the tape in the waning days of her illness, and the track list was a sort of poem. That didn't make sense to me until I saw the whole sequence written out, in her mother's delicate handwriting, on the liner notes of the cassette itself:

Nothing's Gonna Change My Love For You
No One is To Blame . . . It's Just the Way It Is
Someday, Someway . . . Against All Odds . . .
Things Can Only Get Better.

Don't Give Up . . . Be Good to Yourself.
I Won't Hold You Back.
Dance the Night Away!

You Know I Love You, Don't You?
(You Were) Always on My Mind
You Are So Beautiful
You Make My Dreams Come True

I could hear Zelinsky muttering at the cash register, cursing the stubborn gears of some ancient typewriter, and I couldn't believe he had ever convinced a woman to love him. And yet here was a mixtape to prove that he had.

I returned the case to Mary. "I can see why you never get tired of it."

Mary laughed. "Oh, I'm sick of it! But my dad and I can't agree on anything else. Picking out the music was always Mom's job."

Mary explained that she had grown up in the store, playing on the hardwood floors with Weebles and Tinker Toys while her parents renovated the interior, painstakingly cutting and sanding and hanging all of the shelves, and hand-lettering all of the signs. The store was a lot busier back then, Mary explained, because so many regulars would stop in just to chat with her mom. "It was like *Cheers* in here. Three hundred people came to her funeral. The priest said that was a Wetbridge record. And so of course I fainted."

She'd lowered her voice to a whisper. There were two women browsing nearby in the stationery aisle, comparing two different boxes of ivory linen resume sheets, and Mary was being careful to not broadcast her story.

"Did you say fainted?"

She nodded. "We're at the Mass, and I'm standing in front of the whole church. And I'm doing okay. Crying a little, but I'm not hysterical. Then I make the mistake of looking at my dad, and *he's* crying, *he's* hysterical. I'd never seen him cry, ever. And that's when I lost it. I fell on this giant spray of flowers from the Merchants Association. Knocked it over and cut my lip on the wire stand. It was awful." She cringed at the memory, and then shook it off, suddenly embarrassed. "I'm sorry. I don't know why I'm telling you all this. You were only asking about the stupid music."

"It's not stupid."

Mary put her back to me and leaned toward her monitor, like she was trying to immerse herself in the code. "Let's get back to work."

We were supposed to be animating the legs of the guards so they would bend their knees when they ran. But within minutes, I found myself telling Mary how my father lived in Alaska, how he and my mother were never even married, how we'd probably be in the poorhouse if it wasn't for my aunt Gretchen. These were my biggest secrets and I was deeply ashamed of them, but I felt like I owed Mary a story in return.

"I wish I knew why he left," I told her. "That's one thing I've never understood."

She had stopped typing and turned to face me. "He's going to come back someday," she said. "Sooner or later, he's going to want to meet you."

I shook my head. "I don't think so." Mom didn't offer a lot of details about my dad, but she'd spent hundreds of hours discussing him with my aunt Gretchen, and I'd become an expert at eavesdropping on their phone conversations. Mom described him as "reckless and irresponsible" and "a narcissist" and (this one hurt the most) "a loser." She insisted he was never coming back, that there was a better chance of Paul Newman showing up on our doorstep.

"Your mother's wrong," Mary said. "One day your dad is going to get curious about you. It's bound to happen. But by the time he gets here, it'll be too late, because you'll already be living in California." She tapped the monitor with the pink eraser at the end of her pencil. "As soon as Fletcher Mulligan sees this code, he's going to insist on adopting you."

I laughed. "I'm not sure my mom will agree to that."

Mary didn't let logic get in the way of her fantasy. "First it'll just be a job offer. He'll want to hire you for Digital Artists. But once you get out there, you'll need a place to stay, so he'll give you a spare room in his mansion. You'll start hanging out, eating dinner with Fletcher and his wife. And once they get to know you, they'll insist on making it legal. So you can inherit the entire company after Fletcher dies. Like *Charlie and the Chocolate Factory*."

I felt like Mary had somehow read my mind. I can't tell you how many times I daydreamed this exact scenario, lying in bed at night in the moments before I drifted off to sleep.

"You're crazy," I told her. "Where do you get these goofy ideas?"

"It's going to happen, Will." She looked at me with absolute certainty, radiating confidence like no one else I'd ever met. "Just promise you'll let me visit the mansion someday. You have to promise you won't forget about me."

13

```
1300 REM *** ERROR BUZZER ***
1310 FOR L=0 TO 24:POKE S+L,0
1320 NEXT L
1330 POKE S+1,100:POKE S+5,219
1340 POKE S+15,28:POKE S+24,15
1350 POKE S+4,19
1360 FOR T=1 TO 1000:NEXT T
1370 POKE S+4,18
1380 POKE S+24,0
1390 RETURN
]█
```

MARY AND I ONLY had one argument. It was our fourth afternoon of working on the game. Zelinsky was at the cash register, talking antique lighters with a pair of collectors from Philadelphia, and Mary was helping a customer with fountain pens, so I found myself alone in the showroom. Howard Jones was on the radio, and I was still working on the guard animation, fine-tuning the movements of their arms, when a girl walked up to my desk and said, "Excuse me."

She was two or three years older than me—a junior or a senior, dressed like a punk mini-Madonna with army boots, ripped stockings, and a skirt made of vinyl. Her eyes were ringed with blue makeup. "Do you work here?"

"No," I said.

She shrugged like it didn't really matter. I was hunched over the keyboard, surrounded by notebooks, printouts, highlighters, and candy wrappers. If I wasn't an employee, I was close enough.

"My dad sent me here to buy disks." She reached into the folds of her skirt for a sheet of notepaper. "He needs 'ten five-one-four-inch floppy disks.'"

"Five and a quarter inch," I corrected. "I can show you."

We walked down the aisle to the computer supplies and I explained the options. "He's got Fuji and Maxwell. They're the same price, but Maxwells are black and Fuji comes in rainbow colors."

"Cool," she said, reaching for the Fujis. "Thanks."

She carried the disks to the front of the store and Zelinsky rang up the purchase. I walked back to the showroom and Mary was waiting at her computer. She grinned at me. "She was awful flirty, huh?"

"What do you mean?"

Mary mimicked the girl in a squeaky singsong voice. "'I need five-one-four-inch floppy disks. Because I'm too cute to understand fractions!'"

"She didn't say that."

"It's the *way* she said it. Like she was some kind of helpless baby animal. That's flirting, Will."

I blushed. "Whatever."

"Oh, God, please tell me she's not your type. Don't tell me you like these punk rock chicks with the raccoon eye shadow."

"I don't have a type."

"*Everyone* has a type."

"Not me. I've never even had a girlfriend."

"But you have a type that you like," she said. "Brunette, redhead, tall, short, goth, cheerleader—"

"I like all those types," I said. "I don't discriminate."

"Everyone discriminates," she said. "Everyone has personal biases and preferences. That's basic human psychology."

I felt like I was back in Hibble's office—no answer was going to satisfy her.

"What about you?" I asked. "What's your type?"

"I like confident people. I like guys who know what they want."

"Like Tyler Bell?"

I don't know why I said it. I didn't believe any of the things Tyler had said about Mary: *I had to beat her back with a stick, all right? She couldn't keep her hands off me.* I knew Mary would never really fall for a goon like Tyler—but suddenly she looked like I'd slapped her.

"You know Tyler Bell?"

"Everyone knows Tyler Bell."

"How do you know Tyler Bell?"

"He goes to my school. He has a Harley."

"What did he say to you?"

"Nothing. I mean, I *barely* know him. I just know he worked here."

"Tyler Bell is an asshole," she said. "The worst employee we ever had."

"So *not* your type?"

"It isn't funny, Will. Don't even joke about him."

"What's wrong?"

And then Zelinsky was standing over us, his apron covered with wet black ink. At the time, I didn't know how many of our conversations traveled to the front of the store. But looking back, I'm pretty sure he heard most of them.

"Is everything all right?"

He stated the question like a fact, strongly implying that no, everything was *not* all right.

"We're fine," Mary said.

"Maybe Will should go home now."

"We're fine," Mary repeated. "I just want to get back to work."

Zelinsky hesitated, then turned and walked back to the cash register. For the next hour, I didn't dare say anything. We read from our respective books and typed on our respective computers. There were no further customers in the showroom and the only sounds came from All Your Favorite '80s Love Songs—Joe Cocker and Willie Nelson and Phil Collins. From time to time I'd look at Mary, but she was typing furiously and avoiding eye contact.

Sometime around six o'clock I realized there were sirens blaring, and a police officer came into the store to tell Zelinsky that Crenshaw's Pharmacy was on fire. We rose from our desks and went outside to take a look.

There were two fire trucks parked in the middle of Market Street and the volunteer firefighters were scrambling to unload their gear; Tackleberry and two other cops were routing traffic away from the train station. Mr. Crenshaw himself was pacing up and down the sidewalk, shaking his head. Gray smoke was venting from the second-story windows of his building; the fire appeared to be coming not from the pharmacy but the apartment above it. We craned our necks for a better view but we were standing at the wrong angle.

"Come on," Mary told me. "I've got an idea."

We went back inside and walked past the showroom to the cramped narrow staircase in the rear of the store. I followed Mary up to the second floor, and we entered a labyrinth of wire shelves and corrugated cardboard. All around us were boxes and shelves. The passage twisted and turned, and the lighting was dim, but Mary obviously knew every inch of the place. She stopped beneath a massive wooden hatch. "I just need to unlock it," she explained.

I watched as she reached in her pocket for a key chain. Tyler Bell hadn't exaggerated the sorry state of the woodwork; the door looked like something you'd see on a sunken pirate ship. A white wire stretched from the base of the hatch to a small crack in the ceiling, where it disappeared behind the wall.

I pointed to it. "Is that an alarm?"

"Yeah, my dad's pretty paranoid. Like crooks are going to scale our walls and steal our envelopes, you know?"

The wooden door was so heavy, we both had to push. It opened outward, pivoting on two ancient hinges that shrieked with surprise. Then we ascended three steep steps and clambered out onto the roof. It was wide and flat but still a little dizzying; seeing Market Street and the train station from this new perspective was disorienting. The sun was setting and the sky was aflame with a crazy pink-and-orange glow. Up on the roof, it seemed close enough to touch.

We walked toward Market Street, stopping four feet short of the edge. This new vantage point gave us a full view of Crenshaw's building; we could see firefighters moving around through the windows but no one was hurrying anymore; the smoke was thinning and it seemed the worst of the drama was already contained. Down on the street, a crowd of kids on dirt bikes had assembled to watch the action, and I could see Alf and Clark standing among them. Alf had the Beast balanced on his handlebars, and they both appeared to be lamenting the lack of destruction.

"I'm sorry about before," Mary said. "About Tyler. I didn't mean to jump down your throat."

"That's all right," I said.

"He stole from the store. Or tried to, anyway. It's still a sore subject for me and my dad."

At once, her behavior made a lot more sense.

"What did he take?"

"You know those antique lighters near the register? Some of them are two or three hundred bucks. Tyler tried to steal one, and I caught him."

"What happened?"

"My dad was pretty mad. He trusted Tyler. We both did. So he fired him, and that was that." She turned away from Crenshaw's, turning west to face the sunset instead. It was a much better view. "This was all last year, right when school was starting up. But like I said, we're both still angry about it, I guess."

Of course they were angry. This version of the story was a lot more believable than Tyler's horndog fantasy. Mr. Zelinsky had zero patience for shoplifters. Tyler was lucky he hadn't been arrested.

"I barely know the guy at all," I told her. "I'm a freshman and he's a senior."

"I know," she said. "I believe you."

"So we're okay? Me and you?"

"Yeah, we're okay."

I put out my hand and we shook on it. Her fingernails were freshly painted, each with its own tiny sunflower.

"Let's get back to work," I said.

She shook her head. "I'm done for the day. I'm going to hang up here for a bit."

So we stood up there for a long while, watching the sunset and discussing how it was one of those things you could never truly capture in 8-bit, not with the 64's simplistic definition of violet (CHR$(156)), orange (CHR$(129)), and yellow (CHR$(158)). There were too many other colors, thousands of colors. The hardware could never do justice to it.

That night I went home worried that Mary was still angry, that she was going to abandon *The Impossible Fortress* and leave me to finish the game on my own. But when I got to school the next morning, there was another floppy disk waiting inside my locker. I brought it to the lone computer in the school library, checked the directory, and saw it contained another mini-game.

```
You are deep inside The Impossible Fortress,
standing at the end of a long, narrow corri-
dor. The stone walls are lined with flickering
```

torches. Blocking the passage to the north is a massive ogre. He is holding a club and staring at you. Saliva drips from his jaws.

>INVENTORY

You are empty-handed.

The ogre takes a step closer. He is three times your size. He looks very, very hungry.

>PUNCH OGRE

Nice try, Will. You hit the ogre with all your might and he barely flinches. Great, now he's hungry AND annoyed.

>KICK OGRE

Big mistake! Now the ogre is really angry. With a swipe of his fist, you're knocked to the ground. The ogre raises his club over his head, ready to crush you.

Suddenly a secret panel in the wall slides open! Out charges Mary Zelinsky, broadsword in hand. She slays the ogre and he topples to the floor.

>STAND UP

You stand and Mary sheaths her sword. "I'm sorry I snapped at you yesterday," she says. "I

```
hope I didn't ruin anything. Will you please
accept this dead ogre as my apology?"

>SAY YES

"Thank you, Will!" Mary says. (Your score just
went up by 100 points, giving you a rank of
Fantabulous.) "I'll see you after school!"

GAME OVER.
```

Then the strangest thing happened. Underneath the words GAME OVER, the cursor was still flashing, inviting me to input another command.

```
>GO NORTH

I just told you, the game is over.

>ENTER SECRET PASSAGE

Sorry, the dead ogre is blocking your way.

>FOLLOW MARY

But Mary is standing right here! She looks
quite fetching in her chainmail armor and iron
breastplate.
```

This had to be a test. Mary wouldn't have programmed all of these responses if she hadn't intended for me to see them. On a whim I tried something crazy:

>KISS MARY

You lean forward, placing your hands on Mary's waist. She stands on tiptoes and closes her eyes, pressing her lips to yours. Suddenly your vision is obscured by fireworks and shooting stars. Your score increases by 50,000,000 points, giving you the rank of The Coolest Guy I Know.

And then the game finally stopped. A librarian walked past me, and I abruptly powered down the computer before she could read the screen. She gave me a suspicious look—I was blushing from ear to ear—but returned to her desk without comment.

After school I went to Zelinsky's and found Mary working in the showroom. Her face was close to the monitor; she was absorbed in a problem. I threw down my backpack and fell into my chair. Waiting beside my computer was a bag of pretzels and a cold can of Dr Pepper, straight from the fridge.

"Thank you," I said. "And thanks for the game. I finished it." She turned to look at me, searching my face for clues, and I realized my statement was vague. I took a deep breath and said, "I got the fifty million points."

Mary turned back to the screen. She tapped a line of code with her pencil. "This part right here is causing tons of lag. What if we moved it to the beginning?"

I leaned over her shoulder for a better look, and maybe I leaned a little closer than usual. Close enough to smell her shampoo, or her perfume, or whatever made her smell so good. Our fight was over and we were back to normal. But normal was a little different from that day forward.

14

```
1400 REM *** ASSIGN RANKINGS$ ***
1410 IF SCORE>=8000 THEN RANK$="FANTABULOUS!"
1420 IF SCORE<8000 THEN RANK$="AWESOME!"
1430 IF SCORE<7000 THEN RANK$="GREAT!"
1440 IF SCORE<6000 THEN RANK$="GOOD"
1450 IF SCORE<5000 THEN RANK$="AVERAGE"
1460 IF SCORE<4000 THEN RANK$="NOT BAD"
1470 IF SCORE<3000 THEN RANK$="FAIR"
1480 IF SCORE<2000 THEN RANK$="UGH!"
1490 RETURN
]■
```

AS THE DAYS PASSED, I saw less and less of Alf and Clark. We still biked to school every morning, but I'd stopped joining them in the cafeteria for lunch; instead I hid in the library and used the extra time to work on *The Impossible Fortress*. The contest deadline was coming up fast; I couldn't waste a single minute. I'd even started bringing stacks of printouts with me into the bathroom.

Friday afternoon I was sitting in the school library, converting binary strings into decimal numbers and tripping all over the math. A binary string looked like a random sequence of zeros and ones—00100100—but each digit in the sequence represented a different value: 128, 64, 32, 16, 8, 4, 2, or 1. So 00010010 had a value of 18 (0+0+0+16+0+0+2+0) and 10000001 had a value of 129 (128+0+0+0+0+0+0+1). Mary was a wiz at binary numbers. She could look at a string like 00111111 and immediately say "sixty-three," but I still had to do all the arithmetic by hand, tallying sums the old-fashioned way.

Someone sat down across from me and placed a wrinkled ten-dollar bill on the table. I looked up and saw Chadwick Melon, captain of the basketball team, treasurer of the student council, and a solid bet for prom king. He was arguably the most celebrated athlete in Wetbridge High School history, and the recipient of eleven different scholarship offers. I'd never actually spoken to him in person, but I'd applauded him in countless assemblies and awards ceremonies.

"You know Alf?" he asked. "Alfred Boyle?"

"Yeah?"

"Tell him Chad Melon wants ten photos. A full set."

I pushed the money back across the table. I don't know where I found the courage to challenge him; I guess I was just annoyed by the interruption. "Just buy it yourself," I told him. "The magazine's only four dollars."

Chad's smile vanished, and I realized I was probably the first person in Wetbridge school history to question his direct orders. He stuffed the money inside my shirt pocket, pushing down hard. "Make sure Alf knows it's from me."

I stopped by the cafeteria on the way to my next class, and our usual lunch table was empty. I found Alf and Clark in the student smoking section, a small outdoor patio littered with butts, just downwind from the teachers' smoking section. Alf was dressed in another one of his *Miami Vice* getups, but Clark just wore a plain white undershirt and denim cutoffs. They were sitting on a bench, taking drags off the skinniest cigarettes I'd ever seen.

"What are you smoking?" I asked.

"Capri 120s," Clark said. "They're new."

Alf flipped me the hard pack, inviting me to try one. "We found 'em by the bus stop. Someone must have dropped them."

None of us were habitual smokers, but when the universe offered us free anything, we were quick to accept.

"These are lady cigarettes," I told them.

"Huh?" Alf said.

"That's why they're so skinny. They're shaped for female hands."

Clark flung away his cigarette like it was a live wasp. "No wonder I'm queasy!" he said.

Alf took another drag off his cigarette, mulling over the flavor, then exhaled. "Tastes fine to me."

"They spray hormones on the wrapping papers," Clark warned him. "To help women lose weight. You're filling your lungs with estrogen."

I gave the ten dollars to Alf and told him about Chadwick Melon. He didn't think the request was strange at all. "I've sold to five different seniors this week," he explained. "I don't care how old you get. No one wants to walk into 7-Eleven and ask for a *Playboy*. It's like saying, 'I'm here to masturbate.' "

I watched as Alf removed a small ledger from his pocket and added Chadwick Melon's name to a list. Then he took out his enormous bankroll and wrapped the ten-dollar bill around its surface. Over the past few days, the wad of money had swollen to the size of a grapefruit.

"Holy crap," I said. "How much is that?"

"Three hundred and eighty-six dollars," he said proudly. "But don't you worry, Billy. I fully intend to share the wealth. We're all in this together, you know?"

"Sure, sure," I said.

"We could end up clearing five hundred bucks."

"That'd be amazing," I said.

Alf took a long drag off his lady cigarette, exhaled the smoke, and then stared at me, like he was waiting for me to say something else. "So now, what about the alarm code?" he finally asked.

The end-of-lunch bell rang but not soon enough to help me. "I'm working on it," I said.

All around us, the other student smokers were stubbing out their butts and popping Tic Tacs.

"We don't have a lot of time," Clark said. "It's May twenty-second. That gives us seven, eight days tops."

I slung my backpack over my shoulder. I was eager to get back to the library, back to working on the game. "Don't worry," I told them. "I'm getting really close."

15

```
1500 REM *** BOOST SCORE ***
1510 IF LIVES=3 THEN SCORE=SCORE+50
1520 IF LIVES=2 THEN SCORE=SCORE+75
1530 IF LIVES=1 THEN SCORE=SCORE+100
1540 PRINT"{HOME}{CSR DWN}SCORE:",SCORE
1550 DG=DG+DX*.15
1560 IF DG>DX THEN DG=DX
1570 IF DG>50 THEN GOSUB 7000
1580 IF DG>100 THEN GOSUB 7500
1590 RETURN
]■
```

ZELINSKY NEVER SAID HELLO, never attempted small talk, never even looked at me—except at seven o'clock, when he stomped back to the showroom and told me to get out. And those were usually his exact words: "Get out" or "Go on, now," he'd say, like he was shooing a dog off his lawn.

"Your dad hates me," I told Mary.

"It's just an act," she insisted. "He actually likes you. He's impressed by your work ethic."

"He said that?"

"Well, not in those exact words."

"In any words?"

"He's impressed," she said. "Trust me."

I tried to get on his good side. I never left cans of soda on the computer desk (even though Mary did so all the time). I kept my voice down, I said "please" and "thank you" and generally tried to stay out of his way. But every time I arrived at the store, Zelinsky looked disappointed.

That Friday, I was working in the showroom while Mary assisted a customer with a typewriter. Once again I was the only person in the back of the store, when out of nowhere this kid wandered past me. He was maybe ten or eleven, dressed in gray denim from head to toe, and carrying a Big Gulp soda. He ducked behind a rack of Energizer batteries, disappearing from view, and I knew right away he was a thief.

He returned a moment later, still holding the Big Gulp and sucking on the straw. Nice detail, kid.

"Can I help you?" I asked.

He shook his head. "I'm good."

I stood up and followed him to the front of the store. I'll give him credit: he was smart enough to stop at the register and buy something—a pack of Bubbalicious chewing gum.

Zelinsky almost didn't even notice him. He was busy repairing a typewriter for a collector in Princeton. "Just the gum? That'll be two bits."

The kid stared back.

"You don't know that expression? Two bits?" Disappointment fell over his face; it was a look I knew all too well. "It means twenty-five cents."

The kid pushed a wrinkled dollar across the counter.

"Where'd you get the Big Gulp?" I asked.

"7-Eleven," he said.

"There's no 7-Eleven on Market Street. The nearest one's five miles away."

He frowned. "Do you, like, work here or something?"

"You're stealing batteries."

The words hadn't finished leaving my mouth and the kid was already out the door. Zelinsky lunged after him, but I told him not to bother. The kid had left the soda cup on the counter. I pried off the lid, revealing six C batteries submerged in a few ounces of warm cola. Zelinsky's eyes went wide, like I'd just performed some kind of miracle.

"Son of a bitch," he said. "How did you know?"

I couldn't tell him the truth—that Alf and I had practically pioneered the Big Gulp stunt, using the 64-ounce cups to steal cellophane-wrapped music cassettes from Sam Goody.

"I heard him messing around by the batteries," I explained. "I figured he was up to something."

That night Zelinsky let me stay an extra half hour, and when the time was finally up, I almost didn't recognize his voice. Instead of "Get out" or "Go" he said, "We'll see you tomorrow, Will."

Mary elbowed me in the ribs.

"You see?" she said. "He's warming up."

16

```
1600 REM *** OUT OF TIME ***
1610 PRINT "{CLR}{12 CSR DWN}"
1620 PRINT "{12 SPACES} YOU ARE OUT"
1630 PRINT "{14 SPACES} OF TIME."
1640 PRINT "{2 CSR DWN}"
1650 PRINT "THY GAME IS OVER."
1660 FOR DELAY=1 TO 1000
1670 NEXT DELAY
1680 IF LIVES=0 THEN 3300
1690 RETURN
]■
```

THE DAYS PASSED QUICKLY. The air turned warm, flowers blossomed, and Memorial Day signaled the official start of summer. Normally Zelinsky closed for the holiday, but he agreed to open the store so Mary and I could spend the afternoon working. Our classmates were off at the beach or movies or fireworks, but we were stuck in the showroom, working away.

Our contest entry had to be postmarked by Friday, May 29—and by Wednesday, May 27, we were nowhere close to finished. We had created the perfect ML subroutine, an elegant loop that scattered the guards in different directions—they ran with bending knees and waved their arms and shook their spears. It was beautifully animated and lightning quick. But when we tried pasting the loop into the main program, the game crashed and crashed and crashed. No matter what we tried, the 64 returned an error message:

```
BAD SUBSCRIPT
DIVISION BY ZERO
ILLEGAL DIRECT
ILLEGAL QUANTITY
FORMULA TOO COMPLEX
CAN'T CONTINUE
CAN'T CONTINUE
CAN'T CONTINUE
CAN'T CONTINUE
CAN'T CONTINUE
```

Mary and I read and reread *How to Learn Machine Language in 30 Days*, desperate to find our mistake, but we were doing everything right; we were following the instructions to the letter. I was tired and frustrated and suddenly All Your Favorite '80s Love Songs were driving me crazy. Phil Collins was singing "Against All Odds" for the millionth time, and his desperation seemed to echo my own lousy mood. We were out of ideas and out of time.

"I'm done," I said. "I give up."

Mary didn't look up from her book. "We're close."

"No, I'm serious. I quit."

"You're going home early?"

"I quit the whole game. I don't want to do this anymore."

"You can't quit," she said. "You have to win the PS/2 so I get your 64. That was the deal. We shook hands."

"We won't win," I said. "We did everything the book told us. It's not working. My eyes are blurry. My wrists hurt. My back hurts. We've been stuck in this store for A days, and I'm tired."

Mary laughed like I made a joke.

"Go ahead and laugh," I told her. "I quit."

"You know what's funny? You just said 'A days' instead of 'ten days.' You're thinking hexadecimally, Will."

I refused to believe her. "I said ten."

"You said 'A,'" she insisted. "That's real progress. We're so close to beating this thing, I can feel it."

And then the lights went out.

The computer died, Phil Collins stopped crying, and suddenly we were in total darkness. There were no windows in the back of the store. I couldn't see my own hand in front of my face.

"Power failure," Mary said with a sigh. "Happens every summer when the stores turn on their AC."

No power meant no computer. No computer meant no progress. I stood up and smashed into a file cabinet.

"Stop," she said. "Where are you going?"

"This is a sign. God just pulled the plug on our game."

Mary reached through the darkness and found my arm, holding me back. Her fingers laced through mine and suddenly I was holding her hand. It was disorienting—like my entire center of gravity had shifted to my arm and the rest of me was adrift, weightless, like one of those giant balloons in the Macy's Thanksgiving Day Parade. I reached out to steady myself and found Mary's shoulder.

"Sorry," I said. "I can't see."

"Give it a few seconds. Your eyes will adjust." Her hair tickled my cheek and she whispered into my ear: "You can't quit now, Will. I won't let you. We're too close."

I leaned forward, pressing against her. Mary's hair was soft and smooth and cool to the touch, and I'd never felt anything quite like it. The store was completely silent; I could hear her breathing. I wrapped my arms around her waist, pulling her closer, reveling in her fresh clean scent.

Then a feeble beam of light cut across the showroom, and Mary sprang away from me. Zelinsky was patrolling the store with a handful of miniature flashlights, the kind that sold next to the cash register for a dollar and ran off a single AA battery. "You kids okay?"

"We're fine," Mary said.

"Uh-huh," I mumbled.

He gave us flashlights and raised his voice, calling out to the rest of the store. "Any customers back here? Anybody need help?"

A frail voice cried out from the typewriter aisle—an elderly woman who'd crouched down at the time of the blackout, fearing she'd suffered a stroke. Zelinsky helped her stand up, and we all walked outside onto Market Street.

The customer scowled at Zelinsky. "You should pay your electric bill on time," she said. "I could have been injured."

"It's not our fault," Mary said, but Zelinsky talked over her. "I'm very sorry for the inconvenience, Mrs. Durham. I hope you'll come back and see us tomorrow."

"Don't count on it," she huffed.

The old lady hobbled down the sidewalk and Zelinsky turned to Mary. "The customer is always right," he said.

"That old kook is never right," Mary said. "She blamed the *Challenger* explosion on the Vietnamese. She calls parachute pants 'the devil's pajamas.' It's like her glaucoma has spread to her brain."

Mary was grinning at me, waiting for me to laugh at her jokes, but my mind was still back in the showroom, I was still holding her hand and touching her hair. I felt like something extraordinary had just happened—like I'd just caught a glimpse of a different world—and the transition back to reality had left me with whiplash.

Up and down Market Street, merchants were flipping their door signs from OPEN to CLOSED—except for General Tso, who stood on the sidewalk handing out 15 percent–off coupons while his staff filled the dining room with hundreds of tiny votive candles.

“I think we're done for tonight,” Zelinsky said, but I barely heard him. I'm pretty sure I stumbled down Market Street without even saying good-bye.

17

```
1700 REM *** HERO ATTACKS ***
1710 FOR I=0 TO 24
1720 POKE L1+I,0:NEXT I
1730 POKE L1+24,15:POKE L1+12,160
1740 POKE L1+13,252:POKE L1+8,80
1750 POKE L1+7,40:POKE L1+11,129
1760 FOR I=1 TO 100
1770 NEXT I
1780 POKE L1+11,128
1790 RETURN
]■
```

ALF AND CLARK AND I lived at the bottom of a hill on a dead-end street called Baltic Avenue. Our classmates loved to remind us that Baltic Avenue was among the cheapest properties in Monopoly, that the rent was a laughable four dollars. On rainy days, the storm drains would overflow, flooding our cul-de-sac and the sidewalks. We'd have to take off our sneakers and cuff our jeans just to wade out the front door—unless we cut through the old cemetery that bordered our backyards. It was the largest Catholic cemetery in New Jersey, ten acres of tombstones, and growing up, we played beside every single one of them.

I found Alf and Clark walking in the center of the road, faces down, like they were counting all of the tiny cracks and divots in the asphalt. They both looked exhausted. I biked alongside them and braked.

"Where the hell have you been?" Alf asked.

"At the store," I said. "What's up?"

"I'm screwed is what's up," Alf said.

"He lost the money," Clark said.

"What money?" I asked, and then it hit me: "The *money* money?"

"I didn't lose it," Alf said. "It just somehow fell out of my pocket."

"So it's the money's fault?" Clark asked. "I *told* you this would happen! But you had to carry it around. Showing it off every chance you got. You had to be Mr. Big Stuff."

"How much was there?" I asked.

"Four hundred and sixty-eight dollars," Alf said.

"Jesus!" Clark exclaimed. "You're so screwed."

"I had it when I left school," Alf told me. "It's somewhere between here and my locker."

"That's a mile and a half," Clark said. "We've checked the whole way. There's no sign of it. The money's gone."

"Let's check it again," I said, but I suspected Clark was right. Our route to school was well traveled by cars, pedestrians, dog walkers, and kids on bikes. And it was a beautiful afternoon. Everyone was outdoors, enjoying the spring weather. No one living in Wetbridge could afford to overlook a fist-size bundle of cash.

We followed Baltic Avenue to its end, crossed over Route 25, then marched up Crystal Street.

"Maybe someone gave it to the police," Alf said. "We could try to claim it."

"Sure," I said. "Let's tell the cops you made four hundred bucks selling porn to kids. I bet they'd love to help us."

We searched every gutter and sidewalk. We got down on our knees and peered into sewer grates. We trudged across lawns, kicking at weeds and turning over rocks until it was too dark to see anymore. But it was no use. The money was good and truly gone.

Walking back to Baltic Avenue, Alf recited a list of the forty-six guys who had prepaid for exclusive photographs of Vanna White. He sorted the names into three different categories: (1) Guys Who Will Definitely Kick My Ass; (2) Guys Who Will Probably Kick My Ass; (3) Guys Who Lack the Physical Strength to Kick My Ass. Unfortunately, this last category had no names in it.

"Everything's going to be fine," Clark assured him. "We'll go in the store like we planned. You just won't make any money."

I didn't like the sound of that.

"What about the guard dog?" I asked. "And Officer Tackleberry?"

"We fixed all that," Clark said. "We'll show you."

We went into Alf's backyard and entered his basement through the storm doors. Alf's family had the nicest house on Baltic Avenue—two bathrooms, a living room, and a family room—but we spent most of our time hanging around his basement. It was one large room with a cold concrete floor, drafty cinder-block walls, and naked lightbulbs hanging from exposed beams. The basement was full of junk: a purple sofa with split cushions, a busted refrigerator, a wobbly table where we sometimes played Risk. A Maytag washing machine was gently humming in the corner, filling the basement with the scent of Tide.

In the center of the basement was a large sheet of plywood resting on wooden sawhorses. For years this was the site of Alf's massive slot-car racetrack, where we spent many a rainy afternoon wrecking cheap Formula One replicas on sharp turns. But now all the tracks were put away, and the plywood displayed a large-scale model of downtown Wetbridge. Some of the buildings were cardboard, hacked out of shoe boxes and milk cartons. Others were constructed from Legos or Lincoln Logs. Remarkably, everything was built to scale. General Tso's, the bike shop, the train station, Zelinsky's—every store and sign had been re-created in miniature. There were tiny cars, tiny trees, and tiny traffic lights. There were even miniature taxi drivers bullshitting inside a miniature taxi stand.

I circled the model, astonished. “How long did this take?”

Clark shrugged. “Forty hours? Maybe fifty?”

“We’re not leaving anything to chance,” Alf said. “Check it out.”

He reached for an old power transformer and flipped a switch. Like magic, a miniature police officer glided down Market Street and turned up Lafayette, patrolling the neighborhood in a figure-eight loop. With his square jaw and crew cut, he was a dead ringer for Tackleberry.

“How’d you do it?” I asked.

“Slot-car tracks,” Clark explained. “They’re glued to the bottom of the plywood.”

“We’ve been watching his route,” Alf explained. “He walks the same figure-eight loop every half hour. Right past General Tso’s, so we need to time our approach just right.”

The policeman made a soft whirring noise as he rounded the curves, looping around the track. I knelt down, peering underneath the table to marvel at the engineering. A series of wires crisscrossed the bottom of the plywood, delivering electricity to lights in all of the buildings. It was the most impressive model I’d ever seen.

Clark pushed an HO-scale locomotive out of the train station. “The last train from New York arrives at midnight, so we’ll start at twelve thirty. We’ll have the whole town to ourselves.”

“What about Arnold Schwarzenegger?” I asked. “What happens when we wake up the Shit Zoo?”

“Not a problem,” Clark said. “Here’s how we handle it.” He placed three plastic action figures in the parking lot behind General Tso’s. “I’m He-Man, you’re Papa Smurf, and Alf’s Alf.”

“Can I be He-Man?” Alf asked.

Clark ignored him. “We all rendezvous behind General Tso’s at twelve thirty. We hide behind the Dumpster until Tack makes his circuit. At that moment, we have exactly thirty minutes to get in and out of the store." He clicked the small digital stopwatch on the side of the table, and red LED numbers began counting down from 00:30:00. "It's way more time than we need," he added. "We can do the whole operation in five minutes."

"But what about the dog?" I repeated.

Alf smiled. "You're going to love this."

"Right, pay attention," Clark said. "He-Man and Papa Smurf start climbing the fire ladder while Alf runs down the alley." He galloped the action figure through the alley to the front of General Tso's. "There's a separate entrance here for the second-floor apartment. With its own doorbell." They had incorporated a miniature doorbell into the model, and Clark pushed it with his claw. A single Christmas-tree light illuminated the second-floor window of General Tso's, and a tiny sound chip (gutted from a stuffed animal) began to bark.

"We tried it for real last night," Alf explained. "It took the General three minutes to get downstairs, and the dog came with him, yapping his head off. While he's distracted, we go up the ladder and across the roof."

"A ding-dong-ditch?" I asked. "That's the plan?"

Clark shrugged. "Sometimes the best solutions are the most obvious ones."

"What about the alley?" I asked. "We still have to get across the alley."

Clark balanced a wooden Popsicle stick between the two rooftops. "We left a two-by-four on the General's roof. We'll use it like a bridge. Cross over to the bike shop and we're home free."

I observed all of this with a slow-building dread. Over the past two weeks, Alf and Clark had approached the plan with all of the energy and ingenuity that I'd brought to *The Impossible Fortress*. They'd anticipated everything—but there was one crucial missing piece.

"The alarm code," Alf said. "How soon can you have it?"

"It's tough," I started.

"Tough?" Alf said.

"What's tough?" Clark asked. "Tough how?"

"I'm trying. I go there every day. Just like we planned. But her dad kicks me out at seven o'clock every night. I never see him work the alarm."

Alf frowned. "You were supposed to screw it out of her, remember? Are you on third base yet?"

"No."

"Second base? Any base?"

"She's not like that."

"Tyler said she was hornier than a baboon. He said he had to beat her off with a stick."

"Tyler's full of shit. All his stories are bogus. Do you really believe he had sex with Señora Fernandez?"

Alf looked crestfallen, like I'd just revealed there was no Santa Claus. "Of course I believe it. He said she came in Spanish."

"He's lying. He's lied about everything. Mary Zelinsky hates Tyler. She wouldn't touch that guy in a million years."

"How do you know?" Clark asked.

"She told me. Tyler tried to steal from their store. They could have had him arrested."

Alf had stopped listening. He was studying the model of downtown Wetbridge, tweaking the placement of Crenshaw's Pharmacy just so. All the color had left his face, and he was shaking his head. "Without the alarm code, we're screwed. There are forty-six guys ready to kick my ass. You have to let me take over."

"Take over what?"

"Getting the code," Alf said. "You can't close the deal, so let me have a chance."

The idea was so ridiculous, I laughed. "You're not her type."

I could tell I'd offended him, that I'd somehow hurt his feelings. "Oh, but you're her type? She likes scrawny guys with tiny dicks?"

"I didn't say *I'm* her type. I said you're *not* her type."

Over in the corner of the basement, the washing machine went to spin cycle and the clothes shifted off balance, making a faint *thump-thump-thump-thump*—

"Maybe I'm not her type," Alf said, "but I don't want to marry the girl. I just need a quick in-and-out. Wham, bam, thank you, ma'am! Oh, and by the way, what's the code to the alarm system?"

My brain conjured a quick image of Alf groping Mary, forcing himself on her, pushing her down to the floor of the showroom.

"You're not doing that," I said.

"What are her turn-ons and turn-offs?"

"I don't know."

"See, that's the problem. You've been there two weeks and you haven't learned anything!"

Clark made some goofy comment to defuse the tension, but we both ignored him. The drum of the washing machine was louder and louder—BOOM BOOM BOOM BOOM—but none of us moved to stop it.

Alf walked over to a wooden shelf where his mother stored extra food that wouldn't fit in their kitchen pantry. It was loaded with an astonishing amount of junk food.

"What's she like better?" Alf asked. "Twinkies or Oreos?"

I didn't answer him. I knew he was trying to goad me into proving a point.

"Never mind," Alf said, reaching for a bottle of Hershey's Chocolate Syrup. "This is the good stuff. I'm going to pour this on some very private places, you know what I'm saying?"

Clark made another silly comment, but his voice was just more noise in the background. I blinked several times, trying to clear the picture in my mind.

"The funny thing is, she's actually got nice boobs," Alf continued. "I won't mind that part of it. Unhooking her bra and watching those giant melons tumble out. What do you think her nipples are like?"

I pushed him, hard. I didn't mean to hurt him. I just needed him to stop talking. But the force sent Alf stumbling backward and he fell onto the model of Wetbridge, collapsing the Lego train station. Miniature cars careened off the sides of the platform. The plywood base slipped off the sawhorses, and all of Wetbridge came crashing down. And not even this could get Alf to shut up.

"What the fuck, Billy? What's wrong with you?" He rolled off the model, crushing Crenshaw's Pharmacy and stepping on the bike shop, a giant Godzilla stomping Tokyo. "This was your idea! You volunteered to do this!"

I was ready to hit him again. As soon as he stood up, I was going to knock him back down. "Stay away from her," I said. "If you go anywhere near Mary, I'll tell Zelinsky what you're planning, and he'll call the cops."

Alf's grandmother came hurrying down the basement stairs, waving a lit cigarette and balancing Alf's baby brother on her hip. "What the hell is going on?"

I ran past her, ran out into the yard and scaled the chain-link fence that led into the Catholic cemetery. It was dark, but I still knew every inch of the place by heart—all the tombstones with the crazy names, and all of the old rabbit holes, and the dried-up creek that twisted and turned through the graves.

I ran to the old oak on the far side of the cemetery, a tree that functioned as our headquarters until we were too cool to climb trees. It was always our secret rendezvous point after any disaster—a place where we could discuss the fallout without being overheard by our parents.

There were fresh footprints and Bazooka gum wrappers scattered around the trunk; some other younger kids had obviously made it their own. The wooden slats we'd nailed into the trunk were still there; I climbed to the highest perch, a curved limb that was wide enough to cradle you like a hammock. From this height, I could see six lanes of interstate traffic thundering past on the nearby Garden State Parkway.

Me and Alf and Clark used to pass entire summers up in this tree, playing James Bond or Indiana Jones or whatever movie happened to be on TV the night before.

This wasn't my fault. That's what I told myself. A long time ago, I'd wanted to see the Vanna White photos—every guy in America wanted to see the Vanna White photos—but I never agreed to all this other stuff: the color Xeroxes, the early-bird orders, the profits. It wasn't my fault Alf lost the stupid money, or that forty-six guys were going to kick his ass. I would not lie to Mary. Not after all the help she'd given me. Not after our sunset talk on the roof, and not after the way she'd touched my hand in the blackout. I knew that something extraordinary was happening and I didn't have a name for it yet, but I wasn't going to let Alf or Clark screw it up.

18

```
1800 REM *** BONUS LIFE ***
1810 LIVES=LIVES+1
1820 FOR I=0 TO 24:POKE L1+I,0
1830 NEXT I:SP=10
1840 POKE L1,150:POKE L1+1,SP
1850 POKE L1+5,0:POKE L1+6,240
1860 POKE L1+24,15:POKE L1+4,17
1870 FOR SP=10 TO 250 STEP 4
1880 POKE L1+1,SP:NEXT:FOR T=0 TO 100
1890 NEXT T: RETURN
]■
```

LATER THAT EVENING, WHEN I finally returned home, I heard familiar voices coming from the kitchen.

"My first choice is MIT, obviously, but that's going to depend on scholarships. Since I'm a girl, if I keep my four-point-oh, I've got a decent shot."

"You have a four-point-oh? Straight As?"

"My backups are Rutgers or Stevens Institute, because they're so close to home. I could still see my dad on weekends."

Mom and Mary were sitting in the breakfast nook, drinking tea and chatting like old friends. I didn't bother to mention this earlier, but our house was pretty old. Mom kept it clean, but the place needed many hundreds of dollars of repairs. The linoleum tiles on the kitchen floor had warped along the seams, and the corners were curling back. The faucet in the sink was broken, so we used a garden hose snaked through a window over the counter. None of this stuff ever bothered me before—I'd lived with it so long, I stopped noticing it. But with the arrival of Mary, I saw it all with fresh eyes.

"Why are you here?" I asked.

"For the game," Mary said. "We don't have much time."

She didn't seem fazed by our kitchen. She sat drinking tea out of a chipped mug at our wobbly Formica table like it was all perfectly normal.

"Mary found our address in the White Pages," Mom explained, like this was a feat worthy of Sherlock Holmes himself. I could tell she was over the moon; it was her first time welcoming a straight-A student into our home. "She says your game is so good, you could use it for college applications. Like a special essay." She hadn't looked so excited since Prince Charles married Lady Diana, and I hated to burst her bubble.

"The game doesn't work," I said. "It's a failure." Mary's copy of *How to Learn Machine Language in 30 Days* was open on the table, and I felt like flinging it across the kitchen. "We did everything that stupid book says. We followed the instructions to the letter. But it doesn't work."

"Exactly," Mary said. She was leaning across the table, her face glowing, bursting with a secret she couldn't conceal any longer. "I kept thinking the same thing: We did everything the book said. We followed the instructions to the letter. And that's when it hit me, Will: What if the *book* was wrong?"

At first I didn't realize what she meant. I was raised to believe that everything in a book had to be true. Books were written by Writers and edited by Editors. They were created by smart, educated professionals who triple-checked everything before the text was printed. This was 1987 and I was fourteen years old, and there was no such thing as a wrong book.

Mary turned the pages to a map of the 64's memory. "We've been putting the ML at 4915," she said, "but that number has to be a misprint. Look at the map. There's a missing digit, a missing two. We want 49152."

This was so obvious, I couldn't believe I didn't realize it sooner. All the type-in programs in my hobby magazines were loaded into 49152. It was the largest swath of free ML storage in the 64's RAM. Of course it was 49152!

"You're totally right," I said.

"I know," Mary said.

"That has to be it."

"I know!"

"Back up a minute," Mom said. "What's 41592?"

There was no time to explain. I wanted to try it immediately, but my copy of the game was back at the showroom.

"I wish I had the disk," I said.

Like a genie, Mary reached inside her purse and produced a floppy disk with the Planet Will logo on it. "Where's your 64?"

I ran back to my bedroom to power up my computer. I hadn't made my bed in a decade. The floor was a minefield of dirty underwear, dirty dishes, and splayed-open hobby magazines, but there was no time to tidy up or to be embarrassed. I kicked a path from the door to the computer desk, and Mary trailed behind me in a sort of awe. The walls and ceiling were covered with posters of swimsuit models—Elle Macpherson and Paulina Porizkova, Kathy Ireland and Carol Alt. They were crawling and prancing and preening all over my walls in various states of undress, a panoramic fantasy surrounding my bed.

Mom followed along, too. "We don't get a lot of guests," she explained to Mary. "Most days, I just keep his door closed and try to ignore it."

I loaded the game into memory and tweaked the code, changing the 4915 to a 49152. When I typed RUN, the screen went black and nothing happened. I braced myself for the inevitable error message.

But then a mountain sprang up from the bottom of the screen, rising above the land with an earthshaking, lava-spitting fury. Seven ogres were scrambling atop its peak—seven different ogres, all moving independently, seemingly with minds of their own. The princess flailed in her cage, suspended by chains over the top of the mountain.

"Holy shit," I whispered.

My mother smacked my shoulder.

"Move the hero," Mary said. "See if the ogres chase him."

The hero was crouched at the bottom of the screen, ready to storm the fortress. I reached for the joystick, and he sprinted forward, racing up the side of the mountain, suddenly evading ogres that swarmed from all directions. It was all a hundred times, maybe a thousand times faster than before. I pressed the fire button, and the hero swung his sword, neutralizing an ogre with a satisfying swish. The game looked and played almost exactly as I'd first imagined it.

"Does it work?" Mom asked.

I turned and hugged her, and she gasped with surprise. It had been many months since I last hugged my mother. But I had to do something. I worried that if I kept looking at the screen, I might start to cry.

19

```
1900 REM *** VICTORY SCREEN ***
1910 PRINT "{CLR}{12 CSR DWN}"
1920 PRINT "YOU ESCAPED THE FORTRESS!"
1930 IF LIVES>3 THEN SCORE=SCORE+500
1940 IF LIVES=3 THEN SCORE=SCORE+300
1950 IF LIVES=2 THEN SCORE=SCORE+200
1960 IF LIVES=1 THEN SCORE=SCORE+100
1970 PRINT "YOUR SCORE IS";SCORE
1980 PRINT "YOUR RANK IS";RANK$
1990 RETURN
]■
```

THE NEXT TWO DAYS, Mary and I worked nonstop. Having fixed the main loop of the game, we started cramming in all of the little design details that made gameplay enjoyable. We created a victory screen for players who rescued the princess before the timer ran out; the hero and the princess hopped up and down, dancing to the chorus of Wang Chung's "Everybody Have Fun Tonight." There was even a bonus round where players could boost their scores.

All of this was tremendously difficult, but it felt like play. The finish line was in sight; now that we were close, nothing could dampen our spirits. We talked, we laughed, and we no longer cared when a customer interrupted our progress, asking where we kept the binder clips. I even sold my first typewriter, to a desperate Rutgers student scrambling to finish a term paper.

In the mornings I biked to school alone. At lunch I worked in the school library, because I knew Alf and Clark wanted nothing to do with me. I'd only seen them once since the fight in Alf's basement. We'd passed each other in the hallway outside the music room, and the guys didn't even look at me. I might as well have been invisible. And that was fine with me.

The night before the contest deadline, Zelinsky kept the store open until ten so Mary and I could work late. He kept busy stocking shelves and polishing the vintage cigarette lighters, but eventually he ran out of things to do. Finally he carried a *Wall Street Journal* to the back of the store, sat down at one of the showroom desks, and smoked a pipe while he read. The mixtape kept cycling its endless loop—Hall and Oates and Howard Jones and Joe Cocker—and sometimes I'd hear Zelinsky from behind the newspaper, mouthing along to the lyrics. It seemed to happen involuntarily—and as soon as he realized it, he'd silence himself. But a few minutes later, he'd start singing again.

Sometime around nine o'clock, Mary got up to use the restroom (she was constantly going to the restroom; she had the weakest bladder of anyone I'd ever met), and Zelinsky spoke to me from behind his newspaper.

"Mary has a trip coming up. One of these summer study programs. She'll be in DC for most of July."

"Right," I said. "She'll be back August first."

I already knew this because Rutgers was announcing the contest winners on August 5, and Mary insisted that we both attend the ceremony to collect our prize.

The newspaper rustled as Zelinsky turned its pages. He continued reading as he spoke to me. "I could use some help while she's gone.

Mostly with the computers. In case people have questions. Plus some stocking shelves and cleaning up. I'm thinking four bucks an hour."

I realized he was offering me a job. My classmates would be lucky to find work at Burger King or Roy Rogers, and Zelinsky was willing to pay me to work with computers. A real job with air-conditioning, and well above minimum wage.

"I can't," I said.

"Why not?"

It was that stupid Cosmex internship. There was no getting out of it, not if I wanted to advance to tenth grade. But I couldn't explain this to Zelinsky. He and Mary had no idea I was one of the dumbest kids in my class, that I was failing Rocks and Streams, and I sure wasn't going to tell them.

"I just can't."

Zelinsky didn't set down the newspaper, so I couldn't read his expression. But I knew I'd offended him. "Suit yourself."

"I wish I could," I added, a little too late. "But I have this other thing."

He cleared his throat and turned another page. "Finish your game, Will. I want to go home soon."

20

```
2000 REM *** VICTORY THEME MUSIC ***
2010 READ Q1:READ Q2:READ Q3:READ Q4
2020 READ Q5:IF Q1=0 THEN 4500
2030 POKE W1,17:POKE W2,17:POKE W3,21
2040 POKE H1,Q1:POKE L1,Q2:POKE H2,Q3
2050 POKE L2,Q4:POKE H3,Q1/4
2060 POKE L3,Q2/4
2070 FOR J=1 TO Q5:NEXT J
2080 POKE W1,16:POKE W2,16:POKE W3,16
2090 RETURN
]■
```

AT FOUR O'CLOCK FRIDAY afternoon, Mary declared the game complete, but I insisted on making one last change to the title screen. I tweaked the code so the game began with the following message:

```
THE IMPOSSIBLE FORTRESS
A Game by Will Marvin and Mary Zelinsky
© 1987 Radical Planet
```

"Aw, come on," Mary said. "I don't need any credit."

"You deserve *all* the credit," I said. "If it wasn't for you, I wouldn't know machine language."

"What's Radical Planet?"

"Our new company," I explained. "I took Radical Music and Planet Will and mashed them up."

"Radical Planet," she repeated, testing the name. "It's not bad."

The store carried all different kinds of padded envelopes, packing peanuts, and shipping supplies, and Zelinsky encouraged us to use whatever we needed—on the house. "After all this work," he said, "you don't want your disk getting mangled by a post office machine."

By the time Mary finished, the package looked ready to survive a nuclear blast, and we stuck on enough postage to send it around the world. We left the store and walked three blocks along Market Street, arriving at the post office with just minutes to spare. The blue mailbox out front had a sign reading LAST PICKUP 5:00.

I reached for the handle. "Here goes nothing."

"Wait," Mary said. "Don't move."

"What's wrong?"

"You've got an eyelash." She reached out and gently swiped my cheekbone, capturing the stray lash on her index finger. Then she held it out so I could make a wish. "Perfect timing."

If only I'd wished to win the contest, maybe I'd be telling a different story here. Maybe I would have gone home and this all would have ended differently. Now that the game was finished, I didn't have a reason to hang around the store anymore—but I wished I did. I wanted to do something, I wanted to celebrate, I wanted to go out. I blew on the eyelash and let the door of the mailbox clang shut.

"We're going to win," Mary insisted. "The eyelash clinched it."

We took our time walking back. Rush hour traffic was inching along Market Street and the sidewalks were full of commuters. The temperature was creeping up into the eighties, and the businessmen all carried their sports coats draped over their arms. Halfway back, we passed the Regal, Wetbridge's tiny one-screen movie house. A large marquee announced the current film, but the Regal rarely had enough letters to spell the complete title, so the owners resorted to abbreviations and weird phonetic spellings. In the past year, they'd screened CROKODYL DUNDY, LITTL SHP OV HORRS, and FERRS BLLR DAY OUGH. Sometimes the challenge of deciphering the title could be more entertaining than the actual movie. Today the marquee promised: SME KND OV WNDRFL.

"*Some Kind of Wonderful*," Mary said.

I'd never heard of it. "Do you want to go?"

"I've seen it three times," she explained.

"Oh."

"But I would totally go again. It's awesome."

I hurried home for a quick dinner, but I was too nervous to eat very much. Mom studied my plate with concern. It wasn't like me to leave meat loaf untouched. "Are you all right?"

"I'm fine."

"What are you doing tonight?"

"Going to the movies."

"With Alf and Clark?"

"With Mary," I said.

She didn't say anything, just nodded, like I went to movies with girls all the time. I took a shower, put on my best Bugle Boy pants with an Ocean Pacific button-down. When I finally came out of the bathroom, I found a crisp twenty-dollar bill on my dresser. No note, no explanation. I went out to the living room to thank my mother, but she had already left for work.

I walked back to the Regal—I didn't want to bike over, I worried the bike would make me seem like a little kid—and found Mary standing under the marquee. She was dressed in the same T-shirt and skirt she'd worn earlier. Suddenly I felt silly for dressing up.

"You look nice," she said.

"I got pizza on my other shirt," I explained. "These were my only clean clothes."

"Let's get our tickets," she said.

The Regal was a small brick building that dated back to the vaudeville era; now it was just a second-run movie theater facing stiff competition from VCRs, cable television, and shopping mall multiplexes. The owner was rumored to be more than a hundred years old. She single-handedly sold the tickets, served up cold popcorn and watery Cokes, operated the projector, and famously refused to admit any latecomers. In flagrant defiance of the Wetbridge fire code (not to mention common sense), she locked the doors at the start of every film to prevent kids from sneaking inside without paying. Everyone I knew called her the Sea Hag because of her hump-backed posture and sharp tongue, but Mary greeted her at the box office window like an old friend. "Hello, Mrs. Beckenbauer," she said. "How was your trip to the optometrist?"

The Sea Hag peered through the smudged Plexiglas and smiled. I'd never seen the Sea Hag smile at anyone. Until that moment, I wasn't even convinced she had teeth. "This is the third time he dilated my eyes," she said, blinking furiously. "Look at my pupils! They're like quarters!"

Mary turned to me. "This is my friend Will."

The Sea Hag studied me with her enormous quarter-size pupils. I'd been to the Regal dozens of times, but she didn't recognize me. "It's very nice to meet you, Will. You kids are going to like this picture, it's a good one." We tried to pay for our tickets but she refused to take our money; instead she passed us a pack of gummy bears, on the house. "Popcorn's ready in a minute, if you're interested."

There were a lot of people still waiting to pay, so Mary and I moved along into the theater. "She's in our store every day," Mary explained.

"Pack of Virginia Slims and a *Wall Street Journal*. She and my mom used to talk for hours."

"Do you know everyone working in this town?"

"Pretty much."

The Regal Theater had a classic old-timey sort of beauty. There was a red velvet curtain, an orchestra pit, and boxed seats for distinguished guests, and the walls were adorned with portraits of silver screen movie stars: Clark Gable, Greta Garbo, Fred Astaire. It wasn't Carnegie Hall, but if you were a fourteen-year-old growing up in Wetbridge in 1987, you could almost believe the experience was classy.

The theater was only half full, and we had no trouble finding good seats in the middle. As we took our seats, a girl across the aisle made eye contact with Mary and offered a flat "hello." She was seated with a man and woman, presumably her parents. They were busy talking and didn't look over.

"Hello," Mary said.

The girl abruptly looked away, choosing to stare at the curtain rather than continue the conversation.

"Friend of yours?" I asked.

"Used to be," Mary said with a shrug. "Her name's Sharon Boyd. We were best friends growing up, but then she sort of ditched me."

"What happened?"

"High school, I guess." She shrugged again. "If you want to know the truth, I don't have a lot of friends right now."

This seemed hard to believe. Everyone at the store loved Mary. There were a half-dozen regulars who stopped in daily for newspapers or cigarettes and they always asked how Mary was feeling—as if her mother's death was two days ago and not two years ago. "You have tons of friends. We just got free movie tickets, didn't we?"

"It's different at school," she said. "St. Agatha's is just like *The Breakfast Club*. They put everybody in these slots. Sporty girls, girly girls, party girls. But they don't have a slot for me. So by default I'm Ally Sheedy."

"The basket case?"

"I'm serious. They avoid me. Like I'm contagious."

I knew exactly how she felt. "Let me tell you something," I said. "Radical Planet is going to change everything. *The Impossible Fortress* is just the beginning. We're going to work together. You and me. We're going to grow it into a giant company, and we're only going to hire cool people. We'll work out of a giant skyscraper in New York. We'll drive around in a limousine, and everyone in Wetbridge will be jealous."

Mary laughed. "Look who's dreaming now," she said. "Are you serious?"

"We're a great team," I said. "If we keep working, Sharon Boyd is going to rue the day she ditched you."

"I doubt it."

"Trust me." I flicked a gummy bear across the aisle; it landed in Sharon's hair, but she didn't even flinch. Mary cupped a hand over her mouth to stifle her laughter. Sharon tilted her head, and the gummy bear disappeared inside her curls.

"You're terrible," she whispered. "She's not going to find that bear until graduation."

I offered the bag to Mary, and she popped one of the candies into her mouth. "Radical Planet," I said, as if simply saying the name aloud made it real. "We should start the next game tomorrow. We should keep working."

"Don't you want to relax for a bit?"

"I do not," I said. "I want to keep going."

By then the lights were dimming and the curtains were parting and it would have been easy for Mary to avoid the topic. But instead she answered me, loudly and clearly.

"All right," she said. "We'll start a new game tomorrow."

There was a crash of cymbals over the Paramount logo and the movie was under way. *Some Kind of Wonderful* opened like a music video, introducing the lead characters in a montage fueled by New Wave synth-pop. The relentless drumbeat rattled the walls of the theater; the bass was so loud, I could feel it thumping in my chest. I looked over at Mary, and she was rapt with attention, eyes wide and smiling. I reached into her lap and took her hand.

It was like jumping off a cliff. I braced myself for rejection. I knew there was a good chance she'd yank away her hand and cross her arms over her chest. But that didn't happen. Instead she laced her fingers through mine, just like she'd done in the blackout.

Within minutes my forearm was numb; I'd twisted it into a weird angle before reaching over, and now I didn't dare adjust my grip. I was afraid even the slightest twitch would spook Mary into letting go. But she didn't let go. She actually reached over and put her other hand on top of my wrist. And the closeness of her made everything on screen seem amplified. The colors were brighter, the sound was louder, the percussion rattled my core. And yet I couldn't process any of it. I spent the next hour thinking only of Mary's hands—the delicate curve of her wrists, the gentle texture of her skin, the smooth, clean surface of her fingernails. All the drama on the screen was secondary.

And then out of nowhere the movie sputtered to a halt. The screen went white and the soundtrack stopped. Up in the projection booth, the Sea Hag howled in frustration. Then the houselights came on, and she walked out on the stage, explaining that the screening was canceled due to mechanical error.

The audience booed but she held her ground. "There's no point in complaining because I can't fix it." As a consolation, she offered to describe the ending to anyone who wanted to know what happened. "Basically, the artsy boy takes the pretty girl to a big dinner at a fancy restaurant, and the drummer girl is their chauffeur . . ."

Mary pulled me out of my seat. "Come on," she said. "We can't let her spoil it."

I didn't particularly care, but I could tell it was important to Mary, so I followed her up the center aisle to the lobby. The main entrance was already unlocked, but once outside we realized we had no place to go. Sometime during the movie, it had started to thunderstorm. Heavy rains were pelting Market Street, pounding the cars with a loud drumming and slowing traffic to a crawl. We huddled with our fellow moviegoers under the marquee, inches from getting soaked.

"My father's not coming for an hour," Mary said. "He's meeting me here." I suggested that she call him from a pay phone but Mary hesitated. Neither of us was ready to go home. There was a crack of thunder, and a woman standing under the marquee yelped with fright.

"The train station's still open," I suggested. "We could wait in the lobby until the rain stops."

"Would you rather go to the store?" Mary asked.

"What store?"

"My store." She reached in her pocket for a key ring. "I can get us in."

"Your dad won't care?"

"I've done it before. He won't mind as long as we clean up after ourselves."

"What'll we do?"

She smiled mysteriously. "We can play some games," she said. Only I couldn't tell if she meant *Space Invaders* or *Asteroids* or . . . something else.

Actually, I was pretty sure she meant something else.

"It'll be fun," she promised.

"What about the rain?"

"I'll race you."

Before I could respond, Mary was already sprinting down Market Street. I ran after her, and within moments I was soaked. The sidewalk puddles were inches deep and my Chuck Taylors filled like sponges. Thunder cracked again and Mary shrieked, running faster. We ran past the bank and the post office; we blew through stop signs and red lights and we ducked in front of idling traffic. A station wagon locked its brakes to avoid hitting me, hydroplaning on the asphalt and nearly colliding with a pickup truck. After three blocks, Mary abruptly switched to walking and I blazed past her.

"What's wrong?" I called back.

She was out of breath. "It's no use," she said. "We're soaked!"

The front entrance of Zelinsky's was shuttered with a large metal grate; Mary knelt down and unlatched the bottom, and then the spring-loaded grate rose up, coiling beneath the awning like a window shade. Then she unlocked the door and went inside. I moved to follow her, but she stopped me.

"You need to stay here."

"But I'm drenched!"

"It's my dad's rule. There's a security code, and no one's allowed to see it."

She pulled the door closed, leaving me out in the rain, and the significance of the moment was lost on me. I wasn't thinking about alarm codes or security systems; I was thinking of the way she'd held my hand in the Regal, gently squeezing my palm whenever anything exciting happened in the movie.

And now we were going back to the store.

To play some games.

A moment later, Mary opened the door, letting me inside.

The store was dark except for a small work lamp beside the cash register. My heart was still pounding from the run. Mary looked at me and laughed. "We've got towels in the back," she told me. "Don't move. If you get water on any of the magazines, we can't return them."

Rain had flattened her hair and made her T-shirt transparent, revealing the outline of her bra; she looked like she'd just stepped out of the shower. She saw me looking at her and bit her lower lip. And that was it. She started to say "I'll be right back—" when I stepped forward, placed my hands on her hips, and kissed her. We toppled against the counter where Mr. Zelinsky repaired his typewriters. Mary was kissing me back, and I had never experienced anything like it. She tasted like thunderstorms and gummy bears. And it was all so natural. It was my first time kissing a girl, but to my astonishment it felt like the easiest thing in the world.

Until Mary pushed me away.

"No, no, no."

I stopped kissing but didn't let go.

"What's wrong?"

"We can't."

"I like you, Mary. I think I—"

"Get off," she said.

I was too surprised to move. I was shocked.

She shook off my hands. "Let go."

"What's wrong?"

She wouldn't look at me. Her eyes were all over the store. She looked at the windows and the newspapers and the floor—at everything but me. "You shouldn't have done that, Will. We had a good thing going and you ruined it. Why did you ruin it?"

Why did *I* ruin it? *Me?*

"I thought you wanted me to."

"I like you as a friend," she said. "None of this other stuff."

All the other stuff raced through my mind: Mary holding my hand in the movie, Mary complimenting my Bugle Boy pants, Mary scooping an eyelash off my cheek with a touch that felt like a kiss. "But I thought—"

"I'm sorry if I gave you wrong signals," she said.

I didn't believe her. I couldn't believe her. We were not just friends. There was something more, I was certain of it.

Mary was shivering. She suddenly looked wet and cold and miserable. She turned to the Ademco alarm panel and pressed EXIT. The LCD screen flashed ENTER ACCESS CODE, and Mary pressed four keys in quick succession. I didn't process what I was seeing; I was still too bewildered by her reaction.

"You're serious?" I asked. Later, I would cringe over the desperation in my voice, the way I practically whined to her. Later, I would feel ashamed of myself, ashamed of my stupid pathetic mumbling: "You really don't like me?"

"Not that way. I can't, Will. I'm sorry."

The panel was *beep-beep-beep*ing, warning us to get out of the store, and Mary elbowed me outside into the rain. Then she locked the door and pulled down the grate and locked that, too. I just stood there watching her as the rain crashed all around us. I had to shout to be heard over the noise.

"Where are you going?"

She nodded to the pay phone at the train station. "I'll call my dad."

"Do you want me to wait with you?"

"I want you to go home."

She didn't wait for me to answer. She just turned and walked to the train station.

Now, you don't get to be a fourteen-year-old boy without getting knocked around a few times. I'd been pummeled in locker rooms, tripped in school hallways, and thrown from my bike; I'd scraped my knees and sprained my ankles and bloodied my nose, but nothing had prepared me for this. This felt worse than all those things combined. This was the kind of hurt that didn't stop; it just kept getting worse and worse.

I trudged off in the downpour, walking the long mile from Market Street to Baltic Avenue. When I finally reached home, the cul-de-sac was flooded and the house was silent. My mother was working, of course, and the bulb over our porch had burned out a week earlier. I sloshed through the knee-deep water, wading up to the front door, fumbling for keys in the dark.

21

```
2100 REM *** PAUSE GAME ***
2110 PRINT "{HOME}{12 CSR DWN}"
2120 PRINT "{8 SPACES} THY GAME IS PAUSED."
2130 PRINT "{2 CSR DWN}"
2140 PRINT "{3 SPACES} HIT Q TO QUIT."
2150 PRINT "HIT ANY OTHER KEY TO CONTINUE."
2160 GET A$
2170 IF A$="" THEN 2160
2180 IF A$="Q" THEN END
2190 RETURN
]■
```

THE NEXT MORNING, I woke to an empty house. My mother had left a note on the kitchen table, explaining that she was getting her driver's license renewed and wouldn't be back until noon. I sat down with a bowl of Frosted Flakes to watch TV, but the shows were all kiddie crap—*Care Bears* and *Punky Brewster* and *Pound Puppies*. Wrestling wouldn't start for another hour, so I stomped up to my bedroom.

I knew Mary had lied to me. I didn't imagine her little game with the 50,000,000 points, with my ranking of MOST AWESOME GUY I KNOW. She'd been toying with me, leading me on, complimenting me. Making me feel good about myself. And then *she* acted shocked when I tried to kiss her?

I'm sorry if I gave you wrong signals.

In a flash of clarity I understood all the stories I'd heard about girls—all the movies and TV shows and pop songs—they were all true! Girls lied. They were manipulative and untrustworthy. David Lee Roth had tried to warn me. So had Eddie Murphy! So had Andrew Dice Clay! But, like a dope, I'd trusted Mary, and gave her half of the credit for MY video game. I'd lost my two best friends—my only two friends—trying to protect her. And now here I was, alone on a Saturday morning with no one to talk to.

My mind went around and around. *The fat bitch.*

It felt good to think of her that way: the fat bitch. I took out a sheet of loose-leaf and wrote the words over and over: *fat bitch fat bitch fat bitch.* It felt great to write it down, great to channel the anger through a pencil. *Fat fat fat bitch bitch bitch.* No wonder all her friends ditched her! She probably lied to them, too! *Fat fucking bitch.*

I put on my Walkman and lay on my bed and cranked up Van Halen's "Panama." I looked up at my posters of Kathy Ireland and Paulina Porizkova and Elle Macpherson, all my gorgeous and willing supermodels with their slender legs and hairless arms and pouting lips. From now on, I would set my sights on one of them like a normal person. My next girlfriend would not be ashamed to walk on the beach in a bikini. My next girlfriend would be gorgeous, a knockout, a perfect 10. And Mary Zelinsky would die a virgin—unloved, unwanted, untouched. I cranked the volume on my headphones all the way up, burning out my eardrums.

Eventually I became aware of a noise behind the music, a rattling behind the melody. I opened my eyes and saw Clark's claw tapping on my window screen. I threw off my headphones.

"We tried the front door," he said. "You didn't answer."

I'd never been so relieved to see him. "I'll be right out."

I pulled on a clean shirt and went out to the backyard, where I kept my bike leaning against the side of the house. Alf and Clark were waiting in my driveway, perched on their bikes and chugging bottles of Mountain Dew.

I braced myself for the worst. They were angry and they deserved to be angry, and I deserved every awful insult they'd hurl at me. But as long as they were sitting in my driveway, I knew I had a chance to make things right.

"Hey," I said.

Alf took another swig of Mountain Dew. He started to say "What's up" but ended up belching, so the words came out: "What's *urrrrg-gghp*?"

He looked tired. There was a large scrape over his left eye—it looked like someone had massaged his face against a concrete sidewalk—plus several smaller scrapes on his neck and a Band-Aid stretched awk-wardly over the top of his left ear.

"What happened to your face?" I asked.

"Rob Castro happened to my face," he said. "Nick Barsanti hap-pened to my neck, and John Simmons happened to my chest." He lifted up his shirt, revealing a massive gash across his ribs. "They want their money back."

"We've got a plan for raising the cash," Clark explained, "but we need your help getting—"

"Yes," I said, astonished and grateful and relieved that forgiveness could come so easily. "I mean, sure, I'll totally help. What we are doing?"

Alf unzipped his backpack and removed a well-worn 64-ounce Big Gulp cup. It was just like the cup that the battery thief had brought to Zelinsky's. "I figured we'd hit the record store. Pick up some new tapes and sell them for cash."

"You're going to steal four hundred dollars' worth of tapes?"

"No," Alf said, "I'm going to steal twenty dollars' worth. Just enough to pay the guys who want to kill me *today*. Tomorrow there will be new guys ready to kill me, and I'll steal more tapes to pay them."

"Baby steps," Clark said, nodding. "Rome wasn't built in a day."

This didn't strike me as a very good plan. Stealing four hundred dollars' worth of tapes would take weeks of careful effort—but this was no time for making arguments. It was my fault we were in this situation, and I didn't have any better ideas, and I was anxious to get things back to normal. "You guys are geniuses," I said. "Let's go."

The Wetbridge Mall was an easy bike ride from Baltic Avenue. Within the hour we were standing next to Cinnabon in the second-floor food court, scoping out Musicland from a safe distance. There were four different stores selling cassettes in the mall, but Musicland was the only one that didn't wrap the cassettes in giant plastic contraptions designed to foil shoplifters. Instead the albums were piled high on giant wire racks, free for the taking.

"The place is packed," Clark said.

"It's looking good," Alf agreed. Even with three cashiers working, there was still a line of customers. The manager would likely open another register soon, which meant one fewer sales associate on the floor.

"So what are we getting?" I asked.

This was always a highly contested topic. The trick was to set aside your personal preferences and find cassettes that would resell quickly, ideally for five bucks to the twelve-year-old girls hanging around the food court.

"How about U2?" Clark suggested.

Alf shook his head. "One-hit wonder," he said dismissively. "I'm thinking Cutting Crew."

"It's fine with me," I said. After hours of listening to All Your Favorite '80s Love Songs, I was feeling out of touch with Top 40.

We entered Musicland one by one to avoid drawing attention to ourselves, but the aisles were so crowded, it probably wasn't necessary.

Most of the store was dedicated to cassettes and cassingles, and Pop/Rock was the large central aisle that ran down the middle of the store, A to M on one side, N to Z on the other.

Whitney Houston was on the stereo system, belting out "The Greatest Love of All." Alf strolled down the center aisle, Big Gulp in hand, fake-sipping just like the kid at Zelinsky's. Clark and I were supposed to be lookouts, but there wasn't much to look out for. You could recognize Musicland employees by their red polo shirts, and they were all up front by the registers.

Alf stopped beside a mom dressed in a baggy white sweatshirt that said I HEART MY PEKINGNESE. She was studying the Eric Clapton and didn't notice him walking up.

Alf reached for a Cutting Crew album, checked the price sticker on the back of the cassette, and glanced at me. I gave him a nod, and the tape went in the cup. Then he reached for two more. I thought he was pushing his luck, but I looked around and the coast was clear. I nodded, and with another flawless bit of sleight of hand, the tapes dropped into the cup. By this point, Clark was already on his way out of the store. I turned to follow and saw Alf reach for *another* three tapes. Yes, it was possible to fit six cassettes into a single 64-ounce cup, if you positioned each cassette just so. But up until that day, none of us had ever mustered the courage to try it. I couldn't bear to watch. I turned and fled.

Clark was waiting five stores away, on a bench outside the Hickory Farms. We only waited a minute for Alf to join us. He hurried over, Big Gulp in hand, grinning with satisfaction.

"Six tapes?" Clark asked. "Are you kidding me?"

"Three Cutting Crews and three Crowded House. That's money in the bank, gentlemen." He uncapped the Big Gulp and removed the cassettes, passing two to each of us. "Let's unload these and we'll go back for Whitney Houston. Some of that 'How Will I Know' crap. We'll sell a ton."

Over his shoulder, through a sea of people saddled with shopping bags, two figures emerged from the crowd, advancing toward us. One was a man in a jacket and tie; the other was the mom in the I HEART MY PEKINGNESE shirt. She spoke into a walkie-talkie and then started to run.

"Shit!" Clark said.

We dropped our tapes and scattered. We knew the goal of loss prevention (as the stores called it) was preventing losses—so if you surrendered the merchandise, you were much less likely to be chased. I never looked back to see if anyone was following me. I just ran like crazy, darting into the Sears, ducking behind racks of men's suits, sprinting down an escalator, and finally diving beneath a queen-size bed, where I waited for ten minutes, practically holding my breath. I had managed to escape—but just barely.

I went outside to the bus stop. All three bikes were still chained to a No Parking sign, but there was no sign of Alf or Clark. After twenty minutes of waiting, I biked home to Baltic Avenue, fearing the worst. Clearly my friends had been caught shoplifting, and now they were on their way to a juvenile detention center. Officer Tackleberry had warned us about these places—he'd spoken of rats and dripping cinderblock walls and basement shower facilities where new inmates were hosed down and dropping the soap had horrific, unimaginable consequences.

Instead of going home, I biked through the cemetery and stopped at the base of our old tree fort. I climbed the tree and waited in its branches, hoping and wishing and praying that my friends were okay. But an hour passed and still they hadn't come.

I felt like I was going to be sick. If I hadn't promised to get the alarm code, if I hadn't expressed so much confidence, if I hadn't lied to Alf and Clark, none of this would have happened. I could trace this whole awful event back to the roof of the train station, back when I promised my best friends I would get the code.

Eventually I got tired of waiting, so I left the fort and went home. I was unlocking my front door when Alf and Clark came coasting down Baltic Avenue on their bicycles.

"You're okay!" Alf exclaimed.

"We thought you were busted!" Clark said.

"I'm fine," I said. "Where have you been?"

Alf produced six wrinkled dollar bills from his pocket. "We hit Sam Goody after you left. The tapes are harder to boost because of those stupid plastic frames, but I managed to stuff a Bon Jovi down my pants."

I couldn't believe it. "You guys went back for *more*?"

"We'll have better luck tomorrow," Clark promised.

"No!" I told them. "You can't keep taking stupid risks. Sooner or later, you're going to get busted."

Alf shrugged. "Sooner or later, Ray Castro is going to kick my ass. Do you have a better idea?"

I took a deep breath. In fact, I *did* have a better idea. I'd been keeping it to myself all day because I was afraid to mention it. But when I realized how much Alf needed my help, I didn't have any choice.

"I can get you Vanna White," I said.

"Where?" Alf asked. "How?"

"I got the code," I said.

"To Zelinsky's?" Clark said. "The alarm code?"

"I got it last night."

I explained that I had watched Mary punch the access code into the Ademco panel. Shame had etched the moment deep into my memory, like a video I could rewind and replay again and again. If I closed my eyes and concentrated, I could still see the exact placement of her fingers across the twelve-button keypad: Top-left, bottom-middle, bottom-middle, top-middle.

"One-zero-zero-two," I said. "That's the code."

"You're sure?" Clark asked.

"Positive. I was standing right next to her."

"No, I mean, are you sure you want to do this?" Clark asked. "Last time we talked, in Alf's basement—"

"I'm sorry about that. You guys were totally right. It's not stealing if we pay for it."

"Exactly!" Alf said. "That's what we told you!"

"But we need to be super careful," I insisted. "We're going to treat this store like a museum. We don't touch anything, we don't disturb anything. We get Vanna White, we leave the money, and we fix the hatch on the way out. So Zelinsky never knows it was us. Is that clear?"

"Absolutely!" Clark agreed. "We'll be like ghosts!"

"Like ninjas," Alf said. "When are we doing this?"

I took a deep breath. It was Saturday, May 30, nearly one month after Alf first spotted the magazine and came running to my house to deliver the news.

"We better go tonight," I said.

22

```
2200 REM *** FORTRESS IS BREACHED ***
2210 FOR I=0 TO 24:POKE L1+1,0:NEXT I
2220 POKE L1,150:POKE L1+1,200
2230 POKE L1+5,8:POKEL1+6,248
2240 POKE L1+24,15:POKE L1+4,17
2250 FOR T=0 TO 100:NEXT T
2260 POKE L1+4,16
2270 FOR T=0 TO 100
2280 NEXT T
2290 RETURN
]■
```

I'M SURE ALF AND Clark staged all kinds of elaborate stunts to sneak out of their houses past midnight. But my mother was working at Food World, so I just sat in front of the TV, watching *Odd Couple* and *Star Trek* reruns until it was twelve fifteen and time to go. I walked out my back door wearing black jeans, black Chuck Taylors, and a black Van Halen T-shirt; I carried a flashlight, an adjustable wrench, a twelve-inch crowbar, and the crisp twenty-dollar bill from the night before.

Wetbridge had a town-wide curfew for teenagers that started at midnight. We agreed to travel to General Tso's independently to reduce the risk of being spotted. I cut through the Catholic cemetery and stayed off the streets; I hopped fences and crossed through backyards and alleys and vacant lots. The town was silent. All I heard were chirping crickets and the soft shuffle of my sneakers. Now and then a dog barked, but I didn't see or hear a single person.

There was a full moon, and I knew the route like the back of my hand, so I kept my flashlight in my back pocket. It felt good to be out in the night, out on a real adventure, away from a computer screen. And I didn't feel nervous at all. Our plan was solid, and I trusted Alf and Clark to follow the plan. This would be the caper to end all capers, a story we'd be retelling for years.

I didn't dare walk down Market Street, not with Tack doing patrols every half hour, so I looped around to the back of General Tso's, clinging to the shadows of the access road until I reached the empty parking lot. Schwarzenegger's second-floor window was closed, but I could see the dog napping on the sill, a mop of white fur smooshed against the glass. On the other side of the fire ladder was another window with an enormous air conditioner; it was groaning and rattling and sputtering, and I couldn't imagine how anyone slept in the same room with it.

I knew the noise would mask my footsteps, but I was careful to approach the building at an angle—avoiding Schwarzenegger's sight line—just in case the dog was awake. There was a twelve-inch gap between the garbage Dumpster and the back wall of the restaurant, and this is where I found Alf and Clark, crouched on their knees and waiting for me. I squeezed in beside them and switched on my flashlight. The pavement sparkled with broken glass, like a bed of glittering jewels.

Clark was dressed in the same T-shirt and jeans that he'd worn to the mall, but Alf had changed into clothes that were full-on Rambo. He wore olive-and-brown fatigues and his face was smeared with grease paint.

"Are we going to Vietnam?" I asked.

"It's called camouflage," Alf said.

"I told him not to wear it," Clark said.

"I'm invisible," Alf said. "No one can see me."

Clark asked me to turn off the light, explaining that Tack would be making his rounds any moment now. We huddled in darkness, forcing ourselves to stay still. An icy needle sliced the back of my neck, and I jumped. It was condensation dripping from the second-floor air conditioner. I was buzzing with adrenaline; we all were.

"Let's go now," I said. "While the coast is clear."

Alf shook his head. "We have to wait for Tyler."

I was certain I'd misheard him. "Who-what?"

"Tyler's coming."

"Tyler Bell? You told him?"

"Of course I told him," Alf said. "This was his plan, remember?"

"This was *not* his plan," I said. "Don't you remember the model? The model had three people: you, He-Man, and Papa Smurf."

"Right, but—"

"There was no Tyler Bell on the model."

"I didn't think he'd actually come," Alf said. "I figured he'd be off in New York City doing cool stuff. But when I called and told him the code—"

"You told him the code?"

"This was *his* plan," Alf repeated. "This was his plan all along."

"I'm with Alf on this one," Clark said. "I think Tyler deserves his own magazine as a courtesy. We wouldn't be here if he hadn't given us the idea."

"Then we'll get him a magazine," I said. "I don't want him coming with us. I don't trust him."

"I said we'd wait," Alf said.

"I'm not waiting. We go now or I quit."

"Then quit," Alf said with a shrug. "I'll get you a magazine and you can pay me back."

This is when I understood my participation in the plan was no longer essential. All they needed from me was the code, and I'd already turned it over.

Clark rested the Claw on my shoulder. "Relax, Billy. Everything's going to be fine. We'll do the plan exactly like we prepared. No changes. We'll just have an extra helper."

But I knew it wasn't that simple. Something about Tyler's story didn't add up. "The guy's eighteen years old. A senior. If he wants a *Playboy*, he can just walk into a store and buy one."

"Stop being a tightass," Alf said. "We finally have a senior on our side—a cool person trying to help us—and you're being a dick."

"Because he's lying," I said. "He was fired from Zelinsky's for stealing."

"So what?" Alf asked.

"So he's dishonest!"

"Of course he's dishonest! We're breaking into a store! To steal *Playboy*! You want to bring a Boy Scout?"

We argued back and forth in whispers, then stopped at the sound of approaching footsteps. Someone was coming. Clark was closest to the end, so he peeked out.

"It's them," he whispered.

"Them?" I asked.

Clark shrugged. "I guess Tyler brought a friend?"

I nudged him aside to see for myself. Tyler and his friend were walking right in the middle of the access road, right where anyone could see them. Tyler recognized me and pointed.

"What's up, pussy?" he called. "Why you hiding?"

Tyler grinned, but his friend had a flat, neutral expression. The friend was a man, a full-grown man, thirty or forty or fifty years old. He had a brown beard and long brown hair braided into a ponytail. He looked like a cross between Willie Nelson and Sasquatch.

"Where's your girlfriends?" Tyler asked.

Alf and Clark stood up, gesturing for Tyler to keep his voice down. "Tack is doing patrols," Clark whispered. "He starts on Liberty Place and walks west on Market Street, then cuts through the alley—"

Tyler waved a hand, cutting him off. "Tack's not catching nobody. That shitbird couldn't catch AIDS at a faggot convention."

"He'll be here any minute," Clark said.

"Then let's get started," Tack said.

Alf nodded at the stranger. "Who's this?"

"My cousin," Tyler said. "This is Rene."

Rene looked at us with dead eyes. He wore a green army jacket and faded jeans, and there was a large canvas bag slung over his shoulder. There was no further explanation. Suddenly this psycho Hells Angels lunatic was part of our gang, and I knew I had to get away.

"There's a problem," I said.

"A problem?" Tyler asked.

I have always been a terrible liar. Alf could spin bullshit all day long and even Clark could stretch the truth now and then, but I was a terrible fibber. "I think Mary changed the code. After I saw her use it. Just to be safe."

Tyler turned on Alf, grabbing his fatigues and pushing him up against the wall. "You told me he had the code. You said it was one-zero-zero-two."

"That's what he told me!" Alf sputtered. He turned to glare at me. "Tell him the truth, Billy!"

"Maybe that's the code, maybe it's not," I said. "That's the problem, I don't know. There's a chance we get in the store and the alarm goes off anyway."

Rene never moved or changed his expression. I was starting to wonder if he even understood English.

"So why are you here?" Tyler asked. "Did you come here to warn us?"

I nodded. "I don't want anyone to get busted."

"That's very thoughtful," Tyler said. "You put on your ninja costume and sneak out here at twelve thirty just to warn us? That's really considerate, Billy."

His right hand swung out, and I braced myself for a punch. Instead he reached around to my back pocket and yanked out the crowbar. "So why'd you bring this?" He shoved me against the Dumpster and pushed the tip of the crowbar into my throat, like he was getting ready to pry off my head. "Why are you lying?"

It was hard to speak with twelve inches of steel pressed into my trachea. "I'm trying to help you," I said, but the words came out like croaks.

"Easy, easy," Alf said, trying hard to keep the peace. "We all want the same thing, guys. We're all here to see Vanna White's hoo-ha, am I right? Let's keep our eyes on the prize. That's the important thing."

Wrong, I thought. Tyler and Rene weren't going through all this trouble just to see Vanna White's hoo-ha. They were clearly after something bigger.

Tyler's eyes were inches from mine. He was searching my face for signs of duplicity. Finally he released me, and I slunk to the ground, clutching my throat, surprised to find that I wasn't actually bleeding, just scratched.

"Get the crates," Tyler said.

"Now you're talking," Alf said. "Let's do this!"

Earlier in the evening, Clark had stolen some milk crates from the loading dock of the Food World and stored them in the Dumpster behind General Tso's. Now Alf was climbing into the Dumpster and passing the crates to Clark, who stacked them under the fire ladder in a pyramid. If I was going to bolt, this was my last chance. I couldn't beat

Tyler in a footrace—but if I made it to the backyards along High Street, I'd have a decent chance of escaping him. I knew all the hidden gaps in the fences; there were plenty of trees and gardens and toolsheds that would conceal me.

But what then? If I managed to escape, they'd just go into Zelinsky's without me. And I couldn't let that happen. Anything that went wrong at the store would be my fault. If I was going to keep it safe, I'd have to help Tyler and Rene break into it.

Up in the second-floor window, Arnold Schwarzenegger rose to his feet, turned around in a circle, and sat down again.

"You guys go to the roof," Alf said. "I'll ring the doorbell."

Tyler pointed me toward the ladder. "Ladies first."

I wiped my palms on my jeans—it wasn't particularly warm, but I was sweating like crazy—and walked up the crates. When I stood on top, I was just tall enough to grab the bottom rung of the ladder, but I didn't have the strength to pull myself up. My arms were shaking too much.

Clark grabbed my legs and gave me a boost. "Plant your feet against the bricks," he said. "Walk yourself up, all right?"

I was surprised by the calm in his voice. From the way he spoke, you'd think we broke into stores every weekend. With Clark pushing from below, I was able to reach for the second rung, then a third, until I was finally standing upright on the ladder.

"Sweet Jesus," Tyler said, marveling at our incompetence. "I can't tell which one of you is more crippled."

I climbed one rusty rung at a time. The ladder shook and rattled like it was breaking away from the wall, but the drone of the air conditioner masked the noise. I was halfway up when I heard the high-pitched chime of the doorbell and the even higher-pitched yapping of the dog. Now the meter was running. We had three minutes to get on the roof and cross over to the bike shop.

Some ten feet below me, Clark grabbed the bottom rung and pulled himself up. Even with the Claw, he was stronger and faster than me, climbing right on my heels and urging me higher and higher. Little bits of concrete and rusty ladder were falling all around me; I climbed as fast as I could and threw myself onto the roof, wriggling onto the surface like a worm. There wasn't much to see—just a flat asphalt surface and a few PVC vents. I walked up to the east edge of the roof—to the alley separating General Tso's from the bike shop next door—and my stomach flip-flopped.

At ground level, the alley looked small, a narrow gap you could easily hop across. But here on the roof it was a vast chasm. You'd need a running start to clear it—but there was a knee-high wall surrounding the roof, designed to keep debris from spilling off the sides. We would have to stand on top of the wall and leap across.

Clark walked up behind me. "Five feet, two inches."

"How do you know?"

"I measured it. When we built the model."

"I'm not sure I can make it."

"You don't have to make it," he said. "We brought a bridge, remember?"

Clark disappeared into the shadows and returned carrying a long wooden plank. He walked to the east edge of the roof and then carefully laid the plank across the alley until the far end rested on the roof of the bike shop. I clicked on my flashlight and realized it was just an old two-by-four—and like most two-by-fours, it only measured three and a half inches wide.

This was a bridge?

Schwarzenegger's bark echoed up through the alley, and I could hear General Tso shouting across Market Street, daring whoever rang his bell to "show your faces like men!" We had a minute, ninety seconds tops, before he returned to his apartment. Everything was happening much faster than I anticipated.

Tyler was next to ascend the ladder. "What are you waiting for?" He stepped onto the plank, took five confident footsteps across the alley, then arrived on the roof of the bike shop. "Let's go. Hurry up."

Clark held out his arms like an acrobat and stepped forward onto the beam. The wood bowed when he crossed the middle, then sprang back like a rubber band when he reached the other side.

Meanwhile, Alf was coming up the ladder.

"Where did you find this board?" I asked.

"Getty Swamp, behind the Ford plant," he said. "Perfectly good lumber just sitting out in the mud, can you believe it?"

Alf was waiting for me to cross but I gestured for him to go first. I wasn't ready yet. He looked down at the chasm and hesitated. "Holy shit."

"Yeah," I said.

"Come on," Tyler called. "Move it."

By this point Rene was climbing up the ladder, and I suspect Alf crossed the chasm just to get away from him. Halfway across the beam, he lost his balance and leapt toward the bike shop. The plank bounced hard, flipping upside down and nearly clattering off the side. Alf hadn't come close to falling, but Clark pulled him to safety anyway. "I'm all right," he said, breathing deeply. "I'm cool." He looked over at me. "It's okay if you don't look down. Just look straight ahead."

Rene went next, stepping past me like I wasn't even there. He tossed his canvas bag across the alley, and it landed on the roof of the bike shop with a terrible clatter. Then he used the toe of his boot to straighten the plank. On his second step, the two-by-four released a loud crack. It sounded like something in the wood had been fatally damaged—its back broken, its spine snapped. Rene took a third step forward—he was easily two hundred pounds, the biggest of our group, and the plank bowed like it was straight out of *Looney Tunes*, stretching in ways that defied the laws of physics. Two steps later, he was safe on the roof of the bike shop. He grabbed his bag and kept walking.

"Come on," Tyler called.

Alf and Clark stared helplessly across the chasm. I realized I was embarrassing them. But still I didn't move.

Tyler knelt down and grabbed the plank. "You come right now or I'm pulling it in," he said. "I'm going to count to three."

Walking out on the bridge was a spectacularly stupid idea. I knew that Rene's weight had pushed the wood beyond its limits. I was trusting my life to a plank that had soaked all year in a fetid swamp. But I couldn't stay behind. I had to keep an eye on them, keep things from slipping out of control. I stepped forward onto the plank.

The first step was easy. But the second step, the step where I fully removed myself from the roof—that was the commitment. The wood trembled beneath my weight, quivering like the edge of a diving board. I made the mistake of looking down, but there was nothing to see—no alley, just a vast black gulf, a bottomless sinkhole.

A third step was impossible. I couldn't step forward or backward, not without something to hold on to. The beam was too wobbly. I was stuck. On the far side of the chasm, Alf and Clark were coaching me with tips and strategies, but it was all noise. They didn't understand my predicament. Nobody understood my predicament. I was balanced, but I needed all of my concentration to stay balanced. If I shifted my weight even an inch, the board would respond, and I'd have no way to steady myself.

I wanted to explain all of this to Alf and Clark, but even talking seemed too dangerous. My muscles were locked and starting to tremble. Sweat was dripping down my sides. Through the clutter of my thoughts I heard Tyler yelling at everyone, saying, "Shut up, shut the fuck up!"

Suddenly the chasm beneath me transformed into a regular alley with concrete walls and a finite depth. A light was bouncing off the sides, bringing size and dimension to the void, illuminating the route for Tackleberry as he arrived for his patrol.

It was a miracle. We could end this all right now. Tack would help me off the plank, and chase Tyler and Rene from the store, and I would explain everything. Yes, there would be consequences, but none of the consequences were going to kill me. Not like the bridge. I tried to open my mouth, but my jaw was clenched. I couldn't unhinge it.

Tack was whistling a song I couldn't quite place—one of those songs you know all the words to, even though you don't particularly enjoy it. He swept his flashlight back and forth, and I suppose the only thing that prevented him from seeing me was the wide brim of his hat. He passed beneath me and darkness followed in his wake, erasing the alley's dimensions, replacing them with more nothing. I didn't dare turn my head to look after him. I focused on his footsteps and his whistling until I couldn't hear them anymore. And then I was alone again.

"Billy," Alf said.

I blinked. He was standing on the edge of the bike shop, reaching for me.

"Can you reach out your hand?"

I shook my head. *Not a chance.*

"Put out your hand," Tyler said, "or I'll throw this crowbar at your goddamn skull."

I put out my hand. Even with Alf leaning off the side of the building, there was still a large gap between our fingers. "Can you step a little closer? Just a half step closer?"

No way. Not happening. Tyler could throw a crowbar at my skull, but I wasn't budging.

Alf stepped onto the far end of the plank, then crept closer, one inch at a time, testing the strength of the wood. The board groaned and shuddered, but Alf kept pressing his luck, advancing while reaching toward me. It was by far the riskiest, most dangerous, and dumbest thing he'd ever done—and I am talking about a guy who once ate a strip of staples on a dare.

"It's okay," he whispered. "I'm going to help you, Billy. I'm going to get you out of here."

By the time his fingers touched my hand, we were standing in the center of a giant V. He kept whispering encouragement, coaxing me along, and with his hand on my wrist I found the confidence to shuffle forward. Clark watched us from the roof of the bike shop. I realized he was gripping Alf's other wrist, holding him steady while he stepped out to retrieve me. If anything happened to the plank, all three of us would have toppled into the void.

Instead they pulled me to safety. I reached the roof of the bike shop and immediately sank to my knees. Tyler pulled in the plank, then looked down at me with disdain. "Are you finished fucking around?"

"He's fine," Alf said, clapping me on the back. "You're okay, ain'tcha, Billy?"

"Sure he is," Clark said. "It's smooth sailing from here."

I was thinking just the opposite—it was not smooth sailing, because I had to cross the bridge again to get home. But that was a problem for later. The guys helped me stand, and we followed Tyler across the roof.

To anyone down on the street, the bike shop, travel agency, and Zelinsky's all appeared to be three distinct buildings with their own unique architecture, but this was just an illusion. In truth, they were three identically sized units within a single large building. The roof was a wide, flat expanse—there was no way to tell where the bike shop ended and the travel agency began—but each unit had its own roof access hatch and each hatch was stenciled with the name of the corresponding business.

Rene had already unpacked his duffel bag and arranged its contents beside the hatch labeled ZELINSKY'S. He had brought a carbon steel crowbar, a cordless power drill with multiple fittings, WD-40, wire cutters, a socket wrench, and (most inexplicably) a knife shaped like a meat cleaver. He wore plastic safety glasses and held a small torch to one of the hinges; it emitted a bright blue flame, and the air smelled like a gas station.

"Almost done?" Tyler asked.

Rene nodded. Rather than carefully removing each bolt so we could reaffix the hatch later, he was slicing the hinges in half, destroying them. When he was finished, we would essentially rip the doors right off the roof.

I pulled Alf aside. "We have to fix everything when we're done. We have to be like ghosts, remember?"

"They know what they're doing."

"This wasn't our plan."

"They're just hinges, Billy. They cost less than the magazines."

"We're *paying* for the magazines."

"What do you want me to do? We can't stop them now."

Clark joined our huddle. "It's safer this way," he assured me. "I don't want to get caught."

Then he pulled the T-shirt up over his nose, choking on the acrid fumes of melted metal. The rooftop was thick with smoke, and I wondered if it was visible from street level. If Tack had finished his loop without interruption, he'd be back at the train station by now. He would see Zelinsky's building in its entirety. He'd likely notice a plume of gray smoke rising above the roofline.

Rene finished cutting the last hinge, then switched off the torch and removed his safety glasses. He called Tyler over, and they spoke to each other in low whispers. Then Tyler called for all of us to stand around the doors.

"Everyone take a corner," he said. "We're going to lift the doors straight up. These fuckers probably weigh a hundred pounds, so watch your fingers."

We moved into position around the hatch, Tyler and Rene across from Alf and Clark. There was no corner for me to lift, so I squeezed between my two friends. Tyler told me to step back. "As soon as we lift, the alarm's going to trip. You'll have forty-five seconds to get downstairs and enter the passcode. Can you do that without fucking up?"

"Yes," I said, speaking with confidence for the first time all night. I knew I could find my way around the store, even in the dark. I could turn off the alarm and take five copies of the magazine. I could bring them to the roof, and we'd all go home, and there was no need for anyone else to get involved. "You guys can sit tight," I told them. "I'll take care of everything."

"Good," Tyler said. "Because if anything goes wrong, we're dropping the doors and leaving you here."

They all squatted down, prying their fingers beneath the doors. Then on Tyler's count of three they all lifted, but it was immediately obvious that we'd overlooked something, because the doors didn't budge. The guys strained and groaned and heaved, but nothing happened. Something in the construction—maybe some mechanism in the lock—was holding them back.

Tyler stopped to crack his knuckles and adjust his grip. "Let's try this again," he said. "Count of three."

On three they lifted again, to no avail. Even with one hand Clark was trying as hard as the others, straining so much his face turned purple. I foolishly allowed myself a moment of hope; maybe the doors would never open, maybe we would go home empty-handed, no harm done except a few damaged hinges.

"I don't know, guys," I said. "Maybe—"

I was interrupted by a horrible, shrieking squeal—the sound of nails being wrested from wood—and Rene's corner sprang away from the roof. A dirty white wire dangled from the door, its copper strands splayed, the connection severed.

"That's the alarm wire," I said.

No one seemed to grasp the importance of my discovery. They

were all busy pulling up on their corners, not wanting to be outdone by Rene.

"You tripped the alarm," I said.

"Almost there," Tyler grunted, veins popping on his sweaty neck.

"It's too heavy," I said. "There's no time—"

Precious seconds were slipping away from us: *One Mississippi, Two Mississippi, Three Mississippi . . .*

"We can do this," Tyler said. "Everybody lift!"

Clark adjusted his grip and then cried out, dropping his corner and stepping backward. He held up four fingers gouged by a thin red line; blood was welling up to the surface of his good hand and dripping down his palm. *Four Mississippi, Five Mississippi, Six Mississippi.* Rene shoved Clark aside and took over his corner. Some distant part of my consciousness recognized that Rene was the only one of us who had taken the precaution of wearing gloves.

Tyler glared at me. "Help, dipshit!"

I squeezed between Alf and Tyler but couldn't get any leverage. We might as well have been lifting a car. Alf's face was beaded with sweat; we were straining so hard that somebody farted. There was another screech of rusty nails, and Rene popped a second corner off the roof. He grinned in triumph, but we were too late, we were already way too late, I was counting off the seconds in my head.

"We have to leave!" I hissed.

No one answered me. Now that two corners were up, Rene and Tyler had some serious leverage. They leaned on the doors together, bending them back at a forty-five-degree angle and revealing three wooden steps leading down into darkness.

"Go!" Tyler grunted.

"It's too late," I said.

Rene grabbed my arm and shoved me into the hole. I spilled down the stairs, landed on my belly, and smashed my face into a metal file cabinet. My flashlight rolled away from me. Somewhere in the store I could hear the steady chirping of the alarm system, counting down the remaining seconds until all hell broke loose. I touched my hand to my forehead, and it came away wet.

Twenty-three Mississippi, Twenty-four Mississippi . . .

I crawled across the floor until I reached my flashlight and stood up. I was back in the labyrinth of shelves and cardboard boxes—but in the dark of night, none of it looked familiar. I wound through the passages, searching for the stairs, but all I saw were boxes and more boxes. My head was throbbing and I couldn't think straight. I couldn't concentrate. I circled the labyrinth, counting off the seconds out loud: "Thirty-three Mississippi, Thirty-four Mississippi . . ."

Something was wrong. Where were the stairs? I traveled in a complete loop and found myself returning to the hatch. The guys looked down at me in astonishment.

"What are you doing?" Alf asked.

"Get the alarm!" Clark said.

"Or I will throw you off this goddamn roof," Tyler said.

I was already too scared to think straight—scared of the alarm, scared of getting caught, scared of crossing the bridge again—but my fear of Tyler Bell trumped everything else. I tried again. My focus sharpened. I realized the passage was blocked by a tower of cardboard cartons. Zelinsky must have carried up a stack of deliveries and left them to deal with later.

I shoved them forward and the boxes tumbled back downstairs, falling end over end with a terrible clatter, and I half fell, half ran after them. The first floor was pitch-dark, but I had my flashlight, and I knew my way around. I ran past the desk where Mary and I programmed *The Impossible Fortress*, past the cash register where Zelinsky offered me a job. If the count in my head (*Forty-three Mississippi, Forty-four Mississippi*) was accurate, the alarm was about to go apeshit.

I ran to the front of the store and hit OFF on the control panel. The display flashed ENTER ACCESS CODE, and I copied the movements I'd seen

Mary use—top-left, bottom-middle, bottom-middle, top-middle—but nothing happened.

In that moment I realized I was doomed, that I'd somehow gotten the passcode wrong.

Then there was a loud BEEEEEEEE-DOOP.

And just like that, the chirping stopped.

I was in.

23

```
2300 REM *** ALARM SOUND ***
2310 FOR I=0 TO 22:POKE L1+I,0
2320 NEXT I:POKE L1+24,15
2330 POKE L1+5,80:POKE L1+6,243
2340 POKE L1+3,4:POKE L1+4,65
2350 FOR I=20 TO 140 STEP5
2360 POKE L1+1,I:NEXT I
2370 POKE L1+4,64
2380 FOR I=1 TO 50:NEXT
2390 RETURN
]■
```

THE STORE SMELLED LIKE wood and ink and tobacco and Zelinsky himself, as if he were puttering nearby, smoking his pipe and restocking shelves. I turned in a circle, aiming my flashlight into corners, making sure I was truly alone.

Then I got down to business. Zelinsky's workbench swung open on a hinge, creating a narrow gap that allowed me to squeeze behind the counter. The space was off-limits to everyone except Zelinsky himself, and I felt a little like I was climbing into his bed. Here were the cigarettes and the cigars, the glass case of antique lighters and the rolls of scratch-off lotto tickets, and a rack with the holy trinity of dirty magazines: *Playboy*, *Penthouse*, and *Oui*.

I grabbed five copies of the Vanna White issue, then pushed my mother's twenty-dollar bill through the slot in the cash drawer. My elbow bumped a small tray labeled "Need a penny, take a penny" and I carefully nudged it back into place, leaving the tray exactly as I'd found it. I didn't dare touch anything else.

I was walking back through the showroom when the rest of the guys came trampling down the stairs.

"Got 'em," I said, holding up the magazines. "One for each of us."

Rene pushed past me, heading to the front of the store.

"We can go now," I told him.

"Take it easy," Tyler said. He was following his cousin, and Alf and Clark were trailing behind them.

With the steel shutters pulled over the windows, the store was pitch-dark, but the glow of our flashlights was enough to guide the way. Or almost enough—Alf stumbled into a display of ballpoint pens and several boxes clattered to the floor. He exploded with nervous laughter.

"Be careful," I told him. "Pick those up."

Earlier in the week, I had watched Zelinsky build the display, carefully sorting the pens by color: blacks and blues and reds. Alf ignored me, so I knelt down and gathered the pens myself, rebuilding the display exactly as we'd found it.

At the front of the store, Tyler and Rene were studying the alarm panel. It was studded with lights and LEDs, but only one was glowing—a tiny green bulb labeled READY.

Tyler saw me and smirked. "You still think she changed the code?"

"It could be a silent alarm," I said. "It could be calling the police right now."

"It could be," Tyler said. "But I don't think so."

Rene unzipped his canvas bag and produced a second canvas bag—nearly identical in size and color. He gave it a shake, snapping it open. Then he raised the workbench and carried both bags behind the counter.

"The cash register's empty," I said. Rene was ignoring me, so I turned to Tyler. "You worked here. You know Zelinsky empties it every night. He walks to the cash to the night deposit box at the Savings and Loan."

Tyler grabbed a Snickers from the candy rack, bit through the wrapper, and spit the shred of paper to the floor. "Relax."

Alf tugged on my arm. "Let's go," he whispered. "We got what we came for."

"Seriously," Clark said. His good hand was wrapped in the bottom of his T-shirt, but this hadn't stopped the bleeding. Tiny red dots were spotting the floor around his sneakers. "I'm pretty messed up. I need a bandage or something. You do, too, Billy. Your forehead's all bloody."

I gave two of the magazines to Alf. "You can go if you want. But I'm staying. If anything happens, it's going to be our fault."

"Nothing's going to happen," Alf said.

Rene swung his crowbar at the case of antique lighters. The glass door splintered but didn't break. It took three more whacks before it shattered. Then Rene set down the crowbar and began plucking lighters out of the case, transferring them one by one to the empty duffel bag. At last I understood why he'd come: the lighters were easy to carry, easy to unload at pawn shops or flea markets, and worth a combined $7,500 or more.

"Stop," I told him. "You can't take those."

Rene ignored me. I was just a gnat in his ear. I turned to Tyler. He picked up the crowbar and was feeling its heft. It was maybe twenty-four or thirty inches long, the sort of wrecking bar used by EMTs to pry the doors off a smashed vehicle. I stepped in front of Tyler and said, "I didn't come here to steal."

"Me neither," Tyler said.

He finished the last of the Snickers and dropped the wrapper. I knelt down to pick it up. Zelinsky was always on me and Mary to keep the showroom neat, to pick up our garbage and recycle our soda cans and get rid of our scrap paper. Tyler watched me reach for the wrapper and grinned. "Don't bother."

"Why not?"

"Because I'm not finished."

He hooked the crowbar on the candy rack, tipping it forward and spilling all the shelves—an avalanche of gums and mints and chocolate falling over my sneakers. Alf and Clark backed away, but Rene didn't even flinch. He kept plucking lighters from the case like he was picking apples.

"That's enough," I said. "Let's go."

But Tyler was just getting warmed up. He twirled the crowbar like a baton and walked toward the aisle with all of the typewriters.

"Six months I worked here," he said. "I swept the floors. I stocked the shelves. I fixed the whole goddamn inventory. That room on the second floor? It was a mess when I got here. I designed that room. I built those shelves."

With the curved end of the crowbar, he hooked the mouth of a Brother portable typewriter and yanked it off the shelf. It landed with a crash and Tyler stepped over it, moving onto the next machine, an old-fashioned black Olivetti. "I showed up on time, I did my work, and the asshole fired me anyway."

"You stole from him," I said.

"Bullshit," Tyler said. "I never stole a thing from this place. But I'll tell you what happened, if you really want to know."

The Olivetti hit the floor and split open like a melon, cracking down the middle and revealing its oily black innards. Tyler looked crazed, and I wondered if he was high on drugs, because what he said next was ridiculous: "First of all, Mary Zelinsky is the horniest bitch I've ever met. From the day I started working here, she couldn't keep her hands off me. Every time Daddy turned his back, she'd start rubbing up against me. Pushing her tits in my face. I'd leave the store and she'd come racing after me on Market Street, hanging on my elbow like I was her boyfriend."

He toppled three more typewriters, knocking them to the floor, then turned to a shelf of Elmer's Glue—twelve white bottles with orange tips, arranged in rows like toy soldiers. With one swing of the crowbar they went scattering across the store. And through it all Tyler kept talking: "For weeks, I put up with her crap. I figure she'll get over it, she'll lose interest. But she doesn't lose interest, she just gets worse! She's sending me letters and song lyrics. So one day I lay it out for her: I say, 'Sorry, but you are never going to be my girlfriend. It's not happening, ever.' And that's when she runs to Daddy. Tells him I tried to steal a lighter. And the asshole fires me on the spot."

By this point Tyler had stopped smashing stuff. He was concentrating on telling his story, holding my eye contact to make sure I was paying attention. I nodded in all the right places but I knew it was bullshit, just like his stories about Señora Fernandez and banging girls on the roof of the train station.

"Now, if that's not bad enough," Tyler continued, "Zelinsky spreads the word in town so no one will hire me. And pretty soon I can't pay the insurance on my bike. And the day after it lapses, I swear to God, Tack pulls me over and there goes my license. Now I've got no job and no way to get around. All because of Mary and her dad. So this is my little way of saying thanks, understand?"

Maybe if I'd answered "Yes," the night would have ended right there. We would have taken the magazines and the lighters to the roof; we would have crossed the bridge and gone home.

Instead I said, "You're full of shit."

Tyler stared back at me, astonished. But I couldn't help myself. Someone had to say it: he *was* full of shit. He knew it, I knew it, anyone who knew Mary knew it.

"Me? *I'm* full of shit?"

"Mary would never go for you," I said. "She's too good for you."

Tyler snorted. "You don't know that girl at all."

"I know who I believe," I said.

And this really set him off. Tyler took aim at the nearest shelf, swinging the crowbar like a baseball bat, toppling jars of ink and paste and rubber cement. He swung again and again, laying waste to everything in sight, smashing calculators and adding machines, flinging merchandise to the floor and stomping it with his shit-kicker boots. And all the while he was working his way toward me. I had my back against the Aiwa stereo that powered the store's music; I pushed the Eject button on the tape deck, pocketed the cassette labeled "All Your Favorite '80s Love Songs," and got the hell out of the way. A moment later the stereo was on the floor; Tyler stomped it with the heel of his boot, smashing it into tiny pieces of plastic, like he was beating the life out of it. I kept telling myself that everything could be righted in the morning—everything could be reshelved—but Tyler was relentless, and my confidence was fading fast. He toppled the spinner rack full of batteries. He smashed dozens of reading glasses. He gouged the walls and shattered the light fixtures and pulled down the hand-lettered signs. If Rene hadn't intervened, I'm not sure he would have stopped. His cousin had both duffel bags slung over his shoulders—they were so full of antique lighters and cigarette cartons, he couldn't zipper them shut—and he stilled Tyler with a single touch on the shoulder. Rene didn't have to say a word. We all understood what he meant: enough was enough. The store was trashed. It was time to go.

Tyler paused to catch his breath. All of the destruction had left him winded. "We'll hit the computers on the way out," he said, turning to the showroom. "She loves those fucking things."

I stepped in front of him. "No."

Tyler pulled back the crowbar, raising it over his head, allowing me a moment to change my mind. "Move."

I lunged for the crowbar but didn't have a chance. Tyler tripped me with his left knee, knocking me to the floor. I fell on the rack of reading glasses, and Tyler brought down the crowbar. It caught me in the side, and everything went white, like I was staring at the sun. The pain was so sharp and sudden, I nearly threw up.

I rolled off the reading glasses and twisted onto my belly. If I could have found the breath to speak, I would have begged Tyler not to hit me again.

He stepped over me and walked toward the showroom.

Alf and Clark grabbed my arms and helped me up. "Let's get out of here," Alf whispered. "The guy's psycho. We can't stop him."

I shook my head. There was still one way to end this.

"Go to the roof," I said. "Run as fast as you can."

"What about you?" Clark asked.

"Go home. Get out of here."

Then I limped to the front of the store and aimed my flashlight at the Ademco keypad. Most of the buttons were too cryptic to understand, especially in the dark, but there was a single red button labeled PANIC that left no doubt to its function. The alarm was instantaneous—loud and piercing, like an ambulance siren at close range. I clapped my hands over my ears, slipped on a roll of Life Savers, and fell face-first on the floor.

White strobes flashed ten times a second, casting my movements in freakish slow motion. I stopped just long enough to grab a *Playboy*—I wasn't leaving without the magazine—and then limped to the back of the store, sidestepping broken typewriters and overturned file drawers. The siren blared nonstop; I knew the sound was reverberating up and down Market Street. Passing the showroom, I saw my tactic had worked. Mary's 64 was spared. Zelinsky's store was destroyed, but the Showroom and all its computers were intact.

I bounded up the stairs and darted through the maze of boxes. Out on the roof, the siren was a few decibels softer, but there were new sirens on top of the old siren—the peel of approaching patrol cars. The

Wetbridge police station was just four blocks away; they would be arriving in seconds, not minutes.

I ran across the roof. The guys had already moved the bridge into position. Tyler was on the roof of General Tso's, and Clark was hurrying across the chasm. Rene and Alf were waiting on the bike shop for their turns to cross. Rene heaved his canvas bags across the alley—first one, then the other. The bags hit the roof of General Tso's and spilled their contents, lighters and hard packs scattering everywhere. Schwarzenegger answered the noise with a frenzy of yapping.

"Hurry up!" Tyler shouted.

Rene took two steps onto the bridge. The wooden board sagged beneath his weight, then snapped. He dropped straight down, vanishing into darkness, like a stone disappearing into a well. A moment later, amid all the sirens, I heard a sharp cry and the faint clatter of broken two-by-fours.

24

```
2400 REM *** CAPTURED BY GUARDS ***
2410 FOR I=L1 TO L1+24
2420 POKE I,0:NEXT I
2430 POKE L1+24,47
2440 POKE L1+5,71:POKE L1+6,240
2450 POKE L1+4,22:POKE L1+1,36
2460 POKE L1,85
2470 FOR T=1 TO 250:NEXT T
2480 FOR T=15 TO 0 STEP-1
2490 POKE L1+24,INT(T):NEXT T:RETURN
]■
```

AFTER I'D BEEN PHOTOGRAPHED and fingerprinted, Tack brought me to a pay phone and handed me a quarter. "One call," he said.

My wrists were cuffed, and I nearly dropped the quarter while fumbling it through the coin slot. I dialed the supermarket, and my mother's boss, Mr. Nanette, answered the phone: "Food World."

He sounded irritable—Mr. Nanette always sounded irritable—so I lost my nerve and hung up.

"What happened?" Tack asked.

"I don't need a call."

He sighed and fished another quarter from his pocket. "There has to be somebody. A grandfather? Maybe an uncle?"

I shook my head. "I'll tell you everything that happened. I don't need anyone to help me."

I'd been trying to explain the situation ever since they'd helped me down from the rooftop. But every time I tried to plead innocence, Tack told me to wait. "We'll get your statement in a minute," he said. "There's a proper procedure for everything."

I hoped that if I told my side of the story, I'd have a good chance of getting home before my mother finished her shift. I hadn't stolen or destroyed anything. Neither had Alf or Clark. Our only crime was buying a dirty magazine—and with Vanna White on the cover, who could blame us? Everything else could be blamed on Tyler and Rene. They were the *real* bad guys, and they were only captured because I was brave enough to trigger the panic alarm. Rene was taken to the hospital in an ambulance. The rest of us were escorted to the police station in separate vehicles and placed in separate cells. My mind went around and around, rehearsing the story as I waited for Tack to return.

But when the door finally opened, it was these two other guys, regular-looking guys. They didn't look like big scary cops at all. One wore a Giants jersey and the other guy had a Members Only jacket. They smelled of cigarette smoke and looked like they'd just stumbled out of the bar at T.G.I. Friday's. The Giants guy was in the middle of telling a story and he didn't even look at me: ". . . my car's still at the hospital, so Pudding offers to drive me back. We get there and it's late, past midnight."

"This is Lincoln Hospital?"

"Yeah, right off 27. And the place is empty. My Mustang is the only car in this big giant lot. And when Pudding pulls alongside it, I see something on the hood. Little glass jar. Like a baby food jar, you know?"

"On your car?"

"Exactly. A baby food jar on the hood of the car. So I get out of Pudding's car and I go to move the jar, and what do you think's inside it?"

Members Only guy looks amused. "I'm going to guess *not* baby food?"

"You're goddamn right it's not baby food."

"Oh, no."

"Dog turds. Little tiny dog turds. Like a jar of black olives."

"On the hood of your car?"

"On the hood of my fucking Mustang."

"Jesus. What are the odds?"

"Odds have nothing to do with this! Someone put it there on purpose. Someone collected dog turds, put them in a baby food jar, transported the jar all the way out to the hospital, and then placed it on the hood of my Mustang."

"Kincaid?"

"He's on my short list. Him and that sneaky fucker Art Wong. Tomorrow I'm going to bring the jar to Forensics, see if McConnell can lift a print."

The guy telling the story turned to face me. He was carrying a Dixie cup full of water and handed it to me. I drank it immediately.

"Thank you," I said.

"Is it Billy or Will?" he asked me.

"Huh?"

"Your friends call you Billy, but Zelinsky calls you Will. Who are you?"

"Billy," I said.

"All right, Billy. My name's Detective Gagliano but you can call me Dante. We're pretty casual here. This is my buddy Hooper."

Hooper gave me a two-finger salute. Then he closed the door, sank into a chair, and pulled the brim of his ball cap over his face, like he was ready to take a snooze.

"You got banged up pretty bad," Dante said, gesturing to the cut on my forehead. "Does that hurt?"

"Not really."

"How about some more water?"

"No, thank you."

"You're sure? You drank that first cup pretty fast."

I was still very thirsty. "All right," I said. "Thank you."

He made a big fuss of scooping up the cup and leaving the room to return to the water cooler. While he was gone, Hooper closed his eyes and took a long, deep breath. I realized that I knew him from the store, I knew both of these guys from the store. They were among the regular group of cops who visited daily to receive free newspapers or razz Zelinsky about the Yankees.

Dante returned with a second cup, and I immediately drank it.

"More?" he asked.

"He's fine!" Hooper said. He shot me a helpless, exasperated look. Then he said, "I'd like to get home before dawn, if that's okay with you guys."

"Sorry," Dante said. "All right, let's start."

He sat in the third chair and immediately sprang up again. "Shit, I nearly forgot. I think this is yours." He reached in his back pocket for a rolled-up *Playboy* magazine. "You left it in the car."

"Is that Vanna?" Hooper asked, sitting up and snatching the magazine. "Howard Stern's been talking up these pictures for weeks. He says they're incredible."

"So let's see them already," Dante said. "What the hell are you waiting for?"

Hooper placed the magazine in the center of the table where all of us could see it. He hesitated for just a moment, toying with us. Then he opened to the pictorial, and there she was, America's Sweetheart, standing before an open refrigerator in black lingerie. She was facing the camera and smiling coyly, like all three of us had entered the apartment and caught her unaware. Hooper turned the pages and the lingerie fell away; Vanna rolled across her bed, whispered into a telephone, and tickled a kitten. And even though I was sitting in a police station at three in the morning, the pictures still left me breathless. In spite of all the trouble they'd caused me, you could almost argue they were worth it.

"I don't know about you guys," Dante said, "but this is what I call a miracle. You put that face on that body? With those legs? And that ass? There's just no other word to describe it. Miraculous."

"I could look at these photos all night," Hooper agreed, then turned to me. "Unfortunately . . ."

"Right," Dante sighed. "Duty calls." He raised the magazine to his lips, kissing some private part of Vanna's anatomy, then placed the magazine to the side of the table. "Let's keep her around for good luck. You can take her when you go."

"All right," I said, and already I felt considerably better. These guys were obviously not like the hard-assed detectives I'd seen in movies like *Dirty Harry* or *Cobra*. Instead they were more like the cool, laidback detectives I'd seen on TV. They were like *Magnum, P.I.*

Hooper reached into his pocket for a small microcassette recorder. "Chief makes us do everything by the book," he explained. "Hope you don't mind." He pressed Record on the device and placed it in the center of the table. "You want to call your mom again before we start?"

I shook my head. "That's okay."

"Anyone else you want to call? We recommend you have a grown-up for this conversation."

"No, I'm cool. I just want to tell you guys what happened."

Dante asked me to state my name and my address and my date of birth. "Very good," he said. "You're doing great, Billy. Now, we've already talked to Alfred and Clark, so we have a pretty good idea of what happened. But we want to hear your version. Start at the beginning and don't leave anything out. We'd rather have too many details than too few, all right?"

I'd rehearsed my story so many times, it came out easily. I explained that we had only come for the Vanna White pictures, that we planned to act like ghosts, but Tyler and Rene had ruined everything. Dante listened attentively, but Hooper had the brim of his cap down over his eyes; I suspected he was sleeping. I finished my story by describing the escape from Zelinsky's and the unexpected crack of the two-by-four. Then I asked if Rene was okay.

"ICU," Dante said. "Broken back."

"Is that serious?"

I don't know why I said that. I knew a broken back was serious.

"Pretty serious, yeah."

Hooper sat up and adjusted his cap. "Listen, we're just about finished. I just need to square away a few details."

"In case the chief asks," Dante added.

"Sure," I said. "I understand."

"First question," Hooper said. "How did you get the alarm code?"

"I saw Mary use it."

"Mary Zelinsky?"

"Yes."

"How do you know her?"

"She's a friend."

"How long have you been friends?"

"Maybe three weeks?"

"How did you meet her?"

"In the store."

"Why were you in the store?"

"I was buying something."

Hooper reached into his back pocket and removed a small memo pad. I recognized it from the store; it was one of those tiny spiral-bound notebooks that fit in the palm of your hand. Zelinsky sold them near the cash register for twenty-five cents a pop. "I'm going to read what your friend Alf told me," Hooper said. "Tell me if this is right:

'Tyler said one of us had to be nice to Mary to get the code. Flirt with her, take her to the movies, make out with her. Tyler wanted Clark to do it, but Clark said no. He thought it was too mean. But Billy said he would do it. He said he would be nice to her. He said he would screw it out of her, if he had to.' "

"I didn't mean that," I said.

"But you said it?" Hooper asked.

"We were all saying crazy stuff."

"Did you flirt with her?"

"No."

"Did you go to the movies?"

"Well, yeah . . . but that was her idea."

"Did you kiss her?"

"Once," I admitted.

"To get the code," Hooper continued.

"No," I said.

"Then why?"

I just stared at my knees. I didn't know how to answer.

"Do you like this girl? You want to be her boyfriend?"

I thought of Mary shoving me away. The revulsion on her face when she said *I like you as a friend*. My humiliation was still fresh like an open wound. I'd never tell anyone about that night; it was a secret shame I'd carry all the way to the grave.

"No," I said, like the idea was ridiculous.

"Then why'd you kiss her?"

"I don't know."

"Look, we get it," Dante interrupted. "You were messing with the fat girl, am I right?" I didn't deny it, so he kept going. "When I was in high school, there was this one girl—Big Alice, we called her. Enormous girl! Built like a buffalo. We used to put Milk-Bone dog biscuits in her locker. Not to be mean! We weren't trying to hurt her feelings. We were doing it for everyone else, you understand? To be funny."

His story didn't seem funny to me—it seemed cruel—but I nodded anyway. Dante and Hooper had been so kind, it seemed rude to disagree.

"We've got to get this answer on the record," Hooper explained. "I know these questions are embarrassing, but you've got to answer honestly. Do you have a crush on this girl?"

"No."

"Are you attracted to her? Have you ever been attracted to her? Do you think she's pretty?"

"No."

"Be honest, Billy."

"No."

"Then why'd you kiss her?"

I couldn't tell him the truth. I'd never tell anyone the truth. It was too embarrassing.

"I did it for the code," I said. "I wanted to trick her into giving up the code."

"Bingo," Hooper said.

"But I didn't want to trash the place. That was all Tyler and Rene."

They had already stopped listening. Hooper pressed Stop on the cassette recorder and removed it from the table. Dante opened the door, and Hooper followed him out.

"Can I go soon?" I called after them. I guessed it was nearly dawn, and I wanted to get home before my mother ended her shift. I still thought that if I was quick enough, I could keep the whole story from her. "How much longer do I have to wait?"

Hooper turned back at me, and his entire demeanor had changed. He was no longer slouching, no longer teetering on the edge of sleep. His eyes were alert; suddenly he was all business. "That'll be up to the judge," he said. "We're talking burglary, B and E, vandalism, destruction of property. I'm going to guess three months, but honestly? I hope it's more."

"More for me? You're mad at me?"

Dante advanced toward me, leaning over the table, squashing my paper cup flat with his palm. He was so close, I could smell the coffee on his breath; I could see the sweat in his mustache. "Any fuckwit can swing a crowbar at a typewriter. That's why stores have insurance. But there's no insurance for what you did to that family. They're going to live with this stunt for the rest of their lives. Especially my niece. You know her mother died two years ago? From stomach cancer? Do you know what it's like watching your mother die from stomach cancer, you stupid piece of shit?"

My knees began to shake. "I want to call my mom."

"Mommy can't help you now," Dante said.

Hooper held up his recorder. "You're fucked."

They left the room and locked the door.

25

```
2500 REM *** RESET SCORE TO ZERO ***
2510 SCORE=0
2520 LIVES=LIVES-1
2530 IF LIVES=0 THEN 3400
2540 PRINT "{CLR}{5 CSR DWN}"
2550 PRINT "YOUR SCORE IS ZERO."
2560 PRINT "HIT ANY KEY TO TRY AGAIN."
2570 GET A$
2580 IF A$="" THEN 2570
2590 RETURN
]■
```

I SPENT THE REST of the night waiting for Dante and Hooper to come back, but I never saw them again. I was alone in the room with Vanna White.

Alone at last.

I turned the magazine facedown. I wished Dante had left it in the back of the squad car. Now I was stuck with it, I couldn't get rid of it. The tiny cell didn't have any hiding places. I stood up, moved the magazine to the seat of my chair, and sat upon it.

When I got tired of sitting, I paced around the cell. I knew I was in trouble, and I'd made the situation worse by lying. But how could I explain the truth? I still didn't understand it myself; I didn't know the words to explain it. I liked Mary and I hated her. She was the coolest person I'd ever met, and she was a total bitch for leading me on. I felt terrible for what I'd done and glad I'd found a way to hurt her back. These feelings were all knotted up like wet shoelaces, impossible to untangle.

Eventually I grew so tired that I rested my head on the table and (to my surprise) fell asleep. I didn't hear Tack when he opened the door; I didn't know anyone was in the room with me until I felt Tack's hand on my shoulder, shaking me awake.

I opened my eyes and Zelinsky was inches away from me. His face was greasy with sweat and the vein in his forehead was throbbing like crazy. I had awakened into a nightmare. I leaned back, but the chair was bolted to the floor; it wouldn't move.

His voice was trembling. "I want my tape," he said. "It's not in the stereo. It's not in the store. Your friends don't have it, so you goddamn better know where it is."

I realized he meant the mixtape—All Your Favorite '80s Love Songs. I'd forgotten it was still in my pocket. "I saved it for you," I explained. "I saw Tyler going for the stereo, so I grabbed it." I put the cassette on the table, and Zelinsky snatched it up, studying it carefully, making sure everything was intact. For a moment, he seemed soothed by the gentle curves of his wife's graceful handwriting: *You Know I Love You, Don't You? * You Make My Dreams Come True.*

Then he turned to Tack.

"Do your worst to this one," he said. "Charge him with everything you've got. Send him someplace awful."

Tack replied in a low voice. "If we charge Billy, we charge everybody. We can't pick and choose who's responsible."

"But you *know* he's responsible," Zelinsky said.

"That's for the courts to decide," Tack said.

I realized Zelinsky was confused about the whole situation. He hadn't heard my side of the story. He somehow thought *I* was responsible.

"I didn't break anything," I said.

"Shut up," Tack said.

"And I didn't steal anything. It was those other guys—"

"Shut up," Tack repeated. "Don't say anything."

"But I'm not responsible—"

Zelinsky's bloodshot eyes bore into me. He'd been roused from his house in the middle of the night; he was still wearing the undershirt he'd slept in. Around his neck was a silver chain; a dainty women's wedding band hung from its bottom like a charm.

"You're completely responsible," he said. "All of this was your fault. You let them into my store."

"I'm sorry," I said. "I'm sorry for all of it."

"You're only sorry you were caught," Zelinsky said. "They told me what happened. How you planned the whole thing. Tricking Mary into giving up the code. And I'll admit you had me fooled. Had us both fooled. You were pretty damn convincing. But here's what you don't know: All this time she's been fooling you right back. You don't know her at all. And you're too dumb to even realize it."

He said this with tremendous satisfaction, as if somehow—at the end of this absurdly long night—he was walking away with the last laugh.

"I don't understand," I said.

"I know you don't," he said. "You never will."

I wanted to ask what he meant, but he was already leaving. Tack followed him out and closed the door. None of it made any sense. Mary was fooling me right back? Why was he singling out me? What about the guy who stole the lighters and cigarettes? Or the guy who smashed all the typewriters?

I didn't have much time to ponder things. Tack returned to my room just a few minutes later, this time accompanied by my mother. She wore her white Food World uniform, and she was clutching a handful of Kleenex. Her face and neck were flushed with hives, like she was having an allergic reaction.

"How did you find me?" I asked.

"Officer Blaszkiewicz called me," she said. It took me a moment to realize she meant Tackleberry. "He said you were too afraid to do it yourself."

"Stand up," Tack said. "Put out your wrists."

I held out my arms, and he undid the cuffs.

Mom took a deep breath. "Mr. Zelinsky is dropping the charges. For all of you." She whispered the words, like she was afraid of jinxing herself.

"Under two conditions," Tack added. "Number one, you don't go anywhere near the store. No General Tso's, no train station, no movies. If I see you anywhere on Market Street, I will arrest you for harassment and bring you back here."

"All right," I said.

"I need you to say it," Tack insisted. "Look me in the eye and say it out loud."

I looked him in the eye and said it out loud: "I will stay away from Market Street."

"Number two, you stay away from Mary. You don't call her, you don't talk to her. You see her at Wetbridge Mall, you turn the other way and run, understand?"

"I would like to apologize," I said.

"Oh, that's real sweet," Tack said. "Suddenly you're concerned about her feelings? Well, forget it. You don't get to apologize. You've bothered her long enough. Move on and harass someone else."

"He understands," Mom said, placing a firm hand on my elbow. "Tell him, Billy."

I looked down at her hand, at the red blotches that were spreading across her arm. I felt all of her weight bearing down on me, like she was about to fall over.

"I'll stay away from Mary," I agreed. "I'll never talk to her ever again."

We left the police station at dawn. Market Street was deserted. Off on the horizon, the sun was rising behind the train station, filling the sky with pink and orange. There were no signs of Alf or Clark or their parents. I wanted to ask about them but didn't dare say a word. I kept my mouth shut and got in the car.

Mom cried all the way home. Halfway to Baltic Avenue, she got so upset she had to stop the car on the side of the road. I said I was sorry and she hit me in the arm with her purse.

We entered the house and Mom told me to sit on the couch. I said I wanted to go to bed. "We're not finished," she said. "You and I, our conversation hasn't even *started*."

I sat on the couch. She sat across from me with a box of Kleenex and took a deep breath. "When Officer Blaszkiewicz called me at the store, I refused to believe him. I thought he was talking about a *different* Billy Marvin. Another kid with the same name. And on the way to the police station, I actually stopped by our house. I was convinced I'd find you asleep in your bed. But I went up to your room and you weren't there. Your bed was empty. And then I saw this."

She unzipped her purse and removed a sheet of loose-leaf paper. I recognized it from earlier that morning, from a million years ago. I must have left it on my desk before running out to the mall. It was covered with the words *fat bitch* and *fat fucking bitch* over and over in a deranged scrawl. I didn't even recognize it as my own handwriting.

"This is not the life I wanted for us," Mom said. "I wish I had more money. I wish I had a better job. Heck, I wish your father hadn't left us. But I don't complain, Billy, you know why? Because plenty of people have it worse. We're surviving. We're healthy, we're capable, we're getting by. And the number one thing that keeps me going is *you*. Your grades drive me crazy and you're squandering all your potential, but I always knew you were a good kid with a good heart, and that sustained me." She looked at the loose-leaf again—*the fat bitch, the fat fucking bitch*. "But now I realize I don't know you at all." Her voice broke, and she covered her face with her hands, taking big, heaving breaths as tears ran down her cheeks. "I welcomed that girl *into our home*. You made me part of this horrible plan. *How could you?*"

There are plenty of things that a teenage boy doesn't tell his mother. As we get older, there are more and more things we hold back, things too hard to say or too embarrassing to explain. We do this to protect our mothers as much as ourselves, because let's face it—most of our thoughts are truly unthinkable.

That morning was the last time I was ever fully candid with my mother about anything. I talked for a good hour. I told her everything. It was hard to tell the truth, but every detail seemed to revive her, even the embarrassing ones. *Especially* the embarrassing ones. It killed me to admit some of this stuff, but the more I talked, the better she looked. She stopped crying and set down her Kleenex, and the red hives slowly faded from her neck. My explanation must have been pretty thorough because she didn't interrupt me with questions. She just sat and listened and nodded until I was finished.

Then she abruptly stood up and went into the kitchen. She returned a moment later with a washcloth, a bowl of warm water, and a first aid kit. She sat beside me on the sofa, pressed the washcloth to my forehead, and fumbled open a bottle of hydrogen peroxide. "That is a nasty cut," she said, and I realized I'd forgotten about the gash on my forehead. "Close your eyes for a second, all right? Sit back."

My mother was an expert at fixing scrapes. She often reminded me that she'd been planning to go to nursing school, before I'd entered her life so unexpectedly. She dabbed a wet cotton ball to my forehead, and I braced myself for a sting that never came. Then she gently blew on the cut and unwrapped a fresh bandage. "I guess I only have one question," she said. "There's one thing I still don't understand."

"What's that?" I asked.

"Why aren't you in jail right now?" she said. "Why did Zelinsky let you go?"

And the truth was, I had no idea.

26

```
2610 REM *** CLEAR MEMORY ***
2620 PRINT "{CLR}{2 CSR DWN}"
2630 PRINT "JUST A MOMENT . . ."
2640 SYS 49608
2650 IF INT(S/43)=S/43 THEN POKE W3,20
2660 POKE H3,PEEK (SP+1)
2670 POKE W3,21
2680 IF NB(.)=. THEN 4000
2690 GOTO 4500
]■
```

I SLEPT ALL THROUGH Sunday. When I finally awoke, it was Monday morning, and my 64 was gone. The disk drive, the paddles and joysticks, all of my games and books, even the power strip—everything had been cleared away.

My mother was in the kitchen. She wished me a good morning and handed me a glass of orange juice. I asked her about the computer, and she explained that she had already placed a For Sale ad in the newspaper's classified section. The money we raised would go to Mr. Zelinsky to pay for whatever his insurance wouldn't cover. "We'll have a yard sale, too. Every penny helps. I'd sell the car if I didn't need it for work."

When I left the house for school, Alf and Clark were waiting in my driveway. Alf had bruises on his face; he explained that his father started kicking his ass in the parking lot of the police station.

I apologized for pulling the alarm. "I didn't want us to get caught. But I couldn't let Tyler trash the showroom."

I'd expected Alf to be angry, but he just shrugged. "That bridge was going to break whether you pulled the alarm or not," he explained. "I'm just glad I wasn't standing on it."

"Plus you're the reason Zelinsky dropped the charges," Clark added. "If he didn't like you so much, we'd all be in jail right now."

I shook my head. "Zelinsky didn't drop the charges because of me." I still remembered his words at the police station: *Do your worst to this one. Charge him with everything you've got.*

"He must have had a reason," Alf said. "My uncle says you can't collect insurance if you don't press charges."

"So what?"

"So he'll have to pay the damages out of his own pocket. Letting us go will cost him a fortune. Why would he do that?"

I tried to imagine the cost of all the repairs—all of the broken shelves, all of the smashed inventory—and my stomach churned like I was back in the police station all over again. "I don't know," I said. I had pondered Zelinsky's decision all weekend, but it still didn't make any sense.

We got on our bikes and pedaled slowly along Baltic Avenue. Our neighbors gawked as we went by; news of our caper had obviously gotten around, and I dreaded the idea of returning to school. I asked Alf how he planned to handle our classmates and all of the money he owed them.

"That's the only good news," he said, skidding to a stop so he could show me the contents of his backpack. Inside were hundreds of glossy photocopies, all neatly stapled and collated. "My grandma Gigi felt sorry for me, so she went to 7-Eleven and bought their last *Playboy*. I can't tell if she's skipping her meds or just being really cool."

Alf may have settled all of his debts, but our first day back at school was a mess. When I arrived in homeroom, I found an obscene stick figure of Vanna White sketched in black ink on my desk. The other boys burst out laughing; they coughed the words *loser* and *pervert* into their fists. The girls were even worse; they turned away from me in disgust, like I'd just arrived with dog poop all over my sneakers. After passing most of my freshman year in relative anonymity, I'd finally made a name for myself.

The only person who mentioned the break-in directly was the principal, Mr. Hibble. I passed him standing outside his office, and he warned me to "keep my rooster straight." He explained that students with criminal records were not eligible for Cosmex Fellowships. " 'The door to a Yankee prison swings one way,' " he said. "Have you heard that saying? Do you understand what it means?"

"Nobody wants to hire a criminal?" I guessed.

"Precisely!" For once, Mr. Hibble seemed pleased with me. "Don't blow this chance, Billy. I can spot a good kid from a mile away, and I know you're a good kid."

It was the only positive human contact I'd have all day. I was so surprised and grateful, I asked if we could speak privately inside Mr. Hibble's office. "Of course!" he said, and I think he was expecting me to reveal some confidential information about Zelinsky's store. Instead I walked behind his desk and rewired the cables behind his computer, linking the printer to the terminal via the disk drive. Then I instructed him to press the F3 key, and he watched in astonishment as the first page of the school directory spooled from his printer.

"How did you know?" he asked.

I shrugged. "Just a hunch."

"More like natural instincts, if you ask me." Hibble grabbed my wrists and forced me to study my palms. "You're a born mechanic! Good with your hands! That's called a *gift*, Billy. And Cosmex will put your gift to work, I guarantee it."

I avoided my locker all day because I was afraid of seeing Tyler Bell. I feared he was planning to take some kind of spectacular revenge on me. But at lunchtime, Alf and Clark explained that I didn't have to worry. Tyler had dropped out of school just three weeks before graduation and enlisted in the United States Army. "They're sending him down to Fort Benning," Alf explained. "It'll be a long time before you see him around Wetbridge again."

Relieved, I finished my lunch and went to my locker. Upon opening the door, I found a black Maxell disk waiting atop my belongings. I recognized it immediately. The label read FORTRESS BACKUP in Mary's pristine cursive handwriting. The night of the deadline, we'd sent the master copy to the Rutgers contest but kept a backup for ourselves at the store. I checked around the disk for a note, some kind of explanation, but there was nothing. Then I remembered who I was dealing with and brought the disk to the library.

The lone computer terminal was available, so I inserted the disk and loaded the directory. There were just two files, a large backup of the game and a smaller file named GOOD-BYE. I loaded GOOD-BYE into memory and typed RUN. At first glance it appeared to be another text adventure, like the other two mini-games Mary had sent me.

```
They told me what you did, "Billy." I can't be-
lieve it's true. But they say you made a full
confession, that you answered to everything.

The Impossible Fortress was an excuse.

Radical Planet was a trick.
```

The plan was to fool the fat girl, make the fat girl think she was pretty. Well, I have to admit, it worked. This fat girl was fooled.

The cursor was blinking, prompting me to input a reply.

>I'M SORRY

But I knew it was a dummy prompt, that it didn't matter what I typed, that there was no way to win or lose this game. More text spilled down the screen.

I can't believe I trusted you.

I told you so many things that I never told anyone.

And guess what, genius? If you'd just asked me for the alarm code, I probably would have told you that, too. I would have wanted you to know the story behind it. October 2 was my mother's birthday, so 10-02 was my lucky number.

And now that's ruined for me, along with everything else.

Again the cursor prompted me for a reply, another dummy prompt. I didn't type anything this time, just hit RETURN.

So now I just need to forget. That's what all the grown-ups keep telling me. "Don't waste another minute thinking about that jerk." And

I know they're right. I just don't know how I could have been so wrong.

Lucky for me, there aren't many reminders of you in the showroom. Just some notes and backup disks that I've already trashed. This is the last backup copy of the game we made together. I just wish all mistakes were this easy to erase.

As I read, the motor in the disk drive started spinning, a familiar sound which usually meant the computer was loading more data. But then the drive made a loud knocking noise—the sound of a disk being reformatted and wiped clean. I popped out the disk and the game was interrupted by a DOS error. I thought that I'd been fast enough, but when I checked the directory, it came up empty, zero files in memory.

The Impossible Fortress was gone.

27

```
2700 REM *** DRAW NEW HERO ***
2710 FOR X=0 TO 62
2720 READ A
2730 POKE 12544+X,A
2740 NEXT A
2750 POKE 2044,196
2760 POKE V+21,16
2770 POKE V+43,1
2780 POKE V+8,HX:POKE V+9,HY
2790 RETURN
]■
```

THAT AFTERNOON, I WENT to my classes determined to make a fresh start. With no computer programming in my future I was free to concentrate on my grades. I decided I would end the year on a high note. I would ace my finals and give my mother a report card worthy of posting on the refrigerator. I arrived at Rocks and Streams and took a seat in the front row. I opened my notebook and put the date at the top of the page. I listened attentively as Ms. Seidel patiently drilled us on the five kinds of igneous rocks: granite, diorite, gabbro, peridotite, and pegmatite. After a minute or so I turned to a new page and started writing a letter to Mary.

The guilt kept sneaking up on me and derailing my concentration. I couldn't stop thinking about what I'd done—or what Mary *thought* I'd done. I needed her to know the truth. *The Impossible Fortress* wasn't an excuse. Radical Planet wasn't a trick. Everything was real, it was all real.

I spent the afternoon sitting in classes and putting these thoughts on paper, drafting a letter to send to Mary. I didn't think anything could be harder than writing machine language, but I was wrong. Again and again, I crumpled my paper into a ball and gave up. But after a few moments my thoughts would return to Mary, and I'd start writing again.

The end-of-day bell rang at two forty-five, and I still wasn't happy with my letter, but it would have to be good enough. I hurried out of wood shop and bolted down the hall, darting around students as they emerged from classrooms, pushing and jostling each other, ready to go home. Everybody had spring fever, but there were still three more weeks of school. I could feel a sort of expanding energy in the hallways, a growing pressure, as if the school couldn't contain us much longer.

I found Ashley Applewhite standing in front of her locker. Ashley Applewhite, ninth-grade class representative, treasurer of the Key Club, deputy editor of the student newspaper, daughter of the school superintendent, and next-door neighbor of Mary Zelinsky. She was gabbing with three of her girlfriends but they all saw me coming and stopped talking.

"What do you want?" said Ashley.

I held up the *Impossible Fortress* disk. "I got your message."

"It's some kind of game," she explained. "You're supposed to put that inside a computer." Then she turned back to her entourage, forcing me to interrupt their conversation.

"I know what it is," I said. "I need to send a message back."

I held out my letter, a single sheet of paper that I'd folded and taped shut. Ashley sprang back like it was radioactive.

"No way," she said. "Mary wants nothing to do with you."

Again she turned to her entourage, and again I interrupted them. "Please," I said. "It's important."

The other girls huffed and sighed. They were the closest thing to royalty in our ninth grade, and I was testing their patience. Ashley snatched the letter from my fingers, then ripped it into halves, quarters, eighths, and sixteenths. She threw the pieces back in my face, a quick poof of confetti that clung to my head and shoulders. Suddenly we had the attention of everyone in the hallway.

"Stay away from her," she said. "Mary doesn't want to hear from you, ever. And if you try to give me another note, I'll take it straight to the police."

28

```
2800 REM *** START BONUS LEVEL ***
2810 PRINT "{CLR}{12 CSR DWN}"
2820 PRINT "{5 SPACES}YOU HAVE ENTERED"
2830 PRINT "{6 SPACES}THE BONUS ROUND."
2840 PRINT "{5 SPACES}FATE HAS GIVEN YOU"
2850 PRINT "{7 SPACES}ONE LAST CHANCE."
2860 PRINT "{2 CSR DWN}"
2870 PRINT "{5 SPACES}DON'T SCREW IT UP!"
2880 FOR DELAY = 1 TO 1000:NEXT DELAY
2890 RETURN
]■
```

THAT NIGHT, I REASSEMBLED the scraps and copied the letter onto a clean sheet of paper. Then I carried it with me for days, trying to think of ways to get it to Mary.

"What's the letter say?" Alf kept asking.

"None of your business," I told him.

This was maybe a week after our arrest, and any notoriety we'd earned among our classmates was almost gone. Now everyone was buzzing about the tenth grader caught masturbating in the library to

Volume K of the *World Book Encyclopedia.* ("Why Volume K?" Alf kept wondering aloud. "Where's the good stuff in Volume K?")

Me and Alf and Clark were sitting at our little table in the back of the cafeteria, finishing our sloppy joes and french fries. No one else was sitting within twenty feet of us, as if our pervert-loser genes were contagious. I was staring at the envelope and turning it around in my hand, trying to brainstorm solutions to my dilemma.

"Can't you CompuServe it to her?" Clark asked. "Do that electronic mail thing?"

"My mom sold the computer," I reminded him.

"Then regular-mail it," he said. "Leave off the return address and send it to the store."

"Her dad will intercept it," I said. "I need to make sure Mary gets it."

"Why? What's the letter say?" Alf asked again.

"None of your business," I repeated.

A few moments later, I made the mistake of looking around the cafeteria, searching the tables for someone, anyone, who might be able to help me. While I had my back turned, Alf reached across my lunch tray and snatched the envelope. I nearly dove across the table to get it back. The only thing keeping me in check was the stern presence of Mr. Hibble, standing at the entrance of the cafeteria, proudly overseeing his domain.

"Give it back," I warned Alf.

"Take it easy. I won't open it, I promise. I'll just use my psychic powers, all right?"

"What does that mean?" I asked.

He held the envelope to his forehead like Carnac the Magnificent, the fake mystic played by Johnny Carson on *The Tonight Show.*

"What the hell are you doing?" I asked.

He closed his eyes and feigned tremendous concentration. "I'm sensing the word *sorry*. It's very strong. This is an apology?"

I decided the easiest way to get my letter back was to endure the stupid game. "Yes."

Alf closed his eyes and resumed his mystic performance. He was a terrible actor; his attempts at concentration looked like constipation. "You feel bad about what happened?"

"Yes."

"Because we trashed the store?"

"Yes."

"We ruined everything?"

"Yes."

"And now Mary hates you."

"Yes."

"And her father hates you."

"Yes."

"And you like this girl."

"Shut up," I told him.

"You like this girl," Alf repeated, more confidently. "It's cool, Billy. I see it all right here in the letter. You were never trying to get the alarm code. You were hanging around the store because you like Mary for real."

I was so startled to hear Alf speaking the truth, I didn't even try to deny it.

Clark's eyes went wide. "Wait, seriously?"

I shrugged. "I don't know. Maybe."

"Maybe?"

"Definitely," Alf insisted. "Come on, Billy. Stop playing dumb. It's so obvious."

"Fine," I said. "It's true."

"But she doesn't know!" Clark said.

"Right."

"You told the cops you faked everything!"

"Right."

"Oh my God!" Clark said, falling back in his chair and holding the Claw to his forehead, reeling from the news. "This changes everything, Billy! Why didn't you tell us sooner?"

"Exactly!" Alf said. "If you told us, we could have helped you."

"You've already helped me plenty," I said. "Thanks to you guys, Mary and her dad hate my guts. They think I'm this giant spectacular asshole." I figured "giant spectacular asshole" was pretty strong, but I was desperate for reassurance; I needed my friends to tell me that things weren't as bad as they seemed.

"I guess you're right," Clark sighed.

"Thanks," I said, pushing away my tray because I'd lost my appetite. "Does anybody want my food?"

Alf plucked a handful of french fries from my tray and dragged them through a smear of ketchup. "Listen, we can make this right," he said. "This letter will clear up everything. We just need to make sure Mary gets it."

He proposed a dozen different scenarios, but none of them were truly viable. I couldn't go to Mary's house. I was forbidden by law to go anywhere near the store. I couldn't count on any classmates to help me. I wasn't even allowed on Market Street anymore.

As we pondered all of the different scenarios, Clark didn't say a word. He just chewed thoughtfully on his sloppy joe, like he was turning around an idea. "There is *one* thing you could do," he finally said. "It's super risky. There's an excellent chance you'll get caught. But I guarantee you won't see Zelinsky. He'll be miles away."

We waited for him to elaborate, but he suggested we meet in the library after school.

"Just tell us your stupid idea," Alf said. "Why are you being so mysterious?"

Clark refused to spill. "I need to research a few things. Make sure it's really possible. I don't want Billy getting busted again."

When Alf and I reached the library, we found Clark in the reference section, sitting at one of the long tables near all of the college brochures. He was reading a map, but it was upside down, so I couldn't make sense of it. At the table next to ours, a group of fifth-grade girls were pretending to study. But every so often they'd steal glances at Clark and squeal with laughter. This seemed to be happening more and more lately—girls would see him and just lose their minds. Even with the Claw right in plain view.

"Well?" I asked. "Are you ready to tell us the master plan?"

"Let me make sure I have her schedule right," Clark said. "Every morning, Zelinsky drives Mary to Market Street. They open the store together, and then she boards the bus to St. Agatha's?"

"That's right," I said.

"And then every afternoon, the bus brings her back to Market Street, and she stays at the store until closing. Then Dad brings her home?"

"Exactly," I said. "That's the problem."

Clark shook his head. "No, I just told you the solution. This is how you reach her." He spun the map right-side-up so we could read the headline at the top of the page: Mount St. Agatha's Preparatory School for Girls.

"Impossible!" Alf said. "No one climbs that mountain."

"Why not?" Clark asked.

"They've got guards and fences. *Electric* fences."

Clark shook his head. "It's a convent, not a James Bond movie."

"You're Presbyterian, so how would you know?" Alf asked. "I'm an altar boy, and I'm telling you nobody gets into St. Agatha's. It's like Fort Knox for Catholic girls."

"It's a school," Clark insisted. "They have visitors. Deliveries. Lots of people coming and going."

The map was part of an admissions application describing the school's remarkable mountaintop campus. One hundred years ago, St. Agatha's was a monastery with a chapel and a simple dormitory. Since evolving into an all-girls' prep school, the campus had expanded to feature a classroom building, a cafeteria, and athletic fields. Everything was bordered by a "verdant forest landscape" rich with the "abundant wildlife" of northern New Jersey.

"They don't show the fences on this map," Alf said, "but they're there." He leaned across the table and scrawled a crazy jagged circle around the map. "These things will fry you like a grilled cheese."

For once, I actually agreed with Alf. I'd heard so many crazy stories about St. Agatha's, the idea of infiltrating the campus seemed ridiculous.

"Zelinsky won't be anywhere near it," Clark reminded me. "He works miles away."

"Fine, walk me through it," I told Clark. "Once I get up the mountain, how do I find Mary?"

"You don't need to find Mary," Clark said. "That's the beauty of this plan. You just need to find any girl and ask her to deliver the note."

"How do I know she will?"

"Because you had the guts to get there! No one's ever done it before. Girls will respect that. She'll know it must be important, and she'll make sure Mary gets it."

When he put it that way, the plan almost sounded easy. I didn't need to search an entire mountain looking for Mary. I just needed to find one Catholic schoolgirl on a mountain filled with Catholic schoolgirls.

Alf just shook his head. "You'll never pull it off," he said. "If you bike up that mountain, I promise you'll come down in the back of a police car."

I knew he was right. But I also knew I couldn't live with the guilt another day. Mary was out in the world, thinking terrible things about me, and it was driving me crazy.

"I'll have to leave early," I said. "If I'm out the door by seven, I can make it to the school before noon."

"And she'll have the letter before lunchtime," Clark said.

"And we'll visit you in jail," Alf promised.

29

```
2900 REM *** DRAW NEW GUARDS ***
2910 FOR X=0 TO 62
2920 READ A
2930 POKE 12608+X,A
2940 NEXT X
2950 POKE 2045,197
2960 POKE V+21,32
2970 POKE V+44,2
2980 POKE V+10,GX: POKE V+11,GY
2990 RETURN
]■
```

WHEN I GOT HOME from the library, Tack was standing on my front steps, talking to my mother through the screen door. By the time I saw him, it was too late to turn back. He saw me coming and waved hello. It seemed like he had somehow developed ESP. He was coming to bust me for the letter before I even tried to deliver it.

"There he is," Mom said, and there was a cheerful lilt in her voice, like everything in our lives was sunshine and roses.

"How are you, Billy?" Tack asked.

I shrugged but didn't say anything. It seemed that any possible answer was likely to get me into trouble:

"I'm fine."

How can you be fine? You were nearly arrested this weekend! You should be miserable!

"I'm miserable."

Why are you miserable? You could have gone to prison! You should be the happiest kid on earth!

"I'm the happiest kid on earth."

You self-centered little creep! Don't you feel any guilt at all?

"Officer Blaszkiewicz wanted to see how you were doing," Mom explained. A strand of hair fell over her face and she pulled it back, tucking it behind her ear. "He wanted to make sure everything was okay."

"Everything's okay," I told him.

"Glad to hear it," he said. "You were lucky to get a second chance, you know." He went on for several minutes about the beauty of second chances. He spoke of clean slates and fresh starts and the turning over of new leaves. The moment he stopped to catch a breath, I thanked him for coming and ducked inside the house.

I sat at the kitchen table and waited for Tack to go away, but he and my mother kept talking and talking. Eventually I went out the back door and crept around the side of the house to eavesdrop on their conversation. To my astonishment, I discovered they weren't even talking about me! They were discussing the season finale of *Dallas*. The show's heroine, Pamela Ewing, had just smashed her car into an oil tanker. Mom was convinced that no one could survive the fiery explosion; Tack insisted it was just a ratings stunt and the producers would bring her back, bandaged and bruised, in September. I was pretty sure that my mother and Tack were the only two people in 1987 who were still watching *Dallas*.

"That was weird," I said to Mom, later, after Tack got in his squad car and drove away.

She remained at the front door, looking out at the lawn. "I'm going to stop by the garden store tomorrow," she said. "Maybe pick up some perennials. Our front yard looks so dreary."

Our front yard looked the way it always did. Our postage-stamp lawn was speckled with dandelions and ringed by a thin ribbon of white gravel that we replenished every spring.

"I said that was weird," I repeated. "Tack coming to our house."

Mom shrugged. "I thought it was a nice gesture. He's taken an interest in you. He wants to make sure you're not doing anything stupid."

"I'm not," I lied.

Then I went to my bedroom, opened a road atlas of New Jersey, and charted the most direct route from Wetbridge to Mount St. Agatha's Preparatory School for Girls.

30

```
3000 REM *** DRAW NEW ENVIRONMENT ***
3010 FOR J=6 TO 14
3020 FOR I=1030+J*40 TO 1036+J*40
3030 POKE I,35:POKE I+SO,9
3040 NEXT I
3050 FOR I=1044+J*40 TO 1056+J*40
3060 POKE I,35
3070 POKE I+BG, 9
3080 NEXT I:NEXT J
3090 RETURN
]■
```

THE NEXT MORNING, I woke up early, scarfed down a bowl of Frosted Flakes, and dressed in the same khakis and button-down shirt that I'd worn to the movie theater. I didn't think I'd actually see Mary—but if I did, I wanted to look my best. I placed the letter in my back pocket and headed out the front door.

Alf and Clark were waiting in my driveway. They were dressed up, too. Alf had ditched his usual Hawaiian shirt for a pristine white Hard Rock Cafe button-down, and Clark was wearing the nicest hand-me-downs of his Georgia relatives—a lime-green short-sleeved button-down shirt and black wool pants.

"We're coming with," Alf said.

"Alf's worried you'll mess up," Clark said.

"I never said that," Alf insisted.

"You said he'd get fried on the electric fence," Clark said. "Those were your exact words."

Alf shrugged, looking sheepish. "You gotta understand, Billy. These nuns mean business. If they catch you on their mountain, they will kick your ass."

"I'll be fine," I said, irritated. "Go to school." If I somehow had the chance to speak with Mary, I didn't want Alf and Clark hanging around, making stupid wisecracks.

"We're coming with," Alf repeated. "You'll need a diversion to get through the security gates. Clark and I can draw attention away from you."

"And then *you'll* get caught," I told him. "You've still got bruises from Saturday. Imagine what your dad will do if you're busted again."

"If I can see St. Agatha's firsthand, it'll be worth it," Alf said. "I've been hearing about this place my whole life. It's legendary. Did you know there's a swimming pool? They say the girls lie around on giant pillows. Sunning themselves, like housecats."

"I don't think that's true," Clark said.

"I've brought everything we need," Alf said. He unzipped his back-pack to show us its contents: binoculars, walkie-talkies, wire cutters, and a solar-powered calculator.

"What's the calculator for?" I asked.

"Math problems," he said. "I forgot to take it out of my bag."

I realized there was no talking them out of it, so we pedaled off down the street. It felt good to be moving, good to have the plan in motion—but after just five minutes of pedaling, I wished I'd worn shorts. The day was warm and muggy, eighty degrees and still early.

I was already sweating, and I still had to pedal fifteen miles on a single-gear dirt bike.

Wetbridge sat at the intersection of the New Jersey Turnpike and the Garden State Parkway, and it was ringed by six-lane highways. None of these roads were designed for bike traffic, but we squeezed into the shoulder lanes anyway, pedaling furiously as Greyhound buses and tractor trailers thundered past, spraying our faces with gravel and exhaust. I kept my mouth shut, but somehow it filled with a grit that tasted like charcoal. By the time we exited onto a smaller two-lane road, I was dripping with sweat—and filthier than I'd been in my entire life.

And we still had thirteen miles to go.

We passed through three different towns, each nicer than the last. We were entering a part of New Jersey I'd never seen before—residential neighborhoods where all the homes had circular driveways and two-car garages, where the hedges were pruned and the gardens were mulched and the flower beds were bursting with vibrant colors. Between the houses, we saw glimpses of crystal-blue swimming pools and private tennis courts. Traffic was light, so we biked down the center of the road, looking around in astonishment.

"This place is rad," I said. "Soon as I grow up, I'm moving here."

"Soon as you grow up?" Alf asked.

"You know what I mean. When I get older."

Clark shook his head. "This street's like Park Place and Boardwalk combined. How are you going to make all that money?"

"Game design," I said. "I'm going to save all my money and get a new computer, and then I'll make games that sell like crazy."

Alf and Clark didn't answer, but I knew what they were thinking: Minimum wage was $3.35 an hour and an IBM PS/2 averaged $4,000. I'd need to save for years and years before I ever wrote another line of code, and who had that kind of willpower?

"I'll tell you one thing I like about Baltic Avenue," Alf said. "Less grass to mow."

"And less snow in the winter," Clark said. "Can you imagine shoveling all these driveways?"

"It'd take forever," Alf said.

We stood up on our bikes and pumped our legs, pedaling faster, leaving behind the neighborhood and talk of our futures.

By eleven o'clock I was farther from home than I'd ever been in my life. We were passing fields full of tomatoes and corn and fir trees; we even passed a stable full of horses. Our teachers had always told us that New Jersey was nicknamed the Garden State, and that day I finally understood why. The relentless heat made everything seem more unreal. The temperature had soared into the nineties. I had a headache and I desperately needed a drink. We biked more than a mile on a dusty two-lane road without passing a single person or automobile.

"You're sure this is the right way?" Clark asked.

I stopped to check the map. "We're almost there," I told them. "Another mile and change."

We stopped at a two-pump Gulf station to buy drinks and clean ourselves up. Clark paid fifty cents for a bottle of something called Evian, which turned out to be plain old water. Alf and I teased him mercilessly. What kind of dummy wasted fifty cents on water when there was a free spigot and hose right outside the building? Clark shrugged and drank it down. "This is fantastic," he insisted. "It's the best water I've ever tasted."

I removed Mary's letter from my pocket and tucked it under my bike seat for safekeeping. Then I used the hose to clean my face and rinse the dirt and gravel from my clothing. Within minutes, I was sopping wet, but it felt tremendous, and I knew the sun would bake everything dry before we arrived at St. Agatha's.

The attendant was an old man in a plaid shirt and oil-stained pants. He dragged a rusty lawn chair into the shade of the garage and sat down. He watched us spraying ourselves with the hose, and I sensed he was getting ready to yell at us.

"Are we close to St. Agatha's?" I asked him.

"Very close," he said. "But you won't make it."

Alf and Clark stopped horsing around.

"What did you say?" Alf asked.

"I said you won't make it. I know what you're trying, and it ain't going to work."

Clark set down the hose and we all walked over to him. "How do you know?"

"I've owned this station since 1969. That's the year Neil Armstrong walked on the moon. And every year when summer rolls around, I sell sodas and Slim Jims to knuckleheads who think they can sneak into St. Agatha's. So I am speaking from experience. Turn your bikes around. You will not get inside. No one gets inside."

"Because of the fence?" Alf asked. "The electric fence?"

The old man smiled. "You won't even reach the fence."

He refused to elaborate. Just shook his head and clucked his disapproval, like we were venturing blindly into a jungle full of quicksand and crocodiles. I retrieved Mary's letter and returned it to my back pocket. Alf and Clark didn't say anything, but I knew what they were thinking: we had come too far to turn back now.

We hopped on our bikes and kept going.

31

```
3100 REM *** DRAW NEW FORTRESS ***
3110 FOR I=1345 TO 1362
3120 POKE I,35:POKE I+BG,9
3130 NEXT I
3140 FOR I=1625+15*40 TO 1642
3150 POKE I,35:POKE I+BG,9
3160 NEXT I
3170 FOR I=1519 TO 1542
3180 POKE I,35:POKE I+BG,9
3190 NEXT I:RETURN
]■
```

A FEW MINUTES AFTER the gas station, the road curved through a small patch of trees. When we emerged on the other side, the mountain was upon us.

No one associates New Jersey with mountains, but there are forty miles of them in the northern part of the state, formed by volcanoes 150 million years ago (apparently I did retain one or two facts after a year of studying Rocks and Streams). Our destination wasn't particularly large. If you were driving past the mountain in a car, you wouldn't give it a second look. But from the sweaty vinyl seat of a dirt bike on the hottest day of the year, it might as well have been Kilimanjaro.

We soon arrived at the base of the mountain and a large sign:

NOW ENTERING MOUNT SAINT AGATHA'S
PREPARATORY SCHOOL FOR GIRLS
PRIVATE PROPERTY
AUTHORIZED VISITORS AND GUESTS ONLY

"Hear ye children, the instructions of a father,
and attend to know understanding."—Proverbs 4:1

"This is it," Clark said. "Are you sure about this?"

"Sure I'm sure," Alf said. "I've come this far, haven't I?"

Clark flipped his empty water bottle at Alf's face, conking him on the forehead. "I'm talking to Billy, numb-nuts."

Alf leapt off his bike, and it clattered to the pavement. He reached his arm around Clark's neck, pulling him into a choke hold. "I'm sure, I'm sure," I said, inserting myself between them and calling for a cease fire. "Knock it off and let's go."

I'd barely separated them when Alf pointed behind us, to the grove of trees we'd just traveled through. A white Volkswagen Beetle was weaving along the road, coming right toward us.

"Hide," I said.

We dragged our bikes off the road and into the surrounding woods, then dove behind shrubs to conceal ourselves. The Beetle motored past, and we saw five sisters in black habits through the windows, crammed inside like clowns in a circus car. We crawled out from our hiding places to watch the VW ascend the mountain. Even with switchbacks cut into the sides, the incline was steep, and the car climbed slowly, gears grinding and engine groaning.

"I can't pedal that," Alf said. "I'm already whipped."

"That's fine," I said. "We'll leave the bikes."

We charged the road at a full-on sprint, but the pitch was brutal and after a minute we were all walking again. The sun beat down on our necks. The black asphalt was broiling, and I was soaked with sweat. But we were close. I touched my back pocket, checking for Mary's letter. Soon she would have it, and that was all the motivation I needed to keep going. In another thirty or forty minutes, she would finally know the truth, and I'd be able to live with myself again.

We had just climbed the second switchback, not even halfway up the mountain, when I peered down to the road below. Another vehicle was emerging from the grove of trees. This one was a brown UPS truck, and it was going well over the speed limit, building momentum before the first ascent.

"Shit," Alf said.

We started running, but I already knew we weren't fast enough. The truck was coming way too fast; it was bound to overtake us before we reached the top. At once I understood why the old man at the gas station had predicted our failure. We were running up the road in plain sight, three boys on private property where boys were expressly forbidden.

"We're not going to make it," I gasped. We'd just rounded the fourth switchback, and the truck had rounded the third. We had to hide, but there was no place to hide. There were no trees or shrubs—just rocky slopes covered with roses and wildflowers, everything in full bloom. We were moments from being spotted. We had to get off the road, had to camouflage ourselves.

"Get down," I told the guys, and then I dove face-first into a bed of pink roses.

Now, up until that moment I guess I'd never seen a rose in real life. I'd watched countless music videos in which half-dressed girls lay down on beds of roses, caressing crimson petals against their milky white skin. But none of these videos prepared me for the fact that real rose stems are covered with hard, brittle spikes. Before I'd even hit the ground, hundreds of thorns were piercing my clothes, puncturing my skin and drawing blood. By the time I realized my mistake, it was too late. I tried to push myself off, but the hooks had me snared. I shrieked. I howled. Everywhere I moved, there were more thorns, biting deeper into my ankles and gouging the soft tender flesh of my forearms. I might have been stuck there forever if Alf and Clark hadn't grabbed my belt and pulled hard, peeling me off the vines like a strip of Velcro.

The three of us lay gasping and out of breath on the side of the road as the UPS truck rumbled past. The driver hadn't even noticed us.

I touched my fingers to my forehead and they came away red. "Am I bleeding?"

"It's just a scratch," Alf said. He pointed to my temple and traced the outline of a large trapezoid. "Right here . . . and here and here and here."

There were more gashes in my shirt and little spots of blood were blooming through my khakis. But I could see we were nearing the top of the mountain, and this gave me a surge of confidence.

"Are you all right?" Clark asked.

"We're almost there. Let's go before another car comes."

We ran up the last two switchbacks without any problems, and finally the pitch of the mountain leveled off, but the road kept going, winding through a dark grove of trees. We followed it from a distance, trampling over ferns and rotting branches, ready to drop at the sound of another car.

I soon realized the school map wasn't drawn to scale. We seemed to be lost in the middle of a primeval forest, not minutes away from a chapel or classroom building.

Alf looked around, skeptical. "Are you sure this is right?"

"It has to be," Clark said. "This is the only road in."

"Up there," I said, pointing. "See?"

Through the trees we glimpsed a large wrought-iron gate that looked like it had risen up out of the earth, all twisting vines and pointed leaves and the words MOUNT SAINT AGATHA'S PREPARATORY SCHOOL FOR GIRLS arched across the top. On either side of the gate was a tall wrought-iron fence. It was seven feet high and stretched off into the forest, forming a boundary around the entire campus.

"If that's an electric fence," Clark asked, "where are all the wires?"

"They bury the wires," Alf said. "That's how they fool you."

I pointed to a cluster of sparrows on top of the fence, happily chirping. "Maybe you should warn those birds."

Clark pointed out that the fence—electric or otherwise—was the least of our concerns. Next to the gate was a small shed that looked like a tollbooth. Inside sat a man reading a newspaper. We crouched behind a fallen tree and studied the man through Alf's binoculars. This was no snoozing old-timer we could easily distract. The guy looked like a Navy SEAL; he sat on a stool that was too small for his huge, hulking frame, sipping coffee from a thermos and reading the Sports pages.

I handed the binoculars to Clark. "Now what?"

He peered through the lenses. "I'm not sure."

"It's easy," Alf said. "We wait for another car to drive up. While the guard's distracted, we make a break for it."

"That's not going to work," I said. I'd seen too many World War II movies where a lone guard radios for help and suddenly the whole prison camp is teeming with Nazi soldiers.

Clark agreed. "Let's follow the fence," he suggested. "Maybe it stops after a while. Or maybe there's another way inside."

Anything seemed better than confronting the guard, so we set off into the woods, trampling through mud and weeds and fallen branches. I carried the map but there were no landmarks to guide us—no buildings or roads on either side of the fence, just tangled forest and an occasional boulder. The fence twisted and turned, weaving its way around the largest trees. Every twenty feet or so, Alf would give the bars a gentle tap, still determined to find an "electrified section." Clark pushed even harder, hoping to find a spot where the fence was weak and we might pull it down. But the fence never budged. It seemed like it was built to repel an army.

Suddenly Clark stopped walking.

"Did you hear that?" he asked.

I stopped and listened. I didn't hear anything.

"It was a girl," he said. "I heard a girl calling for someone."

Alf looked skeptical, and I guess I was skeptical, too. We were so hot and tired and thirsty, it seemed possible that Clark might be hallucinating.

"Keep walking," I said.

We kept walking. The fence led us all the way around the campus, but we never saw a single student or even a building. The school and its entire population were hidden well beyond the perimeter. After twenty minutes of hiking I realized we were approaching the gate again, this time from the opposite direction. Some fifty yards ahead of us, I could just make out the guard booth through the trees.

"Careful," Alf said, grabbing my arm.

I was so busy looking for the security guard, I'd nearly walked into a small stream. Alf and Clark hopped across, but I stopped to take a closer look. The running water had eroded a narrow gorge beneath the fence, maybe twelve inches deep.

"Forget it," Alf said. "We won't fit."

"We might," I said.

Clark teased the water with the toe of his shoe, poking around at the mud. "It's not deep enough, Billy. Maybe if we had a shovel. But not like this."

He didn't seem to understand we were out of options, that we'd reached the end of the line. I kicked off my sneakers and hurled them over the fence. They landed on the other side, far beyond my reach. "You can turn back if you want," I said, "but I'm going in."

Alf and Clark watched, skeptical, as I climbed down into the creek and lay flat on my back in the cool muddy water. At the base of the fence was a rusty horizontal bar with jagged edges. By turning my face to the side, I was able to pass my head underneath—but my chest wouldn't fit. I sucked in my gut and pulled on the fence, wedging myself further and further until I was completely and totally stuck.

Alf watched me flail for a minute before offering to pull me back out. "Should I grab your feet?"

"Hang on," I said. By pushing up on the fence, I found I could press myself deeper into the mud, carving a deeper trench through the ooze. Something small and slimy fluttered against the back of my neck—a fish? A tadpole? I ignored it and kept pushing, using my legs to propel me along. The rusty base of the fence raked the front of my shirt, slashing the cotton and popping buttons. But soon my waist was through and the rest was easy. I crawled out of the creek, caked with mud and slime, and stood up. Through the bars of the fence, Alf and Clark observed me in a sort of horror.

"You look like Swamp Thing," Clark said.

"It'll wash off." I dipped my hand into the shallow water of the creek, demonstrating how easy it would be to clean up. All I really managed was to smear the mud around my skin. "Come on, now. Let's go."

They both hesitated, and I knew what they were thinking: This sort of thing never happened to James Bond. Somehow he always managed to breach the perimeter without getting a speck of dirt on his white tuxedo.

But then a sound cut through the forest—a girl's voice, laughing. "That's it!" Clark said. "That's her!"

"I hear it now," Alf said.

He kicked off his sneakers and knelt down in the mud. All of my squirming and thrashing had made things easier for him; once he was halfway under, I grabbed his arms and pulled, dragging his pristine Hard Rock Cafe shirt through the mud. Clark had a somewhat harder time because he had to do most of the pushing with one hand, but Alf and I splashed around him in the mud, heaving and pulling until he was all the way through.

It wasn't until Clark stood up that we realized Alf had forgotten his socks and sneakers—they were back on the other side of the fence, out of reach. Alf fished a branch through the wrought-iron bars, trying to snare them, but all he managed to do was push the sneakers farther out of reach.

"We have to go back," he said.

"Are you kidding?" Clark asked.

"There's no time," I said. "We'll get them on the way out."

Alf took a step forward, wincing as his bare heel came down on a pinecone. "I'm not going to make it," he said, but then there was more girlish laughter echoing through the woods, a siren's song calling us forward. Clark and I followed the sound, and Alf had no choice but to limp after us, hopping and complaining the whole way.

Through the trees, we began to discern a large athletic field. Some thirty girls were running, shouting, and swinging nets on long sticks. It was a sport I'd never seen before; they all seemed to be chasing a small rubber ball.

"Is that polo?" Alf asked.

"You play polo on horses," I said.

Alf shook his head. "No, that's jousting."

"It's lacrosse," Clark said. "They're playing lacrosse."

We lay flat on the ground to avoid being spotted, then crept closer on our bellies for a better look. These girls didn't look anything like the bikini models on my bedroom walls; none of them would ever make the pages of the *Sports Illustrated* Swimsuit issue. They were too short or too tall, too fat or too freckled, too sweaty and too flushed and too imperfect. But they were real, they were gloriously alive—laughing and shouting and sprinting across the field. I watched them in quiet astonishment and realized that the rumors about St. Agatha's were true: these were the most beautiful girls I'd ever seen.

"I bet they all get their periods together," Alf said.

"Please don't talk right now," Clark said. "Just let me enjoy this moment."

"It's true!" Alf said. "When girls live together, their menstrual cycles sync up automatically. To protect the herd."

I had listened to Alf's bullshit stories all my life but this seemed like a whole new level of absurdity. "Protect the herd from what?" I asked.

"It's a biological safety check," Alf said.

"What does that mean?" I asked.

"Charles Darwin, Billy! Don't you pay attention in science?"

"Keep your voice down," Clark hissed, but it was too late. Out in the field, one of the girls stopped running, lowered her net-stick, and turned toward the tree line. We got down as low as we could, crouching behind skimpy shrubs and trying to disappear into the ground. Alf was still mumbling about natural selection and gorilla tribes until I elbowed him in the side.

The girl on the field was maybe twenty feet away from us. She stepped closer to our hiding place, and I felt certain we were busted. Then a rubber yellow ball streaked past her and she turned to sprint after it.

"That was close," Clark whispered. "Let's keep going."

We fell back into the forest, weaving through the trees until we saw the tall spire of the chapel. I checked my map and saw we had arrived at the north end of the campus, just behind a large two-story classroom building and a garden ringed by tall hedges. It was our only lucky break all day—the hedges were enormous, nine or ten feet tall, and shielded us when we emerged from the tree line. Any students or teachers glancing out the windows of the classroom building wouldn't see us.

"What is this thing?" Alf asked.

I pointed to a narrow gap between two hedges—an entrance. There was a small stone tablet embedded in the ground. It was engraved with the words IN LOVING MEMORY OF SISTER BEATRICE (1821–1857). A PLACE OF BEAUTY AND SILENT CONTEMPLATION. Clark raised a finger to his lips, gesturing for us to be quiet, and slipped through the gap.

Inside the garden was a labyrinth of smaller hedges, all waist-high, guiding us through flower beds on paths lined with white gravel. Alf cringed with every step, tiptoeing like a little baby, hopping and yelping and crying out in pain. I glared at him. "Do you need to be carried?"

Alf lifted his right foot and plucked three jagged stones from his sole. "It's like broken glass," he said.

"Keep your voice down," Clark said. The garden was full of shady nooks with stone benches and statues of angels and cherubs, and Clark reminded us that a sister could be lurking in the shadows.

"You should have left me at the polo field," Alf said. "I'm no good without sneakers."

"We're almost through," Clark said. "If we get closer to the classroom building, I bet we find someone."

But the garden was more complicated than it looked—the paths doubled back on themselves, splitting into dead ends and infinite loops. I don't know how anyone was supposed to relax in this place; it was a giant exercise in frustration, and Alf's nonstop griping just made it worse.

Then we turned a corner and nearly collided with a girl on a bench. She was taking notes in a paperback and listening to a Sony Walkman—but at the sight of us, she dropped everything and scrambled backward, reaching for a silver whistle that hung from a chain around her neck.

"Wait," I said.

"Please," Alf told her.

The girl pressed the whistle to her lips.

"Video City!" Clark exclaimed.

And the girl hesitated.

"You work at Video City!" he said. "You're Lynn Scott. You do Lynn's Picks, the staff recommendations near the cash register. Don't you recognize us?"

Our faces were covered with mud. Our clothes were ruined. Of course she didn't recognize us.

"We were just there last week," Clark said.

Alf nodded. "We rented *Kramer vs. Kramer*."

Lynn blinked. "Wait a second—you're *those* guys? The guys who keep renting *Kramer vs. Kramer* over and over?"

"Maybe once or twice," Clark admitted.

"Eighteen times!" she said. "The owners keep a tally on a sticky note next to the register. They're taking bets on how soon you get to twenty."

I noticed Clark had already hidden the Claw inside his pocket. Every time we went to Video City, he was always careful to hide the Claw from Lynn and her coworkers. He'd manage to show his membership card *and* pay for the movie *and* accept his change *and* carry out the video using just one hand, which is a lot more awkward than it sounds.

Clark started to introduce us but Lynn cut him off. "You guys aren't allowed to be here," she said, kneeling down to retrieve her book and Hi-Liter. "I'll get expelled just for talking to you."

"We need your help," Clark said.

She shook her head. "I'm here on scholarship. I can't take any chances. My parents will kill me."

"Please," I said. "I have a letter for Mary Zelinsky. I just need you to give it to her."

I reached in my back pocket for the envelope, only to find a limp, soggy mess, saturated with muddy water. I'd ruined the letter while crawling through the creek. I peeled open the envelope and saw all of my words blurred together. Mary would never be able to read them.

Lynn observed the dripping envelope, skeptical.

"Maybe you could find Mary?" I asked. "Can you bring her here?"

"No."

"It's important," I said.

"Then go to the store. Or go to her house. Knock on her door like a regular person."

"I can't."

"Why not?"

Lynn was already walking away from us, and we had no choice but to follow her. She clearly knew the fastest route to the exit. In just moments she would be out and gone.

"It's a long story," Clark said. "Billy can't go anywhere near her."

Lynn glanced back at me. "Your name is Billy?"

"That's right."

"And Mary knows you?"

"Yes."

She shook her head. "I don't believe it. I talk to Mary all the time. She's never mentioned any Billy."

Now, right there, I should have known something was wrong. I was certain my name would have come up once or twice. Especially after I led a gang of thieves into her father's store and destroyed the place.

"Maybe a Will?" I asked. "Did she ever mention a Will?"

"Never."

"Never?"

"Raoul, she brags about Raoul all the time. But she's never mentioned any Will."

"Who the hell is Raoul?" Alf asked. He was limping along behind me, clutching my shoulder for support.

"I don't know," I said. It was my first moment of doubt all day. *You don't know her at all*, Zelinsky had warned me. *All this time she's been fooling you right back*. Maybe this was why Mary had pushed me away in the store. Maybe she was secretly in love with some asshole named Raoul.

"Please," Clark told Lynn. "Just find Mary, and tell her Will is here. He wants to see her. She can come, or she can ignore him. But let her decide. Give her the choice, okay? That's all we're asking."

It was the most Clark had spoken to a girl in years, and I don't know where he found the courage. But in that moment I realized he was blessed with a remarkable gift. Even with his muddy hair and weird hand-me-down clothes and one hand shoved deep in his pocket, there was something about the way Clark looked or the way Clark spoke that made him impossible to refuse. In the span of just fifteen seconds, Lynn went from looking pissed off to anxious and concerned. Suddenly our mission had become her mission.

"All right," she said, "but you won't have much time. Lunch is almost over."

Even Clark seemed surprised by her turnaround. "But you'll actually get her? You'll bring Mary here?"

"I better not get in trouble." She pointed to a shady nook in the garden with a large statue of the Virgin Mary. "Go hide over there. Behind the statue. Keep your voices down because Sister Ellen comes here all the time, and you do not want to cross Sister Ellen."

"Thank you," Clark said.

"Don't thank me. Just hide," she said.

We all moved behind the statue and crouched down.

Clark was whispering excitedly about the way Lynn had spoken to him. "I am totally asking her out," he said. "As soon as I get my surgery, as soon as they hack off this stupid freak show, I am totally asking her out!"

"She likes you already," Alf said. "Why are you going to wait four years?"

"I don't want to spook her."

"You've already spooked her! By renting that stupid movie eighteen times!"

Their bickering was making me tired. Or maybe it was just the sun—directly overhead and beating down on us. I could feel parts of my skin crisping up; the rest was slathered in mud. My heart was pounding.

Clark took the Claw from his pocket and tucked it under his shirt. He looked like a portrait of Napoleon. "Is this less obvious?"

"You're just calling attention to it," I said.

Clark shook his head. "I wish I brought gloves."

Alf was exasperated. "You need to get over this, Clark. The girl's here on scholarship. She's not stupid. You're not fooling her."

Clark wouldn't relent. He kept the Claw hidden beneath his shirt. "If she sees it too soon, she'll be repulsed. It's better this way."

Footsteps passed nearby, on the other side of the hedge wall, and we all stopped taking until they were gone. I was feeling anxious, and I asked if the guys would mind giving me a little privacy. "I'd like to meet with Mary one on one."

"Sure, totally," Alf said. He suggested that we meet by the gap in the fence, where we crawled through the creek. "If you're not there in twenty minutes, we'll know something's wrong and we'll leave. Does that sound all right?"

"That sounds great," I said. "And thank you, guys. Thanks for helping me get this far. I owe you big-time."

"You don't owe us nothing," Alf said. "Just promise you'll make this count, all right? Tell her what you came to say. No wussing out."

He put out his hand and we shook on it. "No wussing out."

"Good luck, Billy," Clark said. "I really hope it goes okay for you. And tell Lynn I said good-bye, all right?"

I promised I would, but this turned out to be unnecessary.

Alf and Clark were just standing to leave when Lynn returned to the garden. Trailing behind her was a tall, slender Asian girl with long dark hair. She cracked her gum and studied us with disapproval.

"Who's this?" Alf asked.

"This is Mary," Lynn said. "From Video City."

"Who the hell are you?" Mary from Video City asked.

"*Zelinsky*," I told Lynn. "I said Mary *Zelinsky*."

"You said Mary from Video City."

"I don't know Mary from Video City." I turned to Mary from Video City. "I'm very sorry to bother you. There's been a mistake. I'm looking for Mary *Zelinsky*."

The girls stared back at me, confused.

"She's short, black hair?" I said. "She paints little pictures on her fingernails? Little binary numbers?"

"Wait, Computer Geek Mary?" Lynn asked.

"Yes," I said.

"From the typewriter store?"

"Exactly!" I said.

"We don't really know her," Lynn said.

"She keeps to herself," Mary from Video City explained.

We were interrupted by a loud chime that echoed across campus. Lynn explained that this was the bell between classes. "You're too late, anyway," she said. "I'm sorry, but I gotta go. I can't miss Trig."

My mind couldn't move fast enough to brainstorm a Plan B. "Where does Mary go after lunch?" I asked.

"I don't know," Lynn said.

"She might have Organic Chem," said Mary from Video City. "On the second floor of the classroom building."

I wasn't leaving now, not after coming this far. I reached into the wall of hedges, pulling apart the leaves and branches and peering out across campus. Girls were spilling out of the cafeteria, dozens of girls talking and laughing and carrying textbooks. They filed across a concrete walkway, walking to the doors of the classroom building.

Clark peered over my shoulder. "There," he said, pointing with his good hand. "Do you see her?"

I saw her.

Mary had just exited the cafeteria, and the trip to the classroom building would take her less than thirty seconds. There was no time to think or make smart choices. If she reached the classroom building, she was gone for good. I lunged forward, bulldozing through the hedges like a cartoon character, pushing and clawing my way through the brambles. Then I ran as fast as I could.

As soon as I left the garden I realized I'd miscalculated. Mary was already halfway to the classroom building, and there was no way I'd reach her in time. I shouted Mary's name, and what followed seemed to happen in slow motion. Every girl on the campus—and by now there were at least a hundred of them—they all stopped moving and turned to stare at me. They gaped and pointed and their mouths formed perfect Os.

Mary heard me yelling and turned around. At first she just seemed confused—but then I came running up and all the color left her face. She looked mortified. And suddenly I felt like an idiot. What the hell was I thinking? What was I going to say, here at the school in front of everyone?

I turned to retreat, and to my astonishment I saw that Alf and Clark were right behind me. They'd left the garden and followed me and now they were beside me. A crowd of girls closed around us, forming a circle. They were pointing at us and laughing, and I remembered how awful we looked. Our clothes were ripped and ruined. My khakis were spattered with blood and muck. Alf was barefoot and Clark had his Claw tucked away like Napoleon and all of us reeked of swamp water. I'm surprised Mary even recognized me.

She was dressed in the St. Agatha's school uniform—a white blouse and a pleated plaid skirt—and she was holding a stack of textbooks like a shield. Her classmates all peeled away, leaving Mary to stand alone. The other girls squealed and jeered at us like monkeys in the zoo. I'd have to shout to be heard over them. Mary looked like she wanted to sink into the ground and disappear.

A nun in a black habit pushed her way through the crowd. She was built like a linebacker, almost as tall as Officer Tackleberry but dressed in a black tunic and a black belt and black orthopedic shoes. "What is this? What's happening here?" I didn't answer, so she turned to Mary. "Miss Zelinsky! Are you talking to these . . . creatures?"

Mary shook her head. "No, Reverend Mother."

She turned to me, and I couldn't hold eye contact. I looked down at my filthy sneakers. It was all too much. It had to be a hundred degrees. I was exhausted and hurting and ridiculously thirsty. "All three of you are trespassing on private property. You're going to follow me to the main office, and we'll wait for the police."

I knew what would happen after that. I knew they would cart us back to the police station and my mother would get summoned with another phone call and this time there would be no second chances. There were no more breaks.

"I need to talk to Mary," I said.

The Reverend Mother's eyes widened. "Did you say something? Are you actually *speaking* to me?"

"Can we please have five minutes of privacy?"

You'd think I'd asked to spend the night with her. "Absolutely not!" she exclaimed. "You'll come to the office right now, and all of these young women will go to class. Go on, now, go!"

The young women didn't disperse. They were too riveted by the drama. This was better than episodes of *Knot's Landing* and *Falcon Crest* combined. More and more students were joining the crowd every moment, and I saw sisters weaving among them, shooing people away.

"Please," I said. "Just one minute."

"Go on!" the Reverend Mother repeated. "Anyone standing here in five seconds is going to face serious consequences!"

They seemed to understand this was no idle threat. They shuffled backward, reluctantly stepping away from the spectacle. Mary looked absolutely miserable. I'd ruined everything.

"Hang on," a voice said, and I realized it had come from the barefoot boy standing beside me. "My name is Alfred Boyle and I've been an altar boy at St. Stephen's for the last seven years. You know me, Reverend Mother. I've seen you at the five thirty Mass. And I biked all morning to get here. We climbed your mountain and crawled through your mud and your thorns. I lost my sneakers and ruined my best Hard Rock Cafe shirt from Cancun, Mexico. And my poor friend Clark—" He grabbed Clark's elbow and yanked the Claw free of the shirt, holding it high for everyone to see. "My poor friend Clark *destroyed his hand* climbing under your fence!" All of the girls gasped, like Alf had just unveiled the Elephant Man. "And we did all of this just so Billy could talk to Mary. So I'm asking you to show a little compassion. Like our savior Jesus Christ taught us in the story of the Good Salmatian."

The Reverend Mother glared at him, and something twitched at the corner of her lips. "Do you mean Jesus and the Good Samaritan?"

Alf nodded. "That's what I said."

The Reverend Mother stepped forward to inspect Clark's hand. Like the rest of him, it was covered in mud, so you couldn't tell precisely what was wrong with it. Clark was mortified, but he endured the scrutiny. What else could he do? He let her look, he let everyone look. The other girls were no longer drifting away; if anything, they had moved even closer.

The Reverend Mother turned to me. "You have one minute," she said. "But no privacy. Say what you need to say, and then we go to my office and call the police."

I turned to Mary. I tried to remember the exact phrasing of my letter. On paper, everything had seemed so clear and concise. But up in my brain, my thoughts were a mess. Mary started shaking. She looked like she was ready to cry. "I'm sorry to come here like this," I said. "I just need you to know the truth. I never lied to you. Not about anything. Especially the last night. After the movie. All that stuff was real. I liked you. I *still* like you."

I looked at her eyes, so she'd see I was telling the truth; I willed her to believe me. *The Impossible Fortress* was real. Radical Planet was real. Everything I felt for Mary was real. She was beautiful and kind and funny. She was better than I deserved, and I was a better person for knowing her. I stuttered and stammered and went well over my allotted minute, but in the end no one could accuse me of wussing out. I said everything I came to say, and then some.

Mary looked like she was ready to throw up. Her forehead was beaded with sweat, and she clung to the handrail to keep her balance.

"Are you all right?" I asked.

The Reverend Mother stepped forward. "That's enough."

"I'm fine," Mary whispered. "You should go."

Water piddled on the concrete steps beneath her feet. A stain spread across the front of her skirt. She was wetting herself.

"Mary?" I asked.

Another sister rushed to Mary's aid, and everyone started talking at once.

"Get back."

"Get the nurse."

"Go to class."

"He doesn't know."

This last voice was Mary's. I could hear her speaking to the other sisters. They were swarming around her, steering her toward the cool shade of the classroom building. I went to follow, but the Reverend Mother grabbed my arm, yanking me in the opposite direction, whispering hot words into my ear.

"Tell the truth," she said. "Are you her father?"

I stared back at her, puzzled. "Her father is Sal Zelinsky."

It was hard to hear anything with all of the shouting. But the Reverend Mother repeated herself, and this time I understood the question clearly: "Are you the father?"

32

```
3200 REM *** REPEAT SIREN SFX ***
3210 FOR I=0 TO 22
3220 POKE L1+I,0:NEXT I
3230 POKE L1+24,15:POKE L1+5,80
3240 POKE L1+6,243:POKE L1+3,4
3250 POKE L1+4,65
3260 FOR I=20 TO 140 STEP5
3270 POKEL1+1,I:NEXT I
3280 POKE L1+4,64:FOR I=1 TO 50
3290 NEXT I:RETURN
]■
```

MY MOTHER INSISTED ON driving me to the hospital. We left our house after dinner, after I'd showered and cleaned myself up. On the drive across town, she tried to manage my expectations.

"This is probably a bad idea," she said.

"I want to see her," I said.

"They might not let you see her. If she's been sedated, or God forbid if anything went wrong—"

"I'll just ask."

Mom squeezed the steering wheel tighter. "And Mary could say no.

She's probably not ready to see you. Labor is labor, it's not like the movies. You need to respect that."

"I know—"

"No, you don't know, Billy. You have no idea. This girl is a *mother*. At age fourteen." She shuddered at some long-ago memory. "Everyone said I was young, and I was a senior."

At the hospital, Mom waited in the car with a Sidney Sheldon paperback while I went inside and got directions to Mary's room. The maternity ward at Wetbridge Memorial Hospital was full of balloons and stuffed animals. There were grown-ups laughing and babies crying and grandparents carrying enormous video cameras that required two hands to operate. Every room was packed with visitors. People spilled out of doorways, talking and smoking cigars and eating food off paper plates. I felt like I'd wandered into a surprise party in the Twilight Zone.

I asked another nurse for Mary, and she pointed down the corridor, to a stretch of dim rooms far from the streamers and celebrations. Zelinsky and the Reverend Mother were seated on folding chairs at the very end of the hallway. Zelinsky saw me coming and stood up, crossing his arms over his chest.

"You're not supposed to be here," he said.

"I came to see if Mary's all right."

"She's not all right. Do you think she'd be here if she was all right?"

"I'm all right," Mary called from inside the room. I couldn't see her from the hallway; I could only see the foot of her bed. "Can you let him in, please?"

Zelinsky didn't budge. I sensed that part of him wanted to drag me kicking and screaming out of the maternity ward. But another part of him was ready to let Mary have anything she wanted.

The Reverend Mother spoke to him in a whisper. "He's the first friend to visit," she said. "I think Mary could stand to see a friend? Just for a short while?"

Zelinsky didn't answer. He sank into his chair, shaking his head, and buried his face in ink-stained hands.

"Ten minutes, love," the Reverend Mother told me. She placed a gentle hand on the small of my back, guiding me through the doorway. "Mary's had a long day, do you understand?"

"Thank you," I said.

I stepped cautiously into the room. I didn't know anything about babies—I'd never even held a baby—so part of me was scared to go any farther. The room was divided into halves by a curtain: The front half was empty. The back half had a bed and a chair and a window overlooking the parking lot. Mary was sitting up in the bed, chewing on a pencil eraser and reading a large binder full of computer code. Her hair was pulled back in a headband, and some of the color had returned to her face. If she hadn't been dressed in a hospital gown, you might not have realized that anything was wrong.

"You're all right?" I asked.

"All the gory stuff is over," she said. "Be glad you weren't here five hours ago."

I looked around the room. There was a dresser and a television, but I didn't see any cribs or boxes or containers that might be holding a baby.

"Where is it?" I asked.

"Where's what?" she asked. "The baby?"

"Yeah."

"She's down the hall. With her parents. They just got here from Scranton."

I took a moment to process this, to understand what she meant.

"Are they nice?"

"Super nice. They're music teachers. And they already have a daughter, so she'll have a sister. They have a house with three bedrooms, and they live across the street from a park. My father and I drove out there a month ago so we could see exactly where she'd live. It's really nice, nicer than Wetbridge."

A month ago. And all this time I had no idea. A month ago, I had walked into the store to buy hearing aid batteries, and Mary gave me a flyer advertising a computer programming contest. And I had no idea.

All this time she's been fooling you right back, Zelinsky told me. *You don't know her at all.*

"Scranton's not very far," I said. "I guess you could visit?"

Mary shook her head. "It's not going to work like that," she said, and her voice cracked. She looked at the open binder in her lap. "But look what they brought me. As a gift." She closed the binder and showed me the cover. It was the operating guide for the new IBM PS/2 computer. "No more messing around on 64s for me. I'm moving on to the big time. VGA graphics and a twenty-megabyte hard disk."

It's crazy: In spite of everything she'd been through, I felt a pang of envy. With a PS/2, Mary would rocket into the big time. Nothing would hold her back now.

"Do you want to sit down?" she asked.

The only seat in the room was a hard-backed metal folding chair, but I took it anyway. "I'm glad you're okay."

"Me too."

"I thought you were dying."

"Dying of embarrassment, maybe."

"I didn't know," I said. "I really had no clue."

"God, it was so obvious," Mary said. "Did you notice how many times I went to the bathroom?"

I shrugged. "I thought that was normal. In movies, girls are always running to the bathroom."

"I guess I did a good job of hiding everything." She gently patted her hips. "The perks of having a full figure."

I didn't know what to say to that.

"At the end of this month," Mary continued, "I was supposed to visit my aunt in Harrisburg. Have the baby out there. You never would have known."

"You could have just told me."

"No, I couldn't have," she said, and I knew Mary was right. I wouldn't have understood. I didn't even understand now. There was only one explanation for all of this, and yet it seemed impossible: "Tyler Bell?"

"Yeah."

"Was it— You know— Did he force himself on you?"

She shook her head. "More like the other way around."

"You forced yourself on Tyler Bell?"

Mary scrambled for the remote control and turned on the television. "Can you keep your voice down?" She raised the volume, concealing our conversation with an ad for Calvin Klein Obsession. "It was stupid, Will. I know it was stupid. He took me out on his motorcycle, and I thought we'd just kiss."

"But you liked him? *Liked him* liked him?"

She didn't answer right away. She looked like she was trying to remember something that happened many years ago.

"My mom had this thing about second chances," she explained. "'Everybody deserves a second chance,' she'd say. Even criminals. Especially criminals. Before she got sick, when she worked at the store, she'd hire part-timers who were straight out of prison. She said it was the Christian thing to do, that Jesus commanded us to forgive them. My father hated this idea. He thought she was crazy. Hiring thieves to stock our shelves. It was nuts, right? But Mom didn't care. She hired ex-cons for years, never had any problems. And then after she died—"

Mary stopped, reached for a plastic cup, and took a long drink of water. "Maybe a year after she died, our part-timer quit, so now it's Dad's turn to hire someone. And he decides he wants to honor Mom's legacy. He wants to do the Christian thing. So he goes to the cops and says, 'Bring me a screwup.' Meaning, bring me some kid who's always in trouble so Dad can straighten him out. The very next day, a cop comes by with Tyler Bell."

"Did you know him?"

"No, I'd never met him. But I'd seen him riding around Market Street on his Harley. Every girl in Wetbridge knows him by sight. They would come by the store and buy crap they didn't need, just for the chance to see him. His hair and his eyes and the whole biker thing. To be honest, I'm not sure if I really liked him, or if I just liked him because everybody else liked him."

She explained that the first few weeks passed without incident. Tyler did his work and kept to himself. "He was nice to me because he had to be," Mary said. "I was the boss's daughter, right? So even though he's three years older, I felt really safe talking to him. Making little jokes. I guess it was flirting. But always when Dad had his back turned. Tyler didn't mind, he just laughed. So every day I got a little bolder."

Then one night Tyler invited Mary to take a ride on his motorcycle. She described how he drove them into the woods behind the Ford motor plant. They sat on blankets and smoked a cigarette. Then they started kissing and didn't stop. "I was so mad at myself, Will. As soon as it ended, I knew it was a mistake. Tyler was nervous. He wouldn't stop talking. He said that out of all the girls he'd been with, I had the nicest hair. Like that was a compliment, you know?"

I didn't say anything. I felt like she was talking about a completely different person, some other Mary, like a character you'd read about in a book. I couldn't believe I knew someone who'd had real sex.

"The next day was awful. He came to work and he kept touching me. Every time my dad turned his back. He wouldn't keep his hands off me. And I just wanted to pretend it never happened. I wanted him to go away. But we were stuck in that store together, every day. So I made up an excuse to get rid of him. I said he tried to steal a lighter."

"You lied?"

"He was so angry. Because no one believed him, you know? Not a single person. It was such a selfish, shitty thing for me to do."

"Did you know you were—" I couldn't bring myself to say the word aloud; I still couldn't believe I was sitting in a maternity ward.

"No, I wasn't sure for another six weeks. I kept hoping I was wrong. By the time I knew for sure, Tyler was long gone."

Up on the television screen, three gorgeous women in cowboy hats welcomed Spuds MacKenzie to a country-western concert on a dude ranch. The dog hopped up behind the drums, grabbed the sticks, and began to play along.

"I waited until February to tell my dad. I couldn't bring myself to tell him. I was too embarrassed. It was such a stupid thing to do."

I thought of Tyler's rampage during the robbery, thought of the blitz of destruction that never totally added up. "Does he know now?"

"My dad told him last week. At the police station. That's why he didn't press charges, by the way. He couldn't send his granddaughter's father to jail. He figures she might want to look up Tyler someday, find out who he is. And it wouldn't be right if he was a criminal. So he told the cops to drop the charges, and they let you all go."

Up on the television, the Bud Light commercial ended and a studio audience shouted WHEEL! OF! FORTUNE! It was seven thirty, and America's favorite game show was starting. I wanted to change the channel, but Mary still held the remote; she seemed grateful to have something to watch, an excuse to stop or at least pause our conversation. Vanna White appeared onstage, resplendent in a designer gown, and the audience applauded as she twirled around, showing off the scooped back and her taut calves.

The first puzzle was a popular phrase consisting of six words. After several spins, the board looked like this:

IF I ___L_ T__N _A__ TI_E

I guess I was grateful to have the TV, too. I was happy to just sit there and hang out like nothing had spoiled between us. For some strange reason my mind kept going back to Tyler Bell, the biggest screwup in Wetbridge and the father of a huge mistake. I knew Tyler was already en route to basic training, and a new life, and I guess the baby was better off without him. But I wondered if he would ever look back and have regrets.

I was still wondering when Zelinsky appeared in the doorway. "Time's up," he said. "Get out." And there was something comforting about his arrival—like we were back in the store and Zelinsky was kicking me out again, just like the good old days.

"Thanks for coming this morning," Mary said. "Your timing was terrible, but I was glad to see you."

"Maybe we could hang out sometime," I said. "The Regal has a new movie. *Which Is Eastwick?*"

"*The Witches of Eastwick*," Mary corrected.

"Maybe we could meet there," I said. "If you felt like hanging out again."

Mary straightened up in bed, neatening the blankets. Her fingernails were painted with tiny ladybugs, little pops of red and black. "I don't think so, Will." She tried clearing her throat, but her voice was still thick. "I got a fresh start today. Things can finally go back to normal. I can pretend this whole awful year never happened." She hesitated, then said, "If I could turn back time . . ."

"Yeah?" I asked.

Mary just nodded at the television screen, and I realized she had solved the puzzle.

33

```
3300 REM *** GAME OVER ***
3310 POKE 53281,0:POKE 53280,0
3320 PRINT "{CLR}{RED}"
3330 PRINT "{9 SPACES}THY GAME IS OVER."
3340 PRINT "{9 SPACES}YOU ARE TRAPPED"
3350 PRINT "{6 SPACES}IN THE FORTRESS"
3360 PRINT "{8 SPACES}FOR ALL OF ETERNITY."
3370 PRINT "{6 SPACES}YOUR SCORE IS ";SCORE
3380 PRINT "{6 SPACES}YOUR RANK IS ";RANK$
3390 RETURN
]■
```

SCHOOL ENDED TWO WEEKS later and I started my Cosmex internship at six forty-five the following morning. The factory was hidden among a sea of warehouses off Route 287; I had to wake at five thirty and take two different buses to arrive on time. My boss was a short, squat Haitian man who never told me his name or asked for mine. He simply thumped his chest and said, "Boss Man."

"Boss Man?" I repeated.

"*Très bon!*" he said.

The factory floor was the size of several gymnasiums, full of quietly humming machines that united to create a dull roar. Within minutes of my arrival, Boss Man had me outfitted with earplugs and a hairnet, and I was standing over a conveyor belt with a box of mascara brush caps. He flipped a switch, and the line groaned to life; a row of open mascara tubes surged toward me. Boss Man grabbed a brush cap, plunged it into the first open tube, and twisted it closed. "Push, twist, yes?" he said.

"Push, twist?"

"Push, twist, push, twist, push, twist," he said, capping the subsequent tubes with a speed that was dazzling. He gestured for me to join in the work, but the tubes moved faster than my hands; I felt like I was chasing them.

"Push, twist, push, twist, push, twist," Boss Man sang, like it was some kind of lullaby he'd learned growing up in Haiti. I hadn't capped more than a dozen tubes when Boss Man abruptly stepped away. "First break ten thirty."

"Hang on," I called. "Can I just—"

"Push, twist!"

He was already gone and the tubes kept coming, hurtling down the line like the march of the wooden soldiers. My heart was racing; my palms were sweating. I needed all of my concentration just to keep up. Some twenty feet to my left, at the end of the conveyor belt, a trio of elderly women collected the finished tubes and placed them in slender cardboard sleeves. They regarded me with suspicion, just waiting for me to screw up.

Gradually my confidence increased. I learned to grab the brushes by the caps (not the bristles) so I could plunge them directly into the tubes. After a while I didn't even have to think about the work anymore—my hands were doing it automatically—and my mind wandered. My perch on the mascara line faced a windowless cinder-block wall. Sometimes people walked behind me and I'd overhear snippets of conversation, but there was never enough time to turn and look. The tubes continued their march down the line, relentless. Eventually I was so bored I looked at my watch, and I realized it was only seven o'clock, that I'd been working on the assembly line for a mere fifteen minutes.

That's when I saw my entire summer falling away from me—ten weeks of mind-numbing, soul-crushing, forty-hour shifts through Labor Day: push, twist, push, twist, push, twist.

There were twelve other interns, all boys. Half of them were mentally disabled; the other half looked like they wanted to kill me. The adult employees were Hispanics, Asians, and Indians with limited English skills; at lunch they divided into factions, like cliques in a high school or gangs in a prison. No one ever said hello or even smiled at me; I might as well have been invisible.

At break time, I took my sandwich outside to the parking lot, crouched in the shade of a Dumpster, and read Stephen King novels. I crammed as much story as I could in the allotted thirty-minute break so I could spend the afternoon chewing over the plot, trying to figure out what might happen next. There was nothing else to occupy my mind. Sometimes I'd try to count the mascara tubes (this required more concentration than you'd think; the highest I ever got was 715 tubes in 47 minutes). But most of the time I just thought of Mary and Zelinsky and how I managed to ruin everything.

Meanwhile, Alf and Clark had joined the closing shift at the Wetbridge McDonald's. They were constantly complaining about the difficulty of their work—the rude customers, the sweltering kitchens, the filthy grease traps. But I could tell they were having the time of their lives. The restaurant was staffed entirely with teenagers, half of them girls, and the night shifts sounded like long, raucous parties. They were staying up until midnight, pigging out on Quarter Pounders and

Chicken McNuggets, and clearing more than a hundred bucks every week.

Most nights I'd walk over to the McDonald's and sit on a playground designed for little kids, reading my Stephen King books until Alf and Clark came outside for their breaks. Over the weeks, I met all of their coworkers—the cute girls on register, the other guys in grill, the friendly geezer who dragged out the trash and swept up the dining room. They entertained me with outrageous stories of crazy customers, like the vegetarian who ordered a Big Mac with no meat, or the guy who paid with a fifty-dollar bill and drove away without his change.

"How about you?" Clark would ask me after they'd carried on for too long. "Tell us a story from the factory. What's going on?"

I never had anything to share. Every day at Cosmex was the same. The factory never stopped; the machines never broke; the giant vats never ran dry of mascara. I spent the mornings dreaming of my lunch break, and my afternoons dreaming of the bus rides home.

And if all that wasn't bad enough, my mother started dating Tack. It took me a while to catch on. Sure, I'd noticed little changes in her behavior: she cut her hair short; she started blending fruit shakes every morning; she was doing her Jane Fonda Workout video again. Apparently Tack would visit the Food World on her break, and they would go across the street to the Wetbridge Diner for coffee. This all became clear one Thursday afternoon when Tack showed up at our house for dinner. He arrived in a shirt and tie, carrying a bouquet of daisies. They tried to act like there was nothing awkward about the situation—"grown-ups can be friends," they assured me—but I saw what was happening, and I didn't want any part of it. Tack tried making conversation over dinner. He said he was thinking about purchasing a home computer and he asked if I could recommend anything. I just shrugged and said I didn't know. I didn't want to encourage him. I didn't like having him at our table with his stiff posture and his silver buzz cut and his loaded gun, like he expected Libyan rebels to come crashing through the windows any moment.

My mother insisted he stay for coffee and dessert, and he even lingered long enough to watch *The Cosby Show* and *Cheers*. I excused myself, went back to my bedroom, and read my computer magazines. I still had all of my old subscriptions, and new issues kept arriving on a monthly basis, advertising all the latest games and programming tricks that I'd never get to try.

Tack started coming for dinner every Thursday. He always brought fresh flowers, and he always stayed until *Cheers* was over. My mother and Tack carried on like *Cheers* was the best thing since *Dallas*. They were constantly debating if Diane Chambers would return to the show in the fall to marry Sam Malone.

July 12 was my mother's birthday. Tack drove us to Seaside Heights, and I spent the night following them up and down the boardwalk. They played mini golf while I just watched. They ate frozen custard, but I didn't want any. They rode through the haunted house on a tiny little buggy, but I chose to wait outside. I knew I was being a jerk, but I didn't care. At one point my mother lost her patience and pulled me aside. "Why are you doing this?" she asked. "It's my birthday. Why do you have to be so miserable?"

"Because I'm miserable," I said.

Through that long, awful, never-ending summer, there was just one thing keeping me going: the Game of the Year Contest for High School Computer Programmers. In the third week of July, I received a letter from the Rutgers faculty, explaining that the 118 games submitted for the award had been culled to five finalists, including *The Impossible Fortress* by Will Marvin and Mary Zelinsky. The faculty hoped we would attend the awards ceremony, where guest judge Fletcher Mulligan of Digital Artists would declare the winner. Every finalist was guaranteed a fifty-dollar college savings bond, and the winner would take home an IBM PS/2, approximate retail value $4,000.

I showed the letter to my mother, and we debated next steps. Technically I was still forbidden to contact Mary, but we both agreed that she deserved to see the letter. And the last time I'd tried to deliver a letter to Mary, things hadn't gone so well. I didn't know what to do.

One Thursday night at dinner, my mother showed the letter to Tack and explained the dilemma. Tack folded the letter in half, then placed it in the pocket of his sports coat. "I'll visit the store in the morning," he said. "I'll give it to Sal."

"He hates me," I said. "You have to give it to Mary."

Tack shook his head. "I can't go behind his back."

"Then you might as well tear it up," I said. "Because that's all Zelinsky's going to do. He'll never let her see it."

Tack paused to take a long sip of coffee. "My goodness, Beth, this is really delicious coffee."

"Thank you," Mom said. "It's Maxwell House."

"Give me the letter," I told Tack.

"Let me help you, Will," he said. "I've known Sal for eight years. He's a reasonable guy. Maybe I can fix this."

I didn't see Tack again for three days. The next time he came to our house, I was out in the yard with my mother, helping her anchor a birdbath in a bed of loose gravel. Her plan to "grow a few perennials" had gradually evolved into a full-blown botanical extravaganza, complete with marigolds and sunflowers, carrots and lettuce, a little trail of stepping-stones. Somehow we'd found ourselves with the nicest lawn on Baltic Avenue.

Tack drove up to our house with a trunkful of compost and fertilizer; he carried it across the yard under my mother's supervision. I knew right away that something was wrong. Most days Tack was quick to say hello and ask how I was doing, but that afternoon he wouldn't look at me. He lifted every bag of mulch with tremendous care, like the job required his complete and total concentration. I waited maybe ninety seconds before asking if he'd delivered the letter.

"I gave it to Sal," he said.

"And?"

"And he gave it to Mary."

"Were you there? Did you see her read it?"

"Yes."

"And? What did she say?"

He shook his head. "She didn't say anything."

Tack reached in his pocket for the letter and returned it to me. I checked the paper front and back, hoping that maybe Mary added some kind of message, but no. Tack sensed my disappointment. He clapped a hand on my shoulder.

"The girl's had a tough year, Will. A real tough year. Sometimes the best thing for people is a fresh start, you know?"

34

```
3400 REM *** PLAY AGAIN?? ***
3410 PRINT "{CLR}{12 CSR DOWN}"
3420 PRINT "{9 SPACES}THY GAME IS OVER."
3430 PRINT "{2 CSR DOWN}"
3440 PRINT "{3 SPACES}WOULD YOU LIKE TO"
3450 PRINT "{5 SPACES}PLAY AGAIN (Y/N)?"
3460 GET PA$
3470 IF PA$<>"Y" OR "N" THEN 3460
3480 IF PA$="Y" THEN GOTO 10
3490 END
]■
```

THE DAY OF THE awards ceremony, I could barely function at work. I kept dropping brush caps, and six of my mascara tubes failed a QC spot check because the tops weren't tight enough. Normally I fell asleep on the bus rides home, but all day I was wired and jumpy. I'd spent weeks waiting for the ceremony, daydreaming about computers I might win and conversations I might have with Fletcher Mulligan. Now that the big moment had finally arrived, everything felt slightly unreal, like I was still in a factory daydream.

I got home from work, and Mom announced that Tack was joining us for the ceremony.

"No," I told her. "No way."

"He's excited for you," she said. "He really wants to be there."

I reminded her that Alf and Clark were already coming to the ceremony, that our tiny Honda couldn't hold more than four people. She assured me there was plenty of space in Tack's car.

"His *police* car?" I asked. "We're taking a cop car?"

"You've seen how big it is," Mom said. "He's got plenty of room for all of us."

Alf and Clark were delighted by the idea, and Mom invited them to join us for a pre-contest cookout. We stood around the backyard, drinking orange soda and eating hamburgers off paper plates while Tack shared crazy stories of Wetbridge's most notorious criminals. Like the woman who stole a Butterball turkey using a baby carriage, and the old man who kept exposing himself to the girls at Crenshaw's Pharmacy.

My friends howled with laughter at every story and the cookout dragged on forever, despite my repeated requests that we get going. The ceremony started at seven o'clock and I wanted to leave the house by five thirty. But at six o'clock we were still in the backyard—now Alf was telling McDonald's stories—and I was fuming. I must have scowled one too many times because Tack set down his hamburger and pulled me aside. "Tell me something," he said. "What time do you want to be at this thing?"

"Seven o'clock," I said. "It starts at seven."

"Then we'll be there at seven," he said. "I'm giving you my word, all right? Now relax and be a good host. These are your friends."

I'd spend a lot of the next twenty-two years making fun of Tack. I'd ridicule his extreme patriotism, his collection of John Wayne porcelain plates, and his insistence on bringing his gun everywhere, even to the zoo, even to the beach. But there's one thing I understood early on: this guy always kept his promises. If Tack said seven o'clock, he'd have you on the campus of Rutgers University with ten minutes to spare, descending the steps of the athletic center to a large basement gymnasium where a dot matrix Print Shop banner hung over the doorway: WELCOME HIGH SCHOOL PROGRAMMERS!

I'd never been to a college before, and I wasn't sure if I was dressed okay. I'd worn turquoise Jams and a white polo shirt with a popped collar, because the preppy kids in movies always popped their collars. But as we got in line with the other kids and parents, I realized I'd worried for nothing. Everybody else was wearing tees—*Pac-Man* tees, *Bloom County* tees, *Far Side* tees.

To most people, I'm sure it looked like a science fair crammed inside a gym. But I felt like I'd arrived at Disney World. There were rows and rows of folding tables with all kinds of computers, and giant bundles of power cables crisscrossing the floor. There were schools and colleges advertising their computer science programs; there were wholesalers and software vendors and computer club representatives. And everywhere I looked, there were kids—hundreds of kids, all of them computer geeks just like me.

Along one wall was a row of coin-op arcade games set to free play, and Alf and Clark drifted off to try them. I walked over to the registration desk and met a man named Dr. Brooks, who introduced himself as a trustee of the university. He wore a navy sports coat with an American flag on the lapel; his face was very tan, almost orange, and he had the whitest, brightest teeth of anyone I'd ever met. He handed me a badge that said FINALIST and said, "I liked your game, Will."

I thought he was mistaken, that he'd confused me with someone else. "My game is *The Impossible Fortress*."

"I know. You're Will Marvin," he said. "I'm judging the winners this evening."

"You're judging? Where's Fletcher Mulligan?"

"His flight was delayed," Dr. Brooks explained. "There were storms over Pittsburgh, and his plane was rerouted to Cleveland."

"So what time is he getting here?"

"I'm afraid he's not going to make it." My disappointment must have been obvious because Dr. Brooks quickly started telling me about his own qualifications. He explained that he was an executive at Boeing, an aerospace company that supplied jets to the air force and rockets to NASA. "I've been working around computers my whole life, so I'm pretty sure I can judge a video game contest." He looked over my head to Tack and winked. "I'm sure Fletcher Morgan would approve of my decision."

"Fletcher *Mulligan*," I said. "His name is Fletcher Mulligan."

"Exactly," Dr. Brooks said. "Go have some fun, Will. This is going to be a great night."

I couldn't believe it. I'd had my share of bad luck over the past three months, but this was ridiculous. How many mascara tubes had I capped waiting for this moment? And now Fletcher Mulligan wasn't even coming? He was in stupid frigging *Cleveland*?

As we walked away from the registration desk, Tack draped a burly arm around my shoulders. "The doc says he likes your game, Will. I don't know much about computers, but I'd call that conversation a good sign."

"It's not," I said. Mary and I had designed *The Impossible Fortress* for the king of video games, not some smug, suntanned corporate executive who didn't even know Fletcher's name. "There's no way I'll win."

"Win, lose, who cares?" Mom asked. "It's 1987 and Robert Redford still hasn't won an Oscar. Do you think he lets that get him down?" Ever since she started dating Tack, my mother saw the bright side of everything.

There was nothing else to do except walk the aisles of the gymnasium—but even this was a disappointment, because the vendors were giving away disks, supplies, and other accessories, and every freebie was a reminder of what I'd lost. My mother insisted I take something, so I accepted a small plastic key chain molded in the shape of a Compaq PC. I knew it was the only computer I'd bring home that night.

Eventually Mom and Tack peeled off to an aisle of colleges offering programs in computer science, and I walked toward the coin-op arcade games, looking for Alf and Clark. Some kids were playing *Ms. Pac-Man* and *Rolling Thunder*, but the biggest crowd had formed around the *Gauntlet* machine, a game that allowed up to four players to compete simultaneously. I assumed a team of players had reached some unprecedented level, and I pushed through the crowd to get a better look. I found myself squeezing past a large man dressed in a white shirt and black tie.

"Sorry," I said.

"Uh-huh," Zelinsky grunted.

I did a double take. He was dressed in his usual work clothes, like he'd come straight from the store. My face must have said "What the hell are you doing here?" because he shook his head slowly: *I honestly have no idea.*

The *Gauntlet* screen flashed GAME OVER and the players turned to face a round of applause. Mary Zelinsky was joined by Lynn Scott, the cashier from Video City, and Sharon Boyd, the girl from the Regal Theater. At that moment, I realized they were the only three girls in a gymnasium crowded with teenage boys. Their very existence seemed a sort of miracle.

Mary recognized me and waved. Her fingernails were painted with a rainbow of zeros and ones, the same binary pattern she'd worn on the day we started working together.

"Hey, Will."

She looked fantastic, a suntanned and more radiant version of the Mary I used to know. Her hair was shorter with blond highlights, a new look for summer. She was wearing an outfit I'd never seen before—a white blouse, khaki shorts, and pink Chuck Taylor sneakers. The new clothes fit her perfectly, now that she had nothing to hide.

"I didn't think you were coming," I said.

"My dad wasn't going to let me," she said, "but then I threatened to have another baby."

Alf gaped at her until I explained this was a joke.

Mary introduced her friends to mine, but of course we already knew Lynn Scott from Video City. "It's been a while," she said to Clark. "You haven't rented *Kramer vs. Kramer* all summer."

Clark had avoided the store ever since our disastrous invasion of Mount St. Agatha's, ever since Alf had exposed the Claw to the entire student population.

"I've been busy at work," Clark explained. He was already stuffing the Claw into his pocket, but Lynn saw what he was doing and stopped him.

"Wait, hang on," she said. "Did you really hurt your hand climbing under the fence?"

Clark laughed, like her question was a joke.

"No, I'm serious," Lynn said. "What happened?"

He took a moment to scan the room—he might have been searching for escape routes—then reluctantly pulled the Claw from his pocket. "I was born like this," he admitted. "It's called syndactyly, and it runs in my family." He turned the Claw left and right, allowing Lynn to take a closer look. "But trust me, as soon as I turn eighteen, I'm paying a doctor to saw it off."

Lynn cringed. "What?"

"They'll slice it clean at the wrist," Clark explained. "Then they can fit me with a rubber hand that looks totally normal."

"That seems extreme," Sharon said.

"No, that's *crazy*," Lynn said. "There's no reason to be self-conscious. All those times you came to Video City, I never even noticed."

"Well, I kept it hidden," Clark admitted.

"But I'd see you other times," Lynn pointed out. "I'd see you walking around Market Street. Or reading in the library. Hanging around the mall. And all those times, I never noticed. Honest to God."

I'm not sure what surprised Clark more: the fact that Lynn hadn't run screaming at the sight of his hand, or the revelation that she'd been noticing him around town, in the library, at the mall. These revelations seemed to trigger an error in his programming; he stood frozen, his circuits freaking out, while Lynn and Sharon waited for him to say something.

"Enough already," Alf said, pushing past them and bellying up to the *Gauntlet* machine. "Can I join next game? Because I am really good. You girls will like having Alfred Boyle on your team."

Lynn took Clark by the hand, encouraging him to come along. "We need a fourth player," she explained. "Mary wants to take a look around."

"That's right," Mary said. "I do."

"I'll come with you," I told her.

We set off quickly before Zelinsky could make any kind of protest. Mary and I walked past rows of vendors selling computer coaching, computer tutoring, and even something called Junior Achievement Sleepaway Computer Camp—four weeks in luxury cabins equipped with state-of-the-art PCs, all meals included, for $2,500. Mary grabbed a brochure and gave it to me as a joke.

I had a million questions I wanted to ask: Where had she been all summer? What was she doing? Did she ever think about me? Did she ever think about her daughter? I'd spent hours on the assembly line preparing for this moment. But Mary just made small talk, so I followed her lead.

"It's a bummer about Fletcher," she said. "I really wanted to meet him."

"Me too."

"Nothing against this guy Dr. Brooks, but he told me his first computer ran on punch cards. In the 1950s. I'm not sure he's actually played a video game."

"I keep telling myself we're going to lose," I said.

"Yeah," Mary said. "Probably."

She didn't sound disappointed. It was obvious she'd already moved on to bigger and better dreams. She was enjoying her new PS/2, hanging out with Lynn and Sharon, buying new clothes and making herself beautiful, while I toiled alone in the cosmetics factory, obsessing over all my past mistakes. *Push, twist, push, twist, push, twist.*

"Have you seen the competition?" I asked.

Mary pointed to the far side of the gymnasium, to a long table full of monitors, joysticks, and keyboards. "You can play all the finalists over there. They set up computers so people can try them. One of them is a total rip-off of *Defender*."

"Is it any good?"

"Yeah, it's great, if you want to play a slower, lamer version of *Defender*."

It was the first time I laughed all summer. I couldn't believe how easily we fell into the old banter, like the last eight weeks had passed in a heartbeat. I wanted to walk past the finalists and see *The Impossible Fortress*, but our conversation was going well, and I didn't want to screw it up. Maybe it was better to leave the past in the past.

"By the way," Mary asked, "is your mom dating Officer Blaszkiewicz?"

"Yeah."

"Is that weird?"

"Very," I said, then thought better of it. "He's not all bad, though. He's super nice to my mom. And he's convinced we're going to win tonight, which is, you know—"

"That's cool," Mary said.

"Exactly."

We were interrupted by a hiss of microphone feedback. At the far end of the gym was a small platform that functioned as a stage; Dr. Brooks stood behind a lectern with two other university trustees. Together they called for quiet, and then Dr. Brooks began to speak. He thanked everyone for coming. He spoke at length about the importance of computer programmers in the near future. He predicted that one day soon, everyone would have computers in their homes. He promised that people would carry computers in their pockets and even wear computers on their bodies. "Imagine a computer no bigger than a candy bar!" he exclaimed, and we laughed at the absurdity of his predictions; they were all straight out of *The Jetsons*.

Finally he turned his attention to the main event—the winner of the Game of the Year contest. "I want to be clear about something. All five of the finalists have terrific code. They're very well programmed. But most are variations on popular arcade games like *Space Invaders*. Only one game tonight aspired to be truly daring, truly original."

Mary shot a hopeful glance at me and I knew what she was thinking. Maybe Dr. Brooks was a better judge than we realized. After all, what could be more daring and original than *The Impossible Fortress*?

Dr. Brooks cleared his throat, looked down at his index cards, and continued. "Tonight's winner is no simple arcade game. It offers a different, more sophisticated kind of fun. With strong graphics and exceptionally catchy music. And it's artfully programmed in a mix of BASIC and machine language, to minimize the lag time in computer calculations. Please join me in congratulating this year's first-prize winner, Zhang Hsu, for his extraordinary game *Five Card Poker*!"

The wall above the platform filled with a screenshot from the winning game, five playing cards on a plain green background. Everyone around me was applauding, but I was too stunned to clap my hands.

Dr. Brooks continued, "Yes, it's impressive when a programmer animates spaceships and monsters and moves them across a screen. But what Zhang Hsu has done is even more remarkable. His poker simulation is powered by a complex artificial intelligence that can outwit human opponents in thirty-five percent of the games I played. It's very well done, and I'm confident it demonstrates a bright future in computer programming. Congratulations, Zhang Hsu!"

Zhang Hsu came to the stage, a short, terrified-looking boy who couldn't be older than twelve. He made a short but gracious acceptance speech, thanking his parents and all of his teachers at Millstone Prep for their patience and support. There was another round of polite applause, and then Zhang Hsu's father helped him carry the enormous IBM PS/2 off the stage.

"Wow," Mary said.

"Yeah."

"We just lost to a nine-year-old?"

"I think so."

I'm not going to lie. I was disappointed. Losing to a terrific game like *Choplifter* or *Space Taxi* would be understandable. But a five-card poker simulation?

To make matters worse, we didn't even collect our fifty-dollar savings bond. Amid all the excitement, the faculty seemed to forget about them. Mary and I asked three different adults about prizes for runners-up, but no one seemed to know what we were talking about.

My mother walked over, followed by Tack and Zelinsky, and gave us hugs. "I'm sorry, kids. You guys gave it a good try. You should be really proud of yourselves."

"I think it's bullshit," Tack said, and he seemed genuinely outraged. "If I want to play poker, why do I need a four-thousand-dollar computer?"

He put this question to Zelinsky, who just shrugged.

"We should go," Zelinsky told Mary.

"It's not over yet," she said. "You said we could stay for the whole thing."

Zelinsky nodded at the stage, where a custodian was already unplugging a microphone and dismantling the podium. "They're wrapping up. Where's your friends?"

Mary looked around the gym, but there was no sign of Lynn or Sharon anywhere. I hoped they would stay lost. I wasn't ready for the night to be over. There was nothing left after tonight, nothing but thousands of mascara tubes in a never-ending stream. I didn't know how I'd find the strength to wake up in the morning.

"Let's go find them," Zelinsky said. "It's late."

Out of nowhere, Clark pushed his way through the crowd.

"You guys have to come with me," he said, gesturing not just to me and Mary but Mom and Tack and Zelinsky as well. "You all need to see this."

Clark led us across the gym to a section designated with a banner as Finalist's Row. There were two long tables full of computers, and the machines were set to play any of the top five contest entries. We could hear the familiar music before we even reached the tables, before we saw that every machine, every single machine, was playing *The Impossible Fortress*. Kids and adults were crowded around the screens, gesturing frantically and arguing about tactics and strategy. Even more people were lined up behind them, waiting to take turns. One guy succeeded in rescuing the Princess, and he danced to the game's victory theme while his friends showered him with high fives.

"Holy crap," Mary said.

"People love it," Clark said. "Look at them!"

"No," Mary said. "I don't mean that."

She put a hand on my shoulder, turning me slightly so I could see what she saw. Standing behind Finalist's Row was a silver-haired man in a purple sports coat and black jeans. He was watching the players carefully, observing how they reacted to the game. I recognized him immediately, of course, the way anyone else might notice if Ronald Reagan walked into a room.

"You're Fletcher Mulligan," Mary said. "You made it!"

He gave a little bow. "Better late than never. We left LA nine hours ago, but Mother Nature was determined to thwart us."

He was accompanied by two younger men and a younger woman—his entourage from Digital Artists. They looked like teenagers themselves—older than me and Mary, but not by much.

Fletcher pointed to the screen. "I'm getting a real kick out of this one," he said. "Look at the animation on those sprites! And the music! Such a clever use of the SID chip, don't you think?"

I was too terrified to answer. I couldn't believe this was really happening. Mary elbowed me in the side.

"We made this," I said. "Me and Mary. This is our game."

"Are you kidding?" Fletcher looked us up and down. "But you guys are just kids! What are you, fourteen? Did your teachers help you?"

Mary laughed. "Definitely not."

One of the players restarted the game, and the title screen popped up. Fletcher leaned closer to the monitor, squinting to read the credits. "What's Radical Planet?"

Zelinsky, Mom, and Tack had wandered up behind us, and everyone was waiting for me to answer the question: What's Radical Planet? I thought back to the night in the store when we coined the name. It seemed like a million years ago.

"It's our company," Mary said. "Will oversees the games, and I handle the music. But we both do a little of everything."

"Who handles your sales?"

"We don't have a publisher yet," Mary said. "We just want to make good stuff and worry about distribution later."

"Exactly, exactly!" Fletcher turned to his entourage and asked Mary to repeat herself, like she'd just summarized the meaning of life. "This is what I keep saying! Nothing ships before it's ready! Just ask Atari. They learned their lesson with that dreadful *E.T.* game."

Fletcher's companions laughed politely while our parents looked on, confused, trying to grasp what extraterrestrials had to do with anything.

"Do you guys have business cards?" Fletcher asked.

I nearly said no, but again Mary was way ahead of me. "We forgot them."

"How can I follow up with you?"

Mary wrote the address of her father's store on a slip of paper, along with the phone number. "We have an office in Wetbridge. Across the street from the train station. It's a really nice setup."

Mr. Zelinsky cleared his throat. "And newly renovated," he said dryly. "All new lights and shelving."

Fletcher gave us business cards. They were embossed with the famous Digital Artists logo, the image stamped on the boxes of all my favorite games. "I want to keep this conversation going, understand? Stay in touch with me." He shook hands with both of us, then shook hands with our parents and Tack, and then spun off into the crowd like a whirling dervish.

As soon as he left, Mary and I exploded with nervous laughter. "Did you hear what he said about the animation?" she asked. "Did you hear *Fletcher Mulligan* complimenting the animation in our game?"

We marveled over the business cards like they were made of gold. They were way better than any trophy, certainly better than any fifty-dollar savings bond. Mary pushed the card in her father's face. She was practically jumping up and down. "Dad, that's the guy I was telling you about! He's like the Willy Wonka of video games! Did you hear what he said about the SID chip?"

"Calm down," Zelinsky said. "What's a SID chip?"

Mary's eyes went wide. "Oh my God. He's coming back!"

"Who's coming back?" I asked.

"Behind you!" she whispered. "Fletcher Mulligan's coming back!"

And the Willy Wonka of video games strolled up like we were old friends, like we'd known each other forever. "I forgot to ask," he said. "What's next?"

"Next?" Mary asked.

"What's the next game?" Fletcher asked. "What are you guys working on?"

I froze. We all froze. I didn't know what to say. I didn't want to ruin anything. Even Fletcher seemed to understand he had asked a delicate question. "You *are* working on a new game, right?"

Mary took a deep breath, like she was getting ready to blow out some candles. "It'll be ready in a month?"

"Perfect!" Fletcher said. "It's good?"

"You'll love it," Mary promised. "It's way better than *The Impossible Fortress*. Better graphics, better music, faster gameplay. It's probably the best thing Will and I have ever made."

Fletcher nodded, like this was the answer he'd been expecting all along. "Then I want to see it as soon as you're finished," he said. "My address is on the card. I'll be waiting, okay?"

We all shook hands again, and he vanished into the crowd.

Mary and I stared after him, dumbfounded.

"One month?" I asked.

"I'm sorry," she said. "I panicked."

"One month to build a whole game from scratch? There's no way. It's impossible!"

"That's what you said about machine language. But we figured it out. We could do it again."

"It's different now. I don't even have a computer!"

Mary looked hopefully to her father, and Zelinsky looked hopefully to the rafters of the gymnasium, as if the perfect excuse might be written on the ceiling.

"Come on, Sal," Tack said.

"Fine," Zelinsky said. "You can use the showroom. But this doesn't change anything." He pointed a finger at me. "I still want you out by seven."

And just like that, we were back in business.

A NOTE ABOUT THE CODE

When I started writing this book, I wanted to program an *Impossible Fortress* video game that would be playable on Commodore 64 emulators (hence the code excerpts at the start of every chapter). But over time I realized that Billy and Mary's masterpiece would find a much larger audience—and would be a lot more fun—if it was designed and programmed for today's computers. Enter the amazing Dan and Jackie Vecchitto of Holy Wow Studios. They read the manuscript at an early stage, spent many hours discussing ideas with me, and created a brilliant faux-8-bit adaptation of *The Impossible Fortress* that you can play for free at my author website, jasonrekulak.com. My high score is 11,358 and I hope you'll leave me a note if you beat it.

ACKNOWLEDGMENTS

Special thanks to my editor, Marysue Rucci, and my agent, Doug Stewart. They are the all-time high-score champions of *The Impossible Fortress*, and I'm incredibly grateful for all of their ideas, energy, and enthusiasm.

Thanks also to TRaSh-80 fan Jonathan Karp, Richard Rhorer, Sarah Reidy, Cary Goldstein, Zachary Knoll, Ebony LaDelle, Tamara Arellano, Lewelin Polanco, Jackie Seow, Dana Trocker, Wendy Sheanin, and everyone else at Simon & Schuster. And thank you to all of the international editors and agents who have embraced this book, including Szilvia Molnar, Caspian Dennis, Hannah Griffiths, Alex Russell, and Tom Harmsen.

I received terrific help and technical support from Luca Fonstad, Will Staehle, Doogie Horner, Dan Vecchitto, Greg Warrington, Ed Milano, Patrick Caulfield, Seth Fishman, Taylor Bacques, Shari Smiley, and just about everybody at Quirk Books. Thank you, all of you.

My parents bought a Commodore 64 for our family in 1984, when a six-hundred-dollar computer seemed like an outrageously expensive luxury. Thanks, Mom and Dad, for everything—and thanks to the developers of VICE (http://vice-emu.sourceforge.net) for keeping the C64 alive and well.

Finally: I couldn't have written this book without the help and support of my wife, Julie Scott, and she's the one person I can't thank enough. *You know I love you, don't you? / You make my dreams come true.*